THE
BEST
FRIEND

Also by Shalini Boland:

THE GIRL FROM THE SEA
a gripping psychological thriller

The OUTSIDE SERIES
a post-apocalyptic mystery thriller

The MARCHWOOD VAMPIRE SERIES
a dark romantic adventure

A SHIRTFUL OF FROGS
a ww2 timeslip adventure

Coming 2017

THE MILLIONAIRE'S WIFE
a twisty psychological thriller

THE
BEST
FRIEND

A Chilling Psychological Thriller

Shalini Boland

Published by Adrenalin Books

ISBN 978-0-9569985-9-0

CHAPTER ONE

2016

It's him again. And I'm pretty sure he's following me. I mean, I can't be a hundred percent sure, but I've seen him here three times already this week, and he was there at the corner shop on Monday, and yesterday at the garage.

'Mummy,' Joe says, tugging on my arm. 'Mrs Landry said my picture was the best in the class.'

'Wow,' I say, taking his small, sweaty hand in mine. 'That's fantastic.'

'Well, maybe not the best in the class,' he amends. 'But she said it was really good.' Joe lets go of my hand again and leaps into the tempting pile of yellow and brown leaves that has drifted up against the school fence. He stamps his feet, a grin on his face, enjoying the crackle and crunch of autumn.

The man is about a hundred yards away, on the other side of the road. He has a scruffy, sandy beard and he's wearing one of those awful sea-captain-type hats. He looks like a tramp, but I don't think he can be very old. I'm sure he's not a parent because I've never seen him with a child. Maybe I should report him.

'Don't go running out of sight,' I call, as Joe spies one of his friends up ahead and abandons the pile of leaves.

'I won't!' he yells back, his sturdy legs stomping off down the pavement.

The man has dropped a little further away from me now, but he's still there. I know it. My skin prickles. I feel his eyes on my back. I curb the urge to turn and double check. I don't want him to know I've noticed him. Maybe I'm just being paranoid. He probably lives somewhere around here. He could be just an eccentric millionaire or something.

'Joe!' I yell. 'Wait for me at the bottom of the hill!' I stride a little faster, squinting in the late afternoon sunshine. I should've worn sunglasses.

Joe has stopped. He's chatting to a tall blond-haired boy on a silver scooter. My heart lifts knowing he's managed to make friends quickly. He's only been at Cerne Manor Prep school for two weeks and yet it feels like he's been here forever. He already loves it. Jared was right – this place is perfect. Okay, it costs an arm and a leg, and we'll be skint forever – finding the termly school fees is going to be a challenge, but Joe is the happiest he's ever been, and that's what matters.

'Who's this?' I ask Joe, finally catching him up.

'Tyler. He's in my class.'

'Hi, Tyler. Where's your mum?' I ask.

He points behind me, up the hill. 'Talking to her friends,

as usual,' he says, rolling his eyes.

I swivel my head to see a group of glamorous mums clustered around a white four-wheel drive vehicle. They're laughing and chatting in a haze of colourful dresses, scarves, shawls and bangles. That's the other thing about starting a new school – it's almost worse for the parents. I'm the new mum on the block and I don't feel quite up to talking to them today. My nail varnish is chipped and I'm sure I must seem dowdy in boring jeans and a plain blue shirt.

My four-year-old niece, Megan, comes here, too. She finishes half-an-hour earlier than Joe, so I never get to see her or my sister, Beth, at school pick-up, which is a shame. It would be nice to have someone to chat with. To not feel quite so much of a newbie.

'Well, it was nice to meet you, Tyler,' I say. 'Have a lovely evening.'

'You, too,' he says politely.

Joe takes my hand again, and we cross the road. I steal a glance behind me, and sure enough, the man is still there following slowly at a distance, his head down. Joe and I turn left down a side-road.

'Okay, Joe,' I say. 'How about you and I have a little race?'

'I thought your knee was bad,' he says. 'When I wanted you to come on the trampoline yesterday, you said—'

'Well, my knee *is* bad,' I say, feeling the joint twinge in anticipation. 'But I can probably run to the end of the road.

7

Winner gets an ice cream.' That's all I have to say to get Joe to move like there's a stick of dynamite under him. He's off. I follow him at a jog. My knee aches, but I ignore the pain and keep going. If that guy really is following me, I don't want him to see where we live. I catch Joe up and we run along the pavement together until we reach the next road. I let him win by a head.

'Yessss!' He pumps his little fist into the air.

'Let's cross over,' I say, taking his hand.

My heart drops as I turn and see the man at the end of the road. He's speeding up now. Not quite jogging, but walking pretty fast. I can hear my heart beating, whether from the run or from anxiousness, I can't tell. Should I call someone? The police? Jared? And say what? No. It'll be okay. Joe and I can lose him. We'll have another "race".

Joe and I cross the road. There's no one else around other than a few cars whizzing past far too quickly – late for school pick-up, no doubt.

'Okay,' I say. 'Ready, steady . . .' He's off again, his rucksack banging against his back, his feet slapping the pavement. I limp along behind him, my poor knee clicking and grinding.

'Does that mean I get two ice creams?' he asks when I finally catch him up again.

'Only if you want to be sick.'

'I won't be. I could have two different flavours. One for

dinner, one for pudding.'

I take his hand and we turn into another side road.

'This isn't the way,' he says.

'We're going a different way, today,' I reply. We jog across the road and turn right and then left. I throw another glance behind us, but I can't see the man any more. The sun has dipped behind the houses and a couple of street lamps flicker on. I shiver even though I'm warm after our exertions.

Finally, we leave the side streets behind and come to Penn Hill Avenue. It's busier here and so Joe and I head towards the crossing. Joe is still chattering away. I'm too preoccupied to pay him any proper attention. I usually love our walk home. It's a chance to catch up on everything he's done that day. A chance to chat without the distractions of TV or video games. But that creepy guy has unnerved me.

The green man flashes at the crossing and we stride across the road, leaving the leafy glamour of Lower Parkstone and heading through narrower streets to our characterful three-bedroom house at the top of the hill. My knee is throbbing. I can't wait to get in and sit down with a cup of tea.

'Mummy, do you want another race?'

'You go ahead. I'll time you. See if you can reach home before I count to ten.'

My phone pings. I pull it out of my bag and swipe the screen to see a new text message, number unknown:

Hi Louisa! Darcy here — Tyler's mom. I got your number from the class list. Wondered if you guys wanted to come over after school tomorrow. Tyler can't stop talking about Joe. We can have a cuppa while they play xxx

I text her back:

That would be lovely. Thank you. Can you text me your address? Louisa X

I smile. Maybe the mums here aren't as snobby as I first imagined.

Even better, I haven't spotted that creepy man again. I'm starting to feel a little silly for worrying about him. Why on earth would I have a stalker? What would anyone want with *me?*

CHAPTER TWO

I stand at the edge of the school playground on my own, waiting for Joe. Darcy and a group of other mums are chatting to the sports teacher, clustered around him, laughing. But it is clearly Darcy who draws everyone's attention, with her willowy figure and honey blonde hair. She has a natural magnetism. She catches my eye and smiles. I feel as though I've been caught spying.

'Louisa!' she calls. 'Come over.'

I dip my head and smile back as all eyes flick over to me and instantly dismiss me as not worthy. Perhaps I'm being unfair. These people don't know me yet.

'Guys,' Darcy says, drawing me into her circle. 'This is Louisa, Joe's mum. They only just started this term.'

I notice Darcy has a subtle American accent.

'Oh, hi.' A woman with a sleek, chin-length brown bob smiles at me. 'I'm Tori. Louie has been talking about Joe all week. Says he's a great football player.'

I recognise the name Louie. I think Joe's mentioned him once or twice. I smile back.

'We'll have to get him playing some matches,' the sports teacher chips in. 'Joe's really impressed me so far.'

I can't remember the teacher's name. I'll have to look it up on the school website when I get home. I'm pleased he's noticed Joe.

'Your husband does the drop off in the mornings, doesn't he?' a woman in sports gear asks.

I nod. 'Yes, Jared. It's on his way to work.'

'Lucky you!' the woman says. 'He's hot.'

I blush, not quite knowing how to respond. 'Thanks . . . I guess.'

Everyone laughs, and I join in, my cheeks burning. Sometimes it's annoying being so fair skinned.

'Here they come,' Darcy says, checking her watch. 'They're a little late out, today.'

I glance over to the double doors to see Joe's teacher, Mrs Landry, followed by a neat line of boys and girls. It's completely different to the sprawling, raucous exit made by the children at Joe's previous school.

The children shake their teacher's hand and are handed off to the parents, one-by-one. Joe's face lights up at the sight of me and I feel a familiar rush of love. He's surrounded by his new friends, Tyler at the forefront proudly proclaiming that Joe's coming to his house tonight.

'Where are you parked?' Darcy asks. 'Do you want to follow me back?'

'That would be great,' I say.

She tells me her address just in case we get separated, and

we make our way back to the cars.

* * *

Fifteen minutes later, we're following Darcy's silver Bentley through a set of electric gates. A workman looks up and winks at me – cheeky sod. He and another guy are painting the eight-foot high boundary wall that seems to run on into infinity. It doesn't even look as though it needs painting. The driveway is so long I haven't glimpsed the house yet. We pass gardeners and groundsmen on our slow cruise.

'Does Tyler live in a castle?' Joe asks from the back seat.

I stifle a giggle. 'Maybe,' I say. 'Let's wait and see.'

We round another bend and finally spy the house up ahead. I had assumed it would be a tacky McMansion, a tasteless pastiche like so many of the other properties in this area. But it's actually a super-modern wood and glass house. Although the word "house" is somewhat inadequate. "Residence" is probably more fitting.

'It's like a sci-fi castle,' Joe says. 'It's way bigger than our house. Not as big as Hogwarts, though.'

I mentally make a note never to invite Darcy over to our house for a playdate, and then shake my head inwardly at my insecurities. Who cares if I live in a normal house and she lives in a glass castle.

Darcy pulls up outside a row of 4 garages. I park my eight-year-old VW Golf next to her gleaming Bentley. Jared would die if he saw this place. I can't wait to tell him about it. Joe and I get out of the car and follow Darcy to the front door.

'Come in,' she says. 'Let's get that kettle on.'

The boys charge ahead, chattering to each other about football. There's no awkwardness or politeness between them, they're just excited to have one another to play with.

'There's a plate of snacks on the counter!' Darcy calls to them. 'Help yourself on your way outside.'

'We probably won't see them for the rest of the afternoon,' I say. 'Not if they're going out to play football. Joe's obsessed.'

'Tyler, too.' We grin at each other and I follow her through to the most magnificent view I've ever seen. Forget that the place is designed like a palace, ahead of us stretches a wall of glass with a view out over the ocean. This is Sandbanks Beach as I've never seen it before. Not from this angle anyway.

'Great view, huh?' she says, as my mouth hangs open.

'Gorgeous,' I say.

'We moved here a couple of years ago. There was an older property on the land and we demolished it and rebuilt. But I know it's all about the view. Let's go out on the deck and watch them play. Marianna will bring our drinks out. Tea?'

'Please.' I nod, noticing a dark-haired woman in a maid's uniform at the far end of the huge kitchen diner.

We step out onto the terrace and sit at a chunky, wooden, square table. Below the deck lies a vast area of emerald grass where the boys are playing football. Beyond that, a white wall, and then the beach. The evening sun is warm on my face, we're perfectly sheltered from any stray breath of wind.

'Are you from America?' I ask.

'Uh huh. Is my accent that obvious? My US friends say I've lost it. They tell me I've gone all British.'

'It's only slight,' I say. 'It's pretty, though.'

'Thanks.' She raises her eyebrows and turns her gaze to the boys. 'So what do you think of Cerne Manor so far?'

'It's amazing. Joe's adapted really quickly. He loves it.'

'Tyler, too.'

'Tyler's really helped him settle in. It's great they get on so well.' I hear a noise behind me and turn my head to see Darcy's maid bringing a tray of tea things – a teapot, china cups, and a plate of biscuits. At my place, she would've got a couple of mugs and a shared teabag. Okay, maybe a teabag each, but still.

'Thanks, Marianna,' Darcy says without looking at the woman.

'Thanks,' I echo with a smile.

Marianna doesn't make eye contact.

We pour our tea. There's no milk jug so I guess I'll have to drink it black. I help myself to a chocolate-chip cookie that tastes homemade.

'How long have you lived in England?' I ask.

She counts on her fingers. 'It'll be eight and a half years now. Mike and I met a year before Tyler was born. It was a whirlwind romance.'

'Wow. Is Mike American, too?'

'No. I met him over here, in London. He's English. He's also a workaholic, which is why you'll hardly ever see him at the school gates. Unlike your divine husband.'

'What does Mike do?'

'Our company deals with commercial property. We buy up buildings and let them out as office space.'

'Cool,' I reply, taking a sip of my tea, which is absolutely delicious. I thought tea was tea. Obviously not. 'Mm, this is so refreshing.'

'Castleton tea,' she says. 'From Darjeeling. I'll give you a tin when you leave.'

'No, no, that's okay,' I say, mortified she might think I was hinting.

'It's fine, I always keep a good supply.'

My eyes keep being drawn by the view, to the dog walkers and joggers on the beach beyond, to the Condor Ferry heading out towards France, the sailing boats like white handkerchiefs in the distance, and seagulls hovering overhead. It's like being on holiday. How can all this be so close to our house, and yet feel so distant?

'How about you?' she asks, pushing a loose strand of hair

behind her ear. 'Do you work?'

'I write a column in a weekend newspaper supplement.'

'How exciting,' she replies.

'Not really. It's only one small piece a week . . . but I do love it.'

'Do you write about people you know? Might I be in it one day?' She leans forward, a gleam in her eye.

'Do you want to be in it?' I laugh.

'Of course!'

'I write about being a mother – schools and being married and all that stuff.'

She gasps. 'You write *Louisa's Life's a Beach*!'

'Guilty,' I say.

'I *love* that column. So, you're famous.' She reaches out a slender, French-manicured hand to squeeze my arm.

'Hardly,' I say, with a swell of pride in my chest.

'I'd brag all the time if I wrote for a newspaper,' she says. 'I write a blog, but it's not the same.'

'What's it about?' I ask.

'Interior design. Hints and tips. That kind of thing.'

'I can see you've got a good eye,' I say, gesturing back to the house. 'Did you—'

'Yeah, I designed the house. Problem is, it's finished now so I'm twiddling my thumbs again. I do enjoy interior design, but my passion is writing.'

'As in books?'

'Mm-hm.'

'Have you written anything yet?'

'Working on a novel,' she says, tossing her hair back behind her shoulder, 'you know, like half the world's population.' She laughs.

I don't mention that I've also been trying to write a novel.

'Mum!' Joe calls from the lawn below.

I shade my eyes and peer down at him.

'Tyler asked if I can have a sleepover. Can I, Mum?'

'Not on a school night,' I call back.

'He's welcome to stay,' Darcy says. 'I have spare toothbrushes, and he can borrow some of Tyler's PJs.'

'Please, Mum!'

'Mum, he can stay, can't he?' Tyler yells.

'That's kind,' I say to Darcy. 'But he'll be too tired tomorrow.'

'Really?' Darcy raises an eyebrow. 'Don't worry, I'll make sure they get to bed by nine.'

I flinch inwardly. Joe's bedtime is normally seven o'clock. He'll be exhausted at school tomorrow if he stays over. Yet I don't want to be a killjoy. I don't want to be the uptight mum who's too strict.

'I'll take them both to school tomorrow,' she says. 'It'll be fine. They'll have a great time.'

'Well, if you're sure,' I say, wishing I could just say no.

'Absolutely!' Darcy replies. 'Sleepover!' she calls down to

the boys, standing and punching her fist in the air. Joe and Tyler go crazy, jumping up and down and high-fiving each other.

Darcy turns and smiles at me. 'I love seeing them so happy and excited.'

I smile back despite my concerns.

One late night can't hurt.

CHAPTER THREE

It's quiet. Nothing apart from the hum of the fridge and the faint purr of traffic in the distance. I've just finished printing out Joe's birthday-party invitations. After much debating and mind-changing on his part, we finally decided on a football party at the park, followed by a pizza picnic. He can take the invitations to school on Monday and hand them out to his new friends.

I suppose, with Joe not here and Jared still at work, I should take this opportunity to make a start on writing next week's column, but I can't settle. I keep thinking about Joe staying over at Tyler's. About whether he'll get enough sleep, or become homesick.

Instead, I begin half-heartedly tidying up the kitchen, loading up the dishwasher, and wiping down the surfaces. That loses its appeal pretty quickly so I plonk myself down at the kitchen table, pick up my phone and start surfing the net. After checking my emails and social media, I tap in a search for "Darcy Lane". Her blog pops up on the front page of my search results, and my eyes widen. Called *The House down the Lane*, it's more than just a blog. The glossy-looking website has interviews and insightful articles on trends and innovations in design. Well written, it actually makes my little newspaper column look a bit pathetic, and I squirm in embarrassment at how pleased I was by her apparent awe.

I hear the familiar click of the key in the front door and my heart gives a little lift. Jared's home early.

The door to the kitchen opens and he breezes in, loosening his tie and dumping his bag on the floor by the table. I rise to my feet and we kiss.

'Hey, Lou,' he says, running a finger down my cheek. 'I missed you today.'

'Missed you, too,' I say, giving him a hug.

'Where's the little man?' he asks.

'Having a sleepover at his new friend's house.'

'Really? Who's that, then? Do we know them?' Jared frowns and heads for the kettle. 'Tea?'

'I'll make it.' I start making tea and fill Jared in on Joe's playdate, and on Darcy's incredible house.

'One day soon,' Jared says, 'we'll live on the beach in one of those houses.'

'I'd rather have an older house with character,' I say. 'Like the one we've already got.'

'You can have whatever house you want if my new idea works out.'

My heart sinks. Every time Jared has an idea, it usually involves buying something we can't afford. 'What do you mean?' I ask, sitting next to him and accidentally slopping some of my tea onto the table. I turn to get a cloth but Jared takes my arm and guides me back down into my seat.

'Leave it,' he says. 'I want to talk to you about something important.'

I hope my mentioning Darcy's swanky house isn't the catalyst for this conversation.

'I've had an idea,' he says.

'Since when?' I ask, making patterns in the spilt tea with my finger.

'I've been thinking about it for a while. You mentioning that place at Sandbanks makes me even more determined to do it. *We* should be living that lifestyle. *We* should have that great big house by the sea.'

Shit, I definitely should have kept my big mouth shut. I look up at my husband, his eyes glittering. 'What's this idea?' I say, trying to inject some enthusiasm into my words.

'Well . . .' He suddenly looks boyish, just like Joe – his excitement spilling out. 'You know how I work crazy long days . . .' He takes a slurp of tea.

'Yeah.'

'And you know I love my job, right.'

I nod.

'Okay, so at the moment I'm the creative director. I do all the work – get everyone motivated, organise the big picture. But all that creativity, all that work, I'm doing it for someone else. I'm lining someone else's pockets.'

I now know where this conversation's heading. My stomach lurches as he continues.

'How about . . .' He takes my hand and squeezes it. 'How about if I set up my own ad agency?'

I'm not sure how to answer. I don't want to dismiss his idea, but I really do think it would be a mistake to set up a new business at the moment. I hear the irregular drip, drip, drip of the kitchen tap. We must get that fixed.

'What do you think?' he prompts.

I have to be careful how I word my answer. He wants my approval. He wants me to confirm that his idea is amazing, when all I can think about is the fact we have this huge mortgage and a child at private school – a school Jared insisted we send Joe because he wasn't doing so well at the state school where he was perfectly happy.

'It sounds interesting,' I say. 'But wouldn't it be a lot more work? We'd never see you.'

'No, that's where you're wrong.' Jared thumps the table and grins.' Gary's always off on some swanky holiday or another. He's rolling in it. We're all working our asses off so he can go on a hundred holidays a year. That could be us.'

'His agency's been going for years,' I counter. 'Surely, in the early days, he never had the time for holidays.'

'Maybe. But we could sacrifice a few years of hard graft for a lifetime of holidays and dosh, couldn't we?'

My heart rate speeds up. I know what Jared's like when

he gets an idea. He won't let it go. He'll force it through with charm, or brute force – whichever works best. It was the same when we bought our house, and it was the same with Joe's school. I remember our ten-year wedding anniversary where Jared arranged a surprise trip to the Caribbean for a two-week, five-star holiday while my sister looked after Joe. Beth didn't feel like she could say no to my husband, even though Megan was only nine-months-old at the time. Jared made it a surprise trip because he knew I would never have wanted to go. Yes, we had a good time, but the guilt and stress marred my enjoyment to the point where I couldn't wait to get back home.

And now we're struggling financially because of all the loans and expenses. I love my husband but his ambition and extravagance leave me edgy and short of breath. 'Why don't we think about it?' I say. 'There's no hurry, is there?'

He grins, leans over and kisses me, his blue eyes twinkling. 'It'll be amazing. You can help me think of a name for the agency.'

'Jared,' I say. 'We really need to think about it first. We've only been in our house a year. Joe's just started a new school. We don't have any spare cash. You'll need money to set it up, a client list, staff . . .'

'Staff's no problem, I know loads of great creatives and account handlers. We can get a business loan to get us off the ground. And I can pitch for new clients. Simple.'

24

He makes everything sound so easy. I want to be swept up in his plans, I really do. But all I can see is the worry of a thousand decisions and the burden of borrowing more money.

'Don't worry, Lou. It'll be good for us. For our little family.' He downs the rest of his tea and gets to his feet, stretching his arms out in front of him. 'Okay, I'm going for a run, then to the gym. I'll be back about nine, okay?'

I nod. 'What do you want to eat tonight?'

'Anything. Something easy. Stir fry?'

I nod, my stomach suddenly knotted with anxiousness. Maybe he's right. Maybe it will be okay, and he'll make a success of it. I shouldn't be such a killjoy. I should be more fun, more laid back. More like Darcy.

CHAPTER FOUR

It's a perfect Indian summer. The sky is a luminous blue, the air bursting with the promise of true warmth. Not a day for cardigans and jackets, but for shorts and swimming costumes, factor-thirty sun cream, and parasols. The beach isn't busy yet so we've managed to nab a great spot down at Branksome, far enough away from the busiest areas, yet not too far from the shop, toilets and café. I'm sitting cross-legged on the rug, under the sun umbrella, head down, engrossed in my novel.

'Sorry we're late.'

I glance up to see Beth, her wife Carys, and Megan laden down with bags. They only live a few minutes' walk from here but they're already red-faced and sweaty.

'Hey,' I say.

'Hi, Aunty Louisa. Where's Joe?' Megan asks, her strawberry blonde curls tumbling out from her sun hat. My niece has similar skin colouring to me, so she has to be extra careful in the sun.

'Hi, sweetie,' I reply. 'Joe and Uncle Jared are out on their paddle boards. Do you want to go out on a board with Uncle Jared?'

She nods, so I put my Kindle down and start to get up. 'I'll take you down to the sea.'

'That's okay,' Carys says, wriggling out of her shorts. 'Stay. I'll take her. I want a swim anyway.'

Beth and I stand together and watch them head down to the water's edge, Megan running ahead, and Carys waving to Jared and Joe.

'What time are Mum and Dad coming?' I ask, sitting back down.

'They should be here any minute – that is if Mum can tear Dad away from the garden.' Beth plops down beside me.

'I was there last week, dropping a book off for Mum, and they were ballroom dancing around the dining room.' I smile at the memory.

'They're doing evening classes,' Beth says.

I nod. They already told me about it.

'Salsa, Bollywood and Ballroom,' we say in unison, dissolving into giggles.

'Well, this is bloody nice,' Beth says, propping herself up with one arm and turning to face me.

It's so not fair – her blonde pixie cut frames gorgeous dark honey-coloured skin, while my pale auburn curls are frizzing around my freckle-spattered face. I coil my hair up on top of my head, holding it off my neck for a moment, wishing I'd thought to bring a hair elastic.

'How are you guys, anyway?' I say. 'How's Megan getting

on at school?'

'Really good. A few wobbles at first, but now she loves it. How about Joe?'

'Yeah, great. We still can't afford it, though.' I laugh, trying to conceal my anxiety.

My sister and her wife are lawyers. They live in a gorgeous three-bedroom apartment, just a few minutes from the beach. Megan started at Cerne Manor last year, which is when Jared got the idea to start sending Joe there. The difference is, my sister and Carys earn a six-figure salary, and we don't.

'Will you have to take him out of the school?' Beth asks, her brow wrinkling. 'I'm sure we can help if—'

'No, no, we're okay. I'm just panicking as usual. Thing is, Jared's got it into his head that he wants to leave his job and set up his own agency.'

'Oh?'

'Actually, he's skipped the "thinking about it" phase. Just wants to do it.'

Beth doesn't respond. She nods with a thoughtful expression on her face.

'In case you can't tell, I'm not thrilled with the idea,' I say.

'Maybe it'll be okay,' she says. 'If anyone can make it work, Jared can. He's a hard worker and people love him. He'll charm the business into a success.'

I force out a smile.

'Don't worry, Louisa. You know what Jared's like. For as long as you've known him, he's always been ambitious. He's always wanted the best – it's why he married *you*.' She grins and pokes me in the chest.

Beth always has a way of making me feel better about things. Making me less anxious. She's only three years older than me, but she's so much more together. I wish I could be more like her.

'Anyway, sorry, let's not worry about that now,' I say, pushing away my anxiety and focusing instead on the sea and the sky. On the image of my family bobbing about on the water, and on the heat of the sun on my skin.

'Hello, girls.'

Beth and I turn at the sound of our father's voice. We both make a move to stand. Mum motions us to stay where we are.

'Hello, darlings,' Mum says. 'We brought chairs. Us old fogies can't get up and down off the rug like you young 'uns.'

'Rubbish,' Beth says. 'You guys are fitter than the lot of us.'

She's not wrong. Mum looks amazing, with her slim figure and swingy, blonde bobbed hair, and Dad is a sprightly sixty-year-old with salt-and-pepper hair and a trim physique. Beth and I get to our feet despite their admonishments for us to stay seated, and we hug and kiss our parents, helping them set out their chairs and parasols.

'Where are my gorgeous grandchildren?' Mum asks as she roots around in her cold-bag.

'In the sea,' Beth answers, 'with Jared and Carys.'

'I remember you two were such water babies,' Dad says. 'Couldn't keep you out of the sea.'

'Watermelon?' Mum asks. 'I cut up some slices. It's nice and cold, just what you want on a scorcher like today.'

Mum and Dad adopted me when I was ten, and yet they always treated me exactly the same as Beth, as though I'm their natural daughter. I love them for it. To me, they are my real parents and I try not to think about the time before I was with them.

The rest of the day passes in a haze of sun cream and picnic food. I'm nicely tired. Ready for a glass of wine at home. Megan is becoming fractious, though. Her voice now a semitone below whiny, her bottom lip quivering.

'We better get this one home,' Carys says, scooping her daughter up and kissing her apple-red cheeks.

'No! I don't want to go,' Megan cries.

'Shh, baby,' Mum says. 'Give her to me while you get your things together.'

Carys gratefully deposits Megan onto Mum's lap.

'We're going, too,' I say to my niece, heaving myself up and surveying our messy encampment. 'We're all going. It's time for baths and beds.'

'Hey, guys.'

I turn my head at the sound of a familiar voice.

'Tyler!' Joe yells. 'Awesome.'

It's Darcy, Tyler and an older guy – balding, but in good shape – who I assume must be her husband. They look like something out of a luxury holiday brochure. Her, in a sheer turquoise kaftan, Aviators, and boho jewellery, hair sun-kissed and lightly tousled. Him, in a white shirt, Ray-Bans, and khaki shorts. By contrast, I must appear crumpled and sweaty. I attempt to brush the sand from my clothes and hair.

'Hey,' Darcy says. 'Fancy seeing you here.'

We kiss on the cheek.

'Hi,' I say.

'This is my husband, Mike.'

'Good to meet you,' he says with a smile. Mike seems as warm and friendly as Darcy.

'This is Jared,' I say with a swell of possessive pride. Next, I introduce my parents – John and Barb – then Beth, Carys and Megan.

'You look like you've had a great day,' Darcy says, eyeing our sandy rug, paddle boards, wet towels and plastic Tesco rubbish bags. 'Nice boards,' she adds. 'We love paddle boarding.'

A tinge of envy needles me. Because of my knee, I can't manage many sports activities any more.

'We're just packing up,' I say.

'Well,' Darcy says. 'You should all come back to our place for a drink. We're just a few minutes' walk along the beach. We can fire up the barbeque. John, Barb, and everyone, you're more than welcome, we'd love you all to come, too.'

'Can we?' Joe asks, turning to me, his eyes round and pleading.

'It's a bit late,' I say. 'You've got school tomorrow.'

'He'll be fine,' Jared says, not picking up on my reluctance. He turns to Darcy and Mike. 'We'd love to come.'

'Thank you for the kind invitation,' my dad says, 'but we'll bow out this time.'

'Dad's itching to get back to his garden,' I say.

He ruffles my hair. 'You know me so well, LouLou.'

Beth gives me a sympathetic glance. 'Thanks for the offer,' she says to Darcy. 'But Megan here is about to have the mother of all meltdowns. We need to get her home, pronto.'

'I totally understand,' Darcy says. 'What a sweetie, though. Another time?'

'Absolutely,' Carys says, expertly folding up their travel rug.

Eventually, we say our goodbyes to my parents, my sister and her family, waving as they leave the beach and head back home.

'We're in the car park,' Jared says. 'We'll pack up and drive round to yours, shall we?'

Mike nods. 'Sure. We'll head back along the beach – take

Joe with us, if you like.'

Joe's face lights up. He and Tyler high five each other and make off down the beach kicking Joe's football to each other as they go.

'Thanks. See you there,' Jared says. He shakes Mike's hand and kisses Darcy's cheek.

It's funny how you can just click with people. It already feels like we've known them for ages. They head off along the beach towards Sandbanks, while Jared and I turn our attention to packing away our gear.

'They seem nice,' Jared says.

'Really friendly,' I agree. 'I wish we had time to go home and get changed. I feel like a right mess.'

'You look fine,' Jared says, brushing sand off his board. 'It's just a barbeque.'

'She's so glamorous, though.' I drag my fingers through salt-encrusted hair.

'Yeah, but you're a natural beauty.' He winks, and my heart swoops. My husband still has the ability to make me blush. Sod it. Who cares if my clothes are creased and my makeup has melted. Like Jared says – it's just a barbeque.

* * *

Half an hour later, Jared and Mike are out on the decking, firing up the state-of-the-art gas grill. Tyler and Joe are on the kitchen sofas, heads together, glued to Tyler's iPad. The house is immaculate but there's no sign of the maid this evening. Darcy's taking some thinly sliced steaks and salmon out of the fridge.

'Surf 'n' turf,' she says. 'I'll make us up a salad, too.'

'Sounds great,' I say. 'Can I do anything to help?'

'No, sit, keep me company,' she says, pointing to a bar stool by the vast black-granite island.

I plonk myself down with my glass of ice-cold beer and watch as she pulls out tub after tub of freshly-prepared salads from the American-style fridge – pasta salad, wild rice salad, green salads and more. She lifts down several glass bowls from a cupboard and spoons out the contents of the tubs. The salads must have all been prepared that day, and I'll bet it wasn't Darcy who made them. Not that I'm criticising. If I had the money, I'd love to have my fridge stocked with delicious, healthy food.

I sip my beer and enjoy the buzz. I'm glad we came. This is the perfect end to a lovely day. 'It's so nice of you to invite us over this evening,' I say.

'Psht.' Darcy waves away my comment with a smile. 'I've got a feeling we're going to be great friends. And look,' – she points outside at Jared and Mike who are chatting away like they've known each other forever – 'our husbands are getting on like a house on fire, and our sons are in heaven.'

'I can't believe Joe has found such a good friend already,' I say.

'He's a lovely boy,' Darcy says. 'We had great fun during the sleepover the other night. I'll just take the steaks outside to Mike.' She picks up the platter. I stand and take it off her.

'I'll go.'

'Thanks,' she says with a warm smile.

I walk out onto the deck, enjoying the glow of the sinking sun on my face and arms. They stop talking and turn to me. Mike's wearing a navy striped apron, and he smiles as I hand him the heaped platter of meat and fish.

'Thanks, Louisa. I think the barby should be hot enough now.'

'Mike's been telling me about the office buildings he's developing in Poole,' Jared says.

'Not talking business are you, boys?' Darcy brings out the covered salads and places them on the table.

'Just making conversation,' Mike says. 'Jared's in advertising. Maybe he could help us with our latest project?'

'Sounds good,' Darcy replies.

'I'm actually thinking about setting up my own agency,' Jared says.

My relaxed mood disappears at his words. He shouldn't be talking about this to other people. Not until we've discussed it properly between us.

'It's still just an idea,' I say. 'Nothing definite.'

Darcy nips back inside and returns with our drinks. I take my beer from her gratefully and gulp down the chilled alcohol. A sudden gust of wind lifts a pile of napkins from the table, scattering them across the deck. I bend down to gather them up.

'You can recommend Jared to some of your clients,' Darcy says to Mike. 'Mike knows everyone who's anyone. If you're setting up a new business, Mike can open a lot of doors.'

I dump the napkins back on the table and watch in dismay as my husband's eyes come alive with the numerous possibilities opening up before him. This is just the green light he needs to go steaming ahead with his plan.

'Yeah, sure,' Mike says, picking up the tongs and transferring the steaks onto the grill. 'I can think of at least a dozen companies who aren't happy with their current ad campaigns.' He turns to Jared. 'Question is – are you any good?' He smiles at my husband but there's an edge to it. He's assessing Jared, waiting for his answer.

I wonder how serious Darcy and Mike are about actually putting Jared in touch with potential clients. Maybe they genuinely do want to help, or perhaps they're simply making conversation. I guess Darcy's words could sound like bragging, but I'm betting they really do know the right people. Maybe their contacts could give us the security we need.

Jared reels off a list of accounts he's successfully pitched for – all prestigious household names. He tells Mike about the awards he's won, and about the calibre of people who'll be working for him.

Mike nods, his mouth quirking upwards. Won over by my husband's enthusiasm and credentials, he claps Jared on the back. 'We'll have a meeting. Call me next week.'

Thankfully, no more business is discussed, and we spend the rest of the evening enjoying the perfect food and the perfect sunset. Joe is excitable and funny. Jared is witty and charming. And I am quiet. Happy that my boys are happy, yet unable to quell the bubbling anxiousness in my stomach. Hoping I'll feel calmer by morning.

CHAPTER FIVE

Winter 1988

Staring at the gross hairs stuck in the carpet took her mind off her sore head. Nicole was sure other carpets didn't look like this. Well, not the ones at school anyway. When they had reading time with Mrs Molesy, they all sat on the blue classroom carpet. It smelled warm and kind of burnt, but it was clean. Not like at home. The carpet at home never got cleaned. It was sticky and smelled of beer and wee.

As she gazed down at the tangled-hair carpet in her and Callum's bedroom, she tried not to wince or cry out. That only made Mummy angry. The hairbrush had caught a knot, and as Mummy yanked the hairbrush down, a bolt of pain flashed across Nicole's scalp with such intensity, she couldn't help gasping.

'If you kept still, it wouldn't hurt, you silly cow.' Mummy tugged the brush through again. The knot had thinned but it was still enough to send splinters of pain firing across Nicole's head.

Once, Nicole had suggested that she might now be old enough to brush her own hair. That had earned her a hard slap across the face. Mummy had said she was a selfish bitch. That it was the one thing she liked to do – to brush her daughter's hair. Then, Mummy had grabbed Nicole by her hair, dragged her across the room and shoved her hard against the wall. Nicole had kept her mouth shut after that. She could put up with a bit of hair brushing if it kept Mummy happy.

A cry from the lounge made Nicole's stomach fall away. It was Callum. He still didn't understand about Mummy, about how important it was not to cry or make a fuss.

'What the fuck does that little shit want now?' The hairbrush stilled.

'Want me to go and see?' Nicole asked, a tremor in her voice.

Mummy gave a last vicious yank of the brush and then threw it on the floor. 'Go on, then. Piss off. You can both go out. I've had enough of you two today. You do my fuckin' head in. I don't know why I bother. Your hair still looks like a bog brush. You must get it from your useless twat of a dad. His mum had shitty hair, too.'

Nicole kept her eyes down, slid off the bed and crept into the lounge. Callum was sitting on the floor crying and stabbing at the buttons of the remote control. He'd somehow accidentally switched channels and couldn't get his programme back.

'You made her cross, Cal, you stupid idiot,' she hissed.

'We have to go out in the car now.'

'Goin' in the car, Nic?' Callum's tear-streaked face brightened.

'Yes,' she whispered, a scowl tugging down the corners of her mouth. 'You made Mummy angry again. It's your fault.'

Nicole grabbed his pudgy hand and dragged him over to the sliding doors which opened out onto a tiny balcony overlooking the main road. Only six of the flats had balconies. There was just enough room for a folding chair and also for Callum's big plastic ride-in car that Daddy had brought home one day last year. He'd got it from the dump where someone had chucked it out. The yellow and red plastic was a bit faded. Apart from that it was okay. It stayed out on the balcony. It would've been great if he could pedal it around on the grass, but they weren't allowed. Mummy said she wasn't about to go lugging it down three flights of frigging stairs. It didn't matter. It was somewhere for them to go when Mummy got shouty.

Callum climbed into the driver's seat and took hold of the plastic steering wheel. Nicole closed the sliding doors to the lounge and squeezed herself into the passenger side of the car. The seat was wet and she felt the water seep through her dress, onto the backs of her legs. She was getting so tall now, she had to sit stooped over. Her sixth birthday was coming up, she hoped that didn't mean she was going to grow even taller. What would she do when she couldn't fit in the car any more?

'Where we goin' today, Nic?'

'Going to Disney World, stupid.'

'Yeah! Dinsley Wowuld!'

Nicole scowled, and glanced back into the lounge where her mother had plonked herself on the sofa, beer in one hand, remote in the other. It was cold outside and she wished she'd remembered to bring a jumper. Never mind. At least Mummy had forgotten about brushing her hair.

CHAPTER SIX

2016

I wish I'd taken the car to pick Joe up from school today, but the storm wasn't forecast, and neither was Joe's disappointment. Finally, we burst in through the front door, soaking wet from the rainstorm, with Joe still in tears. The hallway is as gloomy as our moods, and so I flip on the light switch, illuminating my son's tear-streaked face.

Joe and Tyler got into an argument at school earlier today and everyone took Tyler's side. Poor Joe had kept his emotions in check all day, determined not to cry, but as soon as we left the school gates, the whole story came flooding out. In between gulping sobs, he told me what happened. He got to school this morning and excitedly handed out his party invitations, but it turns out Tyler's birthday is on the same day, and Tyler said that everyone would be going to *his* party, not Joe's.

'Let's go upstairs and get changed,' I say, kissing my son's wet cheek. 'We'll get into nice, dry clothes and I'll make you something to eat, okay?'

'I'm not hungry,' Joe sobs. He flings his coat on the floor, kicks off his shoes and stomps upstairs. I go to follow him, then change my mind. No. I'll give him a few minutes alone to calm down. He's had a terrible disappointment and a difficult day. I need to try to make this right. I need to call Darcy.

I shrug off my sodden coat and hang it on the wooden coat stand. My clothes are soaked through, but I'll sort this out before I get changed. I take my phone out of my bag and wince as Joe's bedroom door slams shut. I'm about to bring up Darcy's contact details when I see I have three missed calls – all from Darcy. Good. She obviously wants to sort this out, too. I walk through to the kitchen and return her call. She answers straight away.

'Louisa? Tyler's come home in tears,' she says.

'Joe, too.' I switch on the kitchen light and sit down at the table, sliding a pile of bills away across its crumb-strewn surface.

'Can you believe our boys' birthdays are on the same day?' she says.

'I know. What are we going to do?' I push my dripping wet hair back off my face and rest my chin in my hand.

'Joint party?' she suggests.

'Genius.' I breathe a sigh of relief. 'We're having a football party at the park, followed by pizza. I can print out new invitations and add Tyler's name. Joe can—'

'Hmm,' Darcy interrupts. 'Sounds cute, but we've already

booked out Bournemouth Football Ground. The boys are going to have some coaching, play a game, then have a tour of the grounds and meet the players. I can't really cancel it now.'

'Oh . . . okay. Um—'

'Would you mind if Joe joined in with Tyler's party instead?' she asks.

'Oh. Well, yes. I mean, that would be great.' I'm a little taken aback. I'd already arranged everything for Joe but I suppose it makes sense if she's already booked such a big event. 'How do you want to do it? We can split the costs and—'

'No, no,' she says. 'It's all paid for. We don't need to split it.'

'I couldn't . . .' I can't let Darcy and Mike pay for my son's birthday party. It doesn't seem right. 'I'd have to contribute something.'

'Please,' Darcy says. 'You'd be doing us a huge favour. We obviously can't have separate parties as they both have the same friends. But I'd hate to cancel Tyler's football stadium tour. He's really looking forward to it. Joe would love it, too, wouldn't he?'

'Of course, but—'

'So that settles it,' she says.

'Well, at least let me do the birthday cake and party bags,' I say.

'The party bags are done,' she says. 'Why don't we bring our own cakes – that way, they each get *Happy Birthday* sung to them by their friends.'

I can see what she's saying makes total sense, and yet for her to organise the whole thing . . . it makes me worry that I'm taking advantage. Or – even worse – like I'm a charity case.

'Well,' I say, unsure how else to solve the issue, 'if you're absolutely sure . . .'

'Awesome.'

'So, what about the invitations?' I say. 'Shall I print some out with both their names?'

'No, that's fine. They're already with the printer. I'll give him a call and get him to add Joe's name. Tyler will bring them in later this week and the boys can hand them out together.'

'Okay, great,' I say, relaxing my shoulders. 'I hope Tyler's okay now. Hopefully, they'll make up tomorrow. I better go upstairs and check on Joe. Tell him about the new plans. I'm sure this will cheer him up.'

'Perfect,' Darcy says. 'Oh, and also, would you and Jared like to come out for dinner with us on Thursday night? We have reservations for Shore View. The table's for two, but we know the manager – he'll squeeze in two more for us. Mike has taken a shine to your hubby and wants to talk business.'

I know for a fact that Shore View is booked up until

sometime next year. The prices are extortionate, but Jared would be thrilled at the opportunity to eat there. We can pick something from the menu that's not too expensive. 'That would be wonderful,' I say. 'What time?'

'Table's booked for eight. We could meet there for drinks first, around seven.'

'Let me just see if I can arrange a babysitter, and—'

'Joe can stay at ours,' Darcy says. 'Drop him round beforehand. Marianna's staying on to babysit.'

'That's okay. I'm sure we can find a—'

'Honestly, it's not a problem. He can stay over and then you don't need to worry about it.'

I don't want to say yes, but I can't think of any excuse to give. 'Okay, well if you're sure . . .'

'Absolutely.'

'Tyler will have to come to ours next time,' I offer lamely.

'Great, he'd love to.'

We haven't even known them a week, and they're showering us with friendship and favours. I decide to organise a sitter anyway. I can unmake plans with Darcy for Joe to stay over. I can't take advantage of her hospitality again.

CHAPTER SEVEN

We park across the road from the restaurant and I wait by the car as Jared heads over to the machine to get a ticket. There's a lull in the rain, thank goodness, but a breeze is gusting off the ocean. I pull my jacket closer around me as my silk dress ripples across my body in deep green waves. Guilt pricks at me, at the extravagance and expense of my new outfit. Jared told me I should buy something new to wear and I have to admit it's nice to feel glamorous for once. My shopping spree was worth it for the confidence boost. I promise myself that after tonight, I'll be frugal for the rest of the year.

Jared returns and sticks the ticket on the inside of the car windscreen. I take his arm and totter beside him, unsteady in towering silver heels that give me the height I've always craved. In the end, we couldn't manage to get a babysitter so I dropped Joe at Darcy and Mike's earlier, giving the boys a few hours to play before bed.

'That dress really suits you,' Jared says. 'You look good, Louisa.'

'Thanks. You too.' I smile up at him and he dips his head to kiss me. The scent of his aftershave making me catch my breath. He grins and quickens his pace. I can't keep up in such impractical footwear.

'Slow down!' I cry. 'These shoes . . .'

'Shall I carry you?' He bends as if to scoop me up, and I hit him with my handbag, laughing at his childish behaviour.

We dodge the lingering puddles and come to an undignified stop at the restaurant. It's one of those places with staff on the door. They nod as we go in, ignoring our stifled laughter. We tell the greeter that we're meeting the Lanes and her snooty expression shifts into a smile.

'Follow me, please.'

We do as she says, and she leads us to the bar where Darcy and Mike are seated on stools, chatting to a man in a dark suit.

'This is the guy I was telling you about,' Mike says to the man. Then he turns to us and smiles. 'Louisa, Jared, good to see you again.'

Darcy and Mike get to their feet. Darcy stunning in a pale blue lace dress, her hair piled into an artfully created up-do. We say hello in a flurry of perfumed, alcoholic kisses and handshakes.

'This is Saul Parnell,' Mike says, introducing the man in the suit. 'He owns Shore View plus several other restaurants along the south coast. I've been talking to him about you, Jared.'

'Good to meet you,' Jared says. 'Your place looks amazing.

That view . . .'

We all turn to gaze at the harbour view, the boats illuminated by the restaurant deck lighting, the distant on-shore lights twinkling in the darkness, the moon casting a silvery wash over the water.

'You should see it during the day,' Saul says. 'Come for lunch, Jared. We'll chat. See Molly on the front desk. She'll schedule you in.'

'Great,' Jared says. 'I look forward to it.'

Saul says goodbye and leaves us to our evening. My husband's face is flushed with excitement. Doors are opening for him without him having to do a thing.

I catch Darcy's eye. She's seen me observing my husband. She's noted his transparent excitement, too. I flush.

She winks and grabs my arm. 'You must try one of the margaritas. They're delicious. I'll order you one.'

'Sounds tempting,' I reply with an apologetic dip of my head, 'but I'm driving tonight.'

'Absolutely not! Leave your car and grab a cab later.'

I turn to Jared and he nods with a smile. 'The parking ticket's good until eight tomorrow morning,' he says. 'I'll cycle down in the morning. Pick it up before work.'

'Nonsense,' says Darcy. 'Leave your car keys with reception and I'll make sure one of the staff drops it back.'

'I didn't know they did that here,' Jared replies.

'They don't, but they will for us.' She winks at Jared and

turns to the barman. 'Four margaritas.'

I catch Jared's eye and he shrugs. It's like we've stepped into a parallel universe. One where nothing is impossible.

Several rounds later, we're shown over to a table by the window. I go to sit next to Jared, but Darcy puts her hand on my arm. 'Come sit by me. Give the boys a chance talk.'

I do as she suggests and sit next to her. She's now seated opposite my husband, and I'm opposite Mike.

Thankfully, no one wants a starter so we browse the menu for main courses. The prices are insane. The cheapest thing on there is vegetarian pasta for twenty-five pounds. I'd prefer fish, but the prices are eye-watering. Mike opts for a steak at over fifty quid, and Darcy's having lobster paella. Jared goes for the chicken and I try to ignore the cost and have the salmon, hoping I don't choke on it. We definitely won't be having dessert. And we'll have to eat beans on toast for the rest of the month.

'It's really good of you to let Joe crash Tyler's party,' I say. 'It sounds like it's going to be an amazing day.'

'Yeah,' Jared says. 'Never mind about the kids – *I'm* excited to go.'

We all laugh as the waitress pours champagne.

Mike raises his glass. 'To new friends.'

'New friends,' we chorus, clinking our glasses.

Despite my horror at the expense of the place, the evening is wonderful. The food is superb and the conversation flows so easily, it's like I almost belong in this glamorous place with these beautiful people. Like maybe what Jared said about us living this lifestyle might actually become a reality. I'm not sure I even want that. I'm happy with what we have, I really am. This evening, this place and all its glitter, it's not real. It's not what truly matters.

The main courses are over and everyone else is clamouring for dessert, so – drunk on margaritas and champagne – I give in and order a passion fruit pavlova which melts on the tongue and tastes like manna from the gods. Mike and Jared are deep in conversation and I'm complimenting Darcy on her design blog. 'Honestly, it's beautifully laid out and the articles are brilliant. Informative and really witty.'

'I should hang out with you more often,' she says.

'No, honestly. You could definitely have a career as a writer,' I say.

'You think?'

'I know.'

'Thank you!' She gives my arm a squeeze. 'God, I'm defeated,' she says laying down her spoon, only having touched about a third of her sorbet. 'So how about Jared? Looks like big things ahead for him – new agency and everything. Exciting for the both of you.'

'Nerve-wracking, more like,' I confide.

'How so?'

'He has a great job already. Chucking it all in to set up on his own is quite a gamble.' Saying the words out loud, I feel a lump of emotion in my throat. I really am quite drunk and probably shouldn't be talking about this to Darcy.

'Going for your dream is always a gamble,' she says. 'Jared has a spark. He'll do it, I can tell.'

'I hope you're right.'

'I'm always right,' she deadpans.

There's a pause, and then we break out into uncontrollable laughter. Jared and Mike look up from their conversation, grinning and shaking their heads at our behaviour. I'm not even sure what's so funny, but I can't seem to stop.

'You'll never believe the time,' Mike says. 'It's twelve thirty already.'

'Shut. Up,' Darcy says. 'How the hell can it be twelve thirty? It only feels like ten o'clock.'

'Shall we get the bill?' Mike asks. 'Don't want to be a party pooper but I've got an early meeting tomorrow.'

'We'll get the bill,' Jared says, without looking at me.

I stop laughing. Has my husband just offered to pay for everyone's dinner? We can barely afford our own.

'No, no' Mike says. 'That's okay, we'll split it.'

Thank god for that.

'No, I insist,' Jared says, before I can take Mike up on his offer to go halves. 'Our son is gate crashing Tyler's birthday party,' my husband says. 'The least we can do is buy dinner.'

Joe's original party was going to be a cheap and cheerful affair. I absolutely dread to think what tonight's meal will cost — the steak, lobster, cocktails, champagne. But I can't find a way to get out of it without embarrassing my husband. In fact, it's already a done deal. Darcy and Mike are already thanking Jared.

'That dress is gorgeous, by the way,' Darcy says to me. 'I meant to say earlier how cute you look tonight.'

'Thanks,' I reply, now bitterly regretting its purchase.

* * *

'Four hundred and thirty quid,' I hiss. 'That's just insane.'

We're halfway home and my earlier good mood has evaporated. I've pushed myself up against the cab door as far away from my husband as I can get, my fists clenched, nails digging into my palms. All I can think of is the mounting credit-card debt that Jared believes will one day magically vanish in a puff of smoke.

'I didn't know the bill would be that much,' he says, squeezing my arm, trying to calm me down.

I shrug him off, shaking my head. 'Well, maybe you should have waited to see it, before offering to pay it.'

'Louisa,' he says, 'I thought I was doing the right thing. You know, with them organising that big birthday party for the boys. It seemed only fair to—'

'We could have had twenty kids' birthday parties for the price of this evening's dinner. And I didn't even want a big party for Joe. I wanted a low-key kick about at the park, followed by pizza.'

'That's not my fault,' he says.

'No, but offering to pay the equivalent of half the national debt for dinner at a snooty restaurant is most definitely your fault.'

He scowls, and slides away from me, across to the other side of the cab. I don't want to have an argument, but I'm unable to swallow down my anger. I'm worried about how badly my husband wants to fit in with these people. I should never have agreed to this dinner date. This whole lifestyle is way out of our league and we shouldn't have pretended otherwise.

We sit in hostile silence as the taxi cruises alongside the harbour, the driver wisely choosing not to make conversation. I'm too angry to feel any embarrassment at what the guy must think of us; I'm sure he's heard dozens of couples arguing in his cab before tonight.

I glance to my right. Jared is angled away from me, his dark expression reflected back in the window. My stomach churns and twists. I hate it when we fight, but I don't know how we're going to get past this. He doesn't think he's done anything wrong. He doesn't see the problem. We already have everything we need, yet it never seems to be enough.

'Mike has offered me free office space for a year,' he says, breaking the silence, turning back to face me. 'I wasn't going to say anything to you about it tonight because I know you're not exactly thrilled about me setting up my own agency. That's the real reason I offered to pay for dinner.'

I don't reply. I'm digesting the information.

His eyes brighten. 'Free office space is worth thousands, Louisa. It's nothing compared with a paltry four hundred quid.'

I take a deep breath. 'Yes, Jared. But, at this moment in time, we haven't got four hundred quid. So hypothetical free office space isn't going to help us pay the credit-card bill next month.'

'You don't get it,' he says.

'No,' I reply. 'You're right. I don't.'

This time, the silence continues right up until the taxi driver drops us outside our front door.

My stomach is still churning. I thought it was anxiety and stress about our argument, but a twist of pain grinds in my gut, followed by a wave of nausea that suddenly sweeps up my back and over my scalp. This is more than just anxiety – I think I'm actually going to be sick. I take a deep breath and pray that I'm going to make it inside the house in time. I really don't want to throw up in this man's cab or on the pavement. Jared sorts out the taxi fare – to add to tonight's mounting expenses – while I fumble for the house keys, stagger out of the vehicle, and lurch towards the front door.

Luckily, we have a downstairs loo and I only just make it there in time before being violently sick into the toilet.

I hear the front door bang shut followed by a tap on the loo door.

'Louisa, are you okay?'

As the toilet door opens, I throw up again. My stomach feels as though someone is screwing it up into a ball.

Jared's hand rests on my back. 'Shall I get you some water?'

'Yes please,' I say, before heaving my guts up once more. Salmon and pavlova. Champagne and stomach acid.

He returns moments later with a glass. I take it from him and use the water to rinse my mouth out. Not yet daring to swallow.

'I didn't think you were that drunk,' Jared says.

'I think it's food poisoning,' I gasp.

'Are you sure?'

I nod. I can tell the different between being drunk and eating a piece of dodgy fish. I bite back any further comments. My husband is worried about me. We've argued enough tonight. And besides, I know I'm about to have a horribly uncomfortable night ahead.

* * *

I spent most of last night throwing up, and most of today

lying on the sofa in my dressing gown. I was supposed to be writing my column today, but I can't get myself motivated so I decide to drag some clothes on and go for a short walk around the block – perhaps a change of scenery will inspire me.

Despite the persistent drizzle, this cool, fresh air is exactly what I need. I gulp down lungfuls of the stuff, trying to clear my head and soothe my tender body. Beth will be dropping Joe back home from school in about an hour so I can't be out for too long. The back roads are quiet, just the wind in the trees and the infrequent hiss of a car cruising by on the rain-slick tarmac.

I decide to head to the local park. I'll walk once around the field and then head home again. I try not to think about last night. About the fight I had with Jared. He was so sweet to me while I was throwing up, so I can't stay mad at him.

A woman with two black Labradors strides past me towards the park. She's wearing a sensible raincoat and wellingtons. The field will most likely be a quagmire. I should have worn boots rather than trainers. Never mind. I don't care about a bit of mud.

I push open the park gate and walk in. The concrete path is covered with wet leaves, and extends along one side of the field, but I ignore it and choose instead to walk on the other side, away from the dogs. I want to be alone.

As my feet squelch through the grass, I gaze up at the

trees flanking the park. At the horse chestnuts, oaks and sycamores swaying in the breeze, their soggy leaves swirling down around me, bright against the slate sky. Joe would love it out here in the rain.

Up ahead, someone steps out of the woods. A man. He pauses, scratches his beard, looks right, and then left, in my direction. After a beat, he turns and begins walking purposefully towards me. I stop dead and my skin goes cold.

It's him again.

CHAPTER EIGHT

What should I do? Should I turn and run? Or should I carry on walking like nothing's wrong? What if he means to do me harm? He's walking towards me, but he's not looking at me any more, his head is down, his hands jammed into his pockets. I'm not taking any chances. The woman with the dogs is just a blur on the other side of the field. There's no one else around. And I'm too weak to run or to even attempt to fight anybody off. I spin on my heel and head back the way I came.

I'm tempted to throw a glance over my shoulder, but I daren't. What if he's running after me? What if he's right behind me? My breath is loud and ragged. I can't hear any footsteps other than the thud of my own heavy feet on the muddy field. I reach the park gate and fumble with the latch. Out of the corner of my eye, I see the man is still a way behind me, walking at a steady pace. He doesn't appear to be in pursuit. I push my way through the gate, letting it bang behind me, and continue along the pavement. My knee aches and my poor delicate stomach isn't happy at my hurried pace, but I can't pause to rest. I have to lose that guy.

Could he have followed me? He came out of the woods so

how would he have known I was headed to the park? Or is it all just a crazy coincidence? He could simply be a local guy who I just happen to keep bumping into. I know that's wishful thinking. I've seen him too many times for it be a coincidence. The way he looks at me, and then quickly turns away again. He's not subtle. I can't tell Jared about him – he'll go mental. Probably want to kill the guy. The police? Maybe. Probably. I'll talk to Beth. She'll know what to do.

The roads are getting busier. The school traffic heavy because of the awful weather. Surely he wouldn't try anything on a busy street. I must be quite safe by now. I stop and turn. He's not behind me. Perhaps I was mistaken and it wasn't even him. No. I know it was him. He had the same sandy beard, the same fisherman's hat. I would know that man anywhere.

I slow down and give an involuntary shudder. My legs have turned to jelly. It was a mistake to come out this afternoon. I should have stayed at home on the sofa. My body trembles and a clammy trickle of sweat slides down my back. I need to get home.

I'm so shaken up, it takes three attempts to fit my key in the lock. I'm constantly whipping my head from side to side, checking the man is nowhere in sight. Does he know where I live? Has he been watching the house? Now I really do sound paranoid. I push open the door and stumble into the hallway, slamming the door behind me. I kick off my muddy trainers, hang up my coat and pad into the front room. The heavy clouds have darkened the skies, but I don't switch on the light. Instead, I creep over to the window and swivel the cord to close the venetian blinds. I leave them open just enough to peek through and see what's happening outside on the rain-drenched street.

My heart thumps. A couple of cars go by. A woman with a flowery umbrella strides past the window. I peer up the road, but no one is there. I stare down the road. My heart stops for a millisecond when I see a man in a hat. I exhale. It's not him. This man is older, stooped, walking slowly. I can't see anyone else. No longer drizzling, the rain now falls in sheets. I close the blinds properly and leave the room, turning on the hall light. I should get out of these damp clothes and dry my hair. Beth and Joe will be here soon.

I'm suddenly fighting fatigue. Last night is catching up with me. My empty stomach gurgles, but I dare not eat anything. I tramp up the stairs as a car door slams outside. I pause on the landing. The doorbell rings. I'm still shaking. If that's Beth with Joe, I need to pull myself together. I can't let Joe see me like this. I trudge back down the stairs. For a second, I think that it might be my "stalker" at the door. I needn't have worried – I can hear my sister out there talking to Joe.

I open the door and the wind catches it, slamming it backwards against the wall. Joe hurls himself at me, flinging his skinny arms around my body.

'Is he okay?' I mouth at my sister.

She shakes her head and makes a sad face.

'You coming in?' I ask.

'I won't, thanks. Megan's in the car. How are you? Feeling any better?'

'Much better, thanks.' I want to tell her about the man with the beard, but now isn't the time. She's obviously in a hurry and there's something up with Joe. 'What's happened?' I ask, glancing down at the top of my son's head.

'Something to do with invitations,' she says. 'I'm not sure. He mentioned it and then clammed up.'

I heave a sigh and give Beth a smile. 'Okay, well, thanks so much for picking him up.'

'No probs. Glad you're feeling better.' She leaves the shelter of the porch and dashes back to her car.

I wave to Megan through the car window and blow her a kiss, before closing the front door and peeling Joe off my body. 'How was last night? Did you enjoy your sleepover with Tyler?'

'Mm. I s'pose.'

'Want something to eat?' I ask.

He shrugs.

Things really are serious if even the thought of food won't bring him round. 'Want to tell me what happened today?'

Another shrug.

'Let's take your wet coat off.' I peel off his rucksack and coat and dump them on the hall floor. Then, I take his damp hand and lead him into the kitchen, turning on the light. 'Okay, Mr Joe Bo, I'm going to prepare my special hot chocolate with mini marshmallows. Do you know anyone who might be interested?'

He murmurs something unintelligible.

'Hm? You say something? Know anyone who might enjoy some delicious hot chocolate?'

'Me,' he says in such a sad voice it breaks my heart.

'Okay, so sit yourself down and I'll start making it, okay?'

He nods.

'But first, let's have another hug.'

He walks into my arms and I press his little body to mine, inhaling his damp brown curls.

'I love you, okay,' I murmur. 'And whatever's upset you, we'll fix it.'

He squeezes me tighter and then lets me go. 'Can I have some hot chocolate now?'

'Of course.' I walk over to the fridge and take out the milk. 'So, how was school today?'

'Bad.'

'You want the Batman mug or SpongeBob?'

'SpongeBob.'

'Why was it bad?' I pour the milk into his mug and place it into the microwave, setting the timer.

Joe slides off the chair and runs into the hall.

'Joe!' I call. 'Where are you going?'

He returns seconds later with his rucksack, swings it up onto the table with a bang, unzips it and starts ferreting around inside. I pull up a chair and sit down next to him just as he pulls out a square piece of card. It's a party invitation – *the* party invitation.

I take it out of his hand and stare at it. Tyler's name is emblazoned across the top. Joe's name is nowhere to be seen.

This is getting more and more ridiculous. Did I somehow misunderstand Darcy? Were we supposed to organise our own invitations? I don't think so.

'Are you sad because your name isn't on the invitation?' I ask.

Joe nods. 'Isn't it my party, too?'

'Yes, sweetie. It is your party, too. Don't worry, I'll sort it out for you.' I realise I'm shaking. I don't know how a straightforward kid's party has descended into such a major hassle. I'm going to have to ring Darcy but I really don't feel like it. What am I going to say? It's all going to sound so petty. The microwave pings. I stick the invitation back into Joe's bag and take Joe's drink out of the microwave, testing the temperature with my finger.

'Tell you what,' I say to my son, 'why don't you curl up in the lounge and watch a movie. Take your hot chocolate with you, okay?'

He nods and I bend down to kiss the top of his head, just as the doorbell rings.

'Daddy!' Joe runs out of the kitchen towards the front door, his sadness momentarily forgotten.

I glance up at the kitchen clock. It's too early for Jared to be home, and why would he be ringing the doorbell? Maybe it's Beth again. I follow Joe into the hall where he's now crouched down, peering through the letterbox.

'Who is it?' I ask.

Joe straightens up and turns back to face me. 'Tyler and his mummy,' Joe says, pulling a face.

God, what are they doing here? It must be to do with the invitations. Shit, I feel like crap, I look an absolute mess, and the house is in a state, too – I eye the chipped paintwork, the basket of wet washing at the bottom of the stairs, and notice that two of the bulbs in the ceiling light need replacing. This is just about the worst time for Darcy to show up. I know I need to talk to her but I don't want to do it here and now.

'Are we going to let them in?' Joe asks.

'Of course,' I say brightly. 'Of course we are.' I turn the handle and pull open the front door.

'Louisa!' Darcy steps into the hallway in a cloud of Chanel and throws her arms around me, kissing both cheeks. Her hair is pulled back into a catwalk ponytail, and she's wearing a stylish cream mac with a silk scarf at her throat.

Tyler sidles around us and stands next to Joe, neither boy saying a word.

'Hi,' I say, dragging my fingers through lank curls in an attempt to magically transform my dishevelled state. 'Sorry, I look such a mess, I haven't been feeling too good today.'

'I heard,' Darcy replies. 'That's why I'm here. I met Beth in the playground and she said you had food poisoning! Poor you. Was it from the restaurant last night? If it is, I shall go in there today and give them a piece of my mind.'

'I think it was the salmon but please don't worry. These things happen.' My stomach gurgles embarrassingly. Darcy is too polite to comment. 'Come into the kitchen,' I say. 'Can I make you some tea or coffee?' I turn to my son: 'Joe, why don't you take Tyler upstairs to your room?'

Joe shakes his head and stands beside me, away from his friend.

Tyler scowls.

'What's going on with you two?' Darcy asks.

Tyler shrugs while Joe looks down at the floor.

'TV?' I ask the boys.

Joe nods.

'Okay, go and put a film on.'

Joe slouches into the lounge and I gesture to Tyler to follow him. Darcy raises her eyebrows and I tilt my head in the direction of the kitchen. She walks through with me.

'I brought you round some goodies to cheer you up,' she

says, handing me a large gift bag.

I'm so taken aback by her kindness that I stand there in the kitchen doorway, my mouth hanging open.

'Just some little things,' she says. 'Magazines, chick-flicks, soup, crackers and Alka Seltzer, ha ha.'

'Thank you so much. That's really thoughtful,' I say as a tear escapes down my cheek.

'Hey, are you okay?' she asks.

I swipe at my tear, but more follow. 'God, I'm so sorry.'

She gives me a hug, then stands back, points to a chair in the kitchen and says, 'sit.'

I do as she asks.

'You're exhausted. I'm going to make you some noodle soup. It'll be gentle on your stomach.'

'No, no, that's okay,' I protest, feeling utterly wretched and useless.

'Nonsense,' she says. She removes her coat and hangs it on the back of a chair, lays her handbag on the table, plucks the gift bag out of my hand and delves inside, pulling out a slim packet of soup. 'I'd rather make it fresh, but actually, these ready-made things are pretty good.'

I'm in too much of a state to protest further. Darcy hands me a tissue from her handbag and I wipe my eyes and blow my nose. 'I'm so sorry for crying all over you,' I say. 'It's been a crappy day.'

'Stop apologising. Everyone's entitled to have a bad day

every once in a while. I know I do.'

'And to top it all off,' I say, 'I still haven't written next week's column. The last thing I feel like doing is writing at the moment. My brain is like mush.'

'Poor you,' Darcy says, tilting her head. 'Just a thought . . . if you want, I can have a go at writing it for you.'

'What? My column?'

'Yeah, sure. Of course, I'd run the finished thing by you first, but I'm pretty sure I know your tone of voice. I can imitate your style if you want . . .'

I can't believe her generosity. 'Thanks so much for the offer. I can't expect you to—'

'It would be my pleasure,' she says.

I'm tempted, yet it feels like I'd be taking advantage of her good nature.

'Before you say no,' she continues, 'it would be *you* doing *me* the favour, not the other way around. You know how much I want to be a writer. This would be a great opportunity for me.'

'Really?'

She nods.

'Oh my God,' I say. 'That would be amazing. I've been stressing about it all day. Only . . . it would have to be done by Monday. Are you able to—'

'Not a problem.' She smiles, and I feel a weight lift off my shoulders.

'And of course I'll pay you for the week,' I add.

'Not necessary,' she says. 'I'll be thrilled enough to see my work in the paper.'

'But—'

'I don't want payment, Louisa,' she says.

'Thank you.'

'Cute kitchen, by the way,' she adds, looking around at the mess.

I don't for one minute believe she means it – we're more shabby than chic. I thank her anyway.

'Pans?' she asks.

I point to a cupboard. 'Thank you,' I say again.

She busies herself with a saucepan, some water and the packet of soup. I think I misjudged Darcy – she really does know her way around a kitchen.

'Any idea why Joe and Tyler are acting funny around each other today?' she asks.

My eyes rest on the party invitation sticking out the top of Joe's rucksack. Should I tell her about it? I feel bad mentioning it while she's being so nice, yet I owe it to Joe to say something. I flex my fingers and take a deep breath. 'I think it's something to do with the birthday invitations.'

Darcy plops a lid on top of the pan and turns to face me, her brow creased in concern. 'Didn't Joe like them? Tyler and I thought they were pretty fun.'

'No, no,' I say, swallowing air. 'Nothing like that. They

look amazing. It's just . . . they don't have Joe's name on.' I pluck the invitation from Joe's bag and hand it to her.

She takes the colourful card in her French-manicured hand and frowns as she examines it. 'Oh my goodness!' she cries. 'What on earth must you think of me? I did tell the printer to add Joe's name, I swear to you. It was all such a rush when the invitations arrived that I didn't think to check . . . Gosh, you must think I'm a terrible person.'

'Of course not,' I say. 'I knew it must be a mistake. It's just . . . now Joe thinks—'

'He must feel awful!' Darcy interrupts. 'Don't worry. I'll get them reprinted.'

'No, no,' I say. 'You can't do that. That's too much hassle and expense. Anyway, they've already gone out to everybody now.'

'Okay,' Darcy replies, pulling up a chair and sitting down. 'What I'll do, is email everyone and tell them about the mistake. That way, they'll know it's a joint birthday, okay?'

'Thank you. I'll tell Joe. He'll be so relieved.'

'Of course,' Darcy says. 'It's the least I can do after I made you abandon your own party and join Tyler's.'

I'm so glad she understands how Joe feels. I knew she would. The aroma of the noodle soup makes my stomach growl once more. Suddenly, I'm feeling much better about everything, and I realise I haven't thought about my stalker once since Darcy got here. Maybe that, like everything else, isn't as sinister as I'm making out. I need to calm down and not worry so much about things. I have a loving husband, a gorgeous son, and a great new friend. Darcy smiles and I smile back. I don't even know why I was in such a state earlier.

'I don't suppose . . .' Darcy starts to say something, then shakes her head. 'No, don't worry.'

'What?' I ask.

'No, honestly, it doesn't matter.'

I wonder what she was going to ask me but I don't press it, she's obviously changed her mind. 'That soup smells amazing, by the way,' I say.

'Should be ready in about five minutes. I'll dish it up and then we'll be off. Let you get some rest.'

'You're welcome to stay for soup,' I say. 'Seeing as how you made it.'

'No, it's fine. I'll eat later with Mike when he gets home.'

I smile. 'Thank you so much, again. It was lovely of you to come over and check up on me.'

'My pleasure.' She gazes down at the scarred surface of the kitchen table, drumming her nails. 'I wonder,' she says, looking up again. 'Do you think . . . Would it be possible to have my name on the column next week? Maybe as a guest writer or something?'

I'm a little taken aback by her request. And I'm not entirely sure how something like that would fly with

Kathryn, my editor.

'Is that cheeky?' Darcy asks. 'It's just . . . I've always wanted to see my name in print in a national newspaper. Kind of an ambition of mine.'

'Well, I could certainly ask my editor,' I say. 'I'm sure it would be fine as a one-off.'

'Awesome! I would love that. Thank you, Louisa. You're a sweetheart. Now let me dish you up some of this soup. Where do you keep your bowls?'

I point to the cupboard where we keep the crockery and I notice Joe's forgotten mug of hot chocolate sitting next to the microwave. It will be cold and congealed by now. I'll have to throw it out.

CHAPTER NINE

'This place is unbelievable,' I say, taking in the high ceilings, exposed brick walls and polished oak floors. It's a dull day outside, yet swathes of light flood in through floor-to-ceiling windows.

'I know, right.' Jared rubs his hands up and down the back of his head and turns to me, his eyes gleaming with excitement. 'I never expected anything like this.'

'To be on the quay is amazing enough, but to be in such a beautiful building is—'

'Yeah,' he says, taking both my hands and squeezing them. 'I thought I might be in a grotty building on the outskirts of town – maybe on a depressing industrial estate. I definitely wasn't expecting a newly refurbed warehouse with views over Poole Quay.'

After getting a decent business loan from the bank, Jared finally handed in his notice at work. His boss asked him to leave the company immediately but Jared didn't mind. He's already been head-hunting staff and building his client list over the past few weeks, with the help of Mike and Darcy.

Jared got the keys from Mike to check out his potential

new offices today, so now we're here to inspect the space before he signs the contract. I can't help being swept up by my husband's enthusiasm. It looks like he's going to make a real success of this. I just wish the butterflies in my stomach would settle down.

'What do you think of these trestles?' he asks, running a hand over one of the chunky wooden tables. 'Would they be okay to work on? Or should I get proper desks?'

'I think they look cool. Not sure how practical they'd be, though.'

'I can keep them for now and then replace them if they don't work out,' Jared says. 'I don't know how I'm going to get any work done with that view.'

We gaze down at the narrow quayside, at the boats and the gulls and the blue-green water.

'So, he's actually letting you have this place free for a year?' I ask.

'That's what he says.'

'What will the rent be after that?'

'I don't know,' Jared replies. 'We can negotiate that nearer the time, I suppose.'

I turn away from the view to face my husband. This is exactly the kind of thing I was afraid of.

'What?' he says, catching my troubled expression.

'You can't wait until "nearer the time" to sort out the rent,' I say. 'You have to sort that out now, before you move in.'

Jared's face darkens. 'Don't spoil it for me, Lou. For once, can't you just enjoy the feeling that everything is working out.'

'I'm not spoiling it. I am enjoying it. But you don't want a nasty shock in a year's time when Mike slaps you with a huge invoice.'

'Mike's not like that. We get on. He's going to help me make a success of this. I know he won't shaft me.'

I dig my nails into the palm of my hand, attempting to stifle my rising temper. 'Chances are, it will be fine. But surely it would be better to know what kind of costs you're looking at. It'll help you to plan. And you need to know how long you'll be tied into the lease. What did you allocate for rent in the business plan? The one you gave to the bank.'

'I don't know. I can't remember off the top of my head.'

I grit my teeth.

'Don't look at me like that, Louisa.'

'I'm just worried, that's all. You need to sort out the details.' I turn away and walk across the empty space, the clop of my boots echoing into the exposed rafters. If I carry on this conversation, we'll end up having a massive row.

'Look,' he calls after me. 'I'll discuss it with Mike when we get home, okay?'

I stop and turn, my gaze drawn by dust motes floating in a shaft of light. 'Okay,' I reply.

'Now,' he says, his mouth twisting into a half smile, 'can we stop with the doom and gloom and go and get some lunch? I'm bloody starving.'

I take a deep breath and nod. 'Fish and chips?'

'Now you're talking,' he says.

We head back down the stairs and out into the chill October air. Jared takes my hand and we walk into the wind towards the end of the quay where a cluster of cafés and restaurants huddle together under striped awnings.

Ten minutes later, we're strolling back along the quay with our warm packets of cod and chips. I open mine up, break off a piece of the crispy fish and pop it into my mouth.

'I've always fancied going fishing,' Jared says. 'Maybe we could get a boat.' He turns to look at me.

I stop walking and raise an eyebrow.

'Not now, obviously,' he adds hastily. 'In a year or two when everything's sorted with the agency. We could moor it here. How cool would that be?'

'I could meet you after work each night with a bottle of champagne and a picnic hamper,' I say, laughing. 'Dressed in all my finery.'

'Mock all you like, woman,' Jared says, tweaking my nose. 'It could be a reality sooner than you think.'

'Next year, boats and champagne, today we'll have to settle for takeaway food on a wooden bench.'

'What about something like that?' He points to a sleek,

white motor yacht moored on the other side of the quay.

'It's a bit flashy.' I pop another chip into my mouth.

'Nothing wrong with flashy,' Jared says with a grin. 'Do you like it, though?'

'Yeah, of course. What's not to like. God, this food really is delish, just what you need on a chilly day.'

'This time next year, we'll . . . Hey!'

A seagull has just swooped down and swiped a chip straight out of my husband's fingers.

'Cheeky little . . .'

I break down into hysterical laughter at the outraged expression on Jared's face. But I soon stop laughing when more gulls begin dive-bombing us for our lunch. I squeal as we run along Poole Quay, flapping our arms in an attempt to scare the squawking birds away. A couple of amused pedestrians glance our way. Apart from them, it's quiet here today. We turn down a cobbled side street, tears streaming down our faces, panting with laughter. Thankfully, the gulls don't follow us and we spy a wooden bench on which to sit and polish off our lunch.

'I still can't believe how gorgeous your new offices are,' I say, breaking off another piece of fish.

'And I can't believe Mike actually came good with his offer,' Jared says. 'Sending Joe to that school has turned out to be one of the best moves we ever made.'

'It wasn't a "move", Jared,' I say, frowning. 'We did it to

help Joe with his reading.'

'You know what I mean, Lou. If we hadn't sent him there, we'd never have met Mike, and my dream of owning my own agency would probably have stayed a dream . . . for a hell of a lot longer, anyway.'

I can't disagree with him. Joe's new school is teeming with wealthy and influential parents. I'm not so keen on that aspect. But the teaching is superb, and I guess it's also helped Jared out. There's no denying Mike has opened doors for my husband.

We sit in silence for a few minutes more, lost in our thoughts, enjoying our lunch.

'I'm stuffed,' I finally say, licking the salt off my fingertips. 'If I eat another mouthful I'll explode.'

'Here, give me that.' Jared takes the fish and chip wrapper from my lap and strolls down the road a little way to dump our rubbish in the bin. I watch him walk. Even from behind he appears confident – his broad shoulders upright, his stride smooth and even. He gives a little leap to the side, clipping his feet together, making me laugh out loud. He screws the wrappers into a ball and shoots it into the rubbish bin. Then, he turns and rubs his knuckles on his jumper, blowing on them to show off his skill. I shake my head at my husband's antics, then I freeze.

A man just crossed the alley behind him. A man with a beard, in a fisherman's hat. He was too far away for me to be absolutely sure, but it looked just like my stalker. Should I run after him to check? I'm with Jared now, so we could go together, confront him. But do I want to ruin our day? Do I want to tell Jared that this man is stalking me? Jared's response will be to punch first, ask questions later. It will be a nightmare. And what if I'm wrong? The man has never approached me. He wasn't even looking my way today. It probably wasn't even him. Anyway, this is Poole Quay – there must be plenty of bearded fishermen wearing hats.

'Okay?' Jared is back, standing right in front of me.

I push the man from my thoughts. 'Yep,' I reply, swallowing my unease. 'I definitely ate too much, though.'

He pulls me to my feet. 'Let's go home.'

I wrap my arms around my husband and give him a salty kiss. Then, we amble back to the car while I try to push all unsettling thoughts of that man from my head.

* * *

Back home, Jared makes us a cup of tea, while I sit at the kitchen table checking emails on my laptop.

My stomach is teeming with nerves – Jared's new offices, the man who may or may not be following me. It's like I'm standing on the end of a moving seesaw trying to get to the middle where things are more stable.

I see a message from Kathryn, my editor. She's been a little off with me these past few weeks. Usually, after I submit my work, she emails me back with glowing praise, pointing out the bits she found funny and occasionally adding suggestions. This month, she's only replied with a simple *Thank you*. Or *Great, thanks*. It's been bugging me, making me insecure about my work. But she hasn't said anything specifically negative, and I haven't plucked up the courage to ask if anything's wrong.

I open the email and read it, the words on the screen hitting me like blows to the stomach. A lump forms in my throat and tears prick my eyes as Jared comes and sits opposite me.

'Louisa?' he says, putting the mugs on the table. 'What's wrong?'

'Kathryn's cancelled my column.'

'Oh no. Why? Surely it's a mistake.'

'She says . . .' I sniff and wipe the tears away with my sleeve. 'She says: *we've loved "Louisa's Life's a Beach", but feel our readership is now looking for something fresh.* Fucking great. So why didn't she ask me if I could try something different? I wouldn't have minded writing something else.'

Jared rushes round to where I'm sitting. He crouches down and wraps his arms around me, kissing the side of my head. 'I'm so sorry. That sucks. Can you email her back, ask if they'll reconsider, or if you can write something else for them?'

'I suppose. But it'll be humiliating. Her email is pretty definite. She's thanked me for the work I've done over the years and wished me good luck for the future. Look.' I swivel my laptop around so Jared can read the rest of the email.

'Shit,' he says. 'Well, okay, fuck 'em. You'll get another writing gig. Something better.'

'Hmm,' I reply, unconvinced. I know how unlikely that is. I was lucky to have held onto this one for as long as I did. I have a horrible feeling this has something to do with the time I let Darcy write for me. I think it pissed Kathryn off. I don't blame her really. I guess I assumed that because I've been writing the column for over three years, she wouldn't mind one guest spot. I was obviously wrong. I thought what Darcy had written was sharp and brilliant – hilarious actually – but maybe the readers hadn't liked it for whatever reason.

'We're going to miss my pay check, too,' I say gloomily. 'Especially now, with you starting your new business and everything.'

'Don't worry about the money,' Jared says. 'We'll be loaded soon.'

I try not to roll my eyes at his words. Hopefully, this time, it really could be more than blind optimism talking.

'Why don't you get back to writing your novel?' he says. 'You've been saying you want to finish it for years. Now you'll have more time.'

'I suppose I could try,' I say. 'I'll need to be more disciplined and write a bit every day, or it'll never get done.'

'So, do it,' he says.

My disappointment lifts a little. Jared's right. I should look at this as an opportunity. And yet I still feel flat. Like someone has steamrollered over my life. Like I've failed somehow, and there's nothing new left out there for me.

CHAPTER TEN

Summer 1990

Nicole's mum lurched into the lounge where Nicole and Callum were sprawled on the carpet watching some boring kids' science programme. It was the only thing on telly apart from sport or the news.

'Go down the shops and get me some crisps,' Mum said, holding out a crumpled five-pound note. 'I got no change so you'll have to take this. And take your brother with you.'

Nicole's stomach rumbled. Did she dare ask Mum if they could get something to eat? There was no food left in the house. Not even any tins of beans or packets of cereal. She stood up and nudged Callum with her toe. He got to his feet, eyes still glued to the TV screen.

'Shall I get us some food?' she asked. 'For tea?'

Mum's eyes narrowed. Nicole's stomach clenched, waiting to see if the question had angered her.

'Get a tin of something,' Mum said. 'Mind it doesn't cost more than 50p, and get some milk and bread 'n' all.'

Nicole relaxed her shoulders and edged over to take the money. Her thumb and forefingers grasped the note, but her mum still held it tight. 'I want change,' she snapped, her gin breath hot and bitter.

Nicole nodded quickly and Mum released the five-pound note. Nicole stuffed the cash into the pocket of her school cardigan, and she and Callum scuttled out of the flat, clattering down the concrete stairs and out into the sunny afternoon.

'We having spaghetti hoops, Nic?' Callum asked.

'Yeah.'

Callum grinned and did a skid on his knees.

'You get a hole in your trousers and Mum will skin your backside.'

Callum got up off the dusty pavement and wiped at the front of his school uniform.

'No hole – look.'

'Yeah, whatever.'

As they walked the half mile to the local Kwik Save, Nicole came up with a plan. She was smiling when they reached the store. Callum made to go inside but she dragged him back by his shirt.

'Wait, dipshit.'

'What?'

'Come over here a minute.' Nicole walked over to a clump of bushes at the edge of the supermarket car park and sat on the wall, kicking at the bricks with the heels of her shoes. Callum climbed up beside her. She took the fiver out of her pocket. Then, she shrugged off her cardigan and held the garment out to her brother. 'Put that on.'

'I ain't wearing that. It's girls' clothes.'

'Put it on or I'll give you a Chinese burn.'

Callum stuck his bottom lip out but did as she asked.

'Right,' she said. 'I'm gonna go in and buy the milk and stuff. You're gonna go in and stick a tin of spaghetti hoops a packet of crisps, and two bars of chocolate inside your cardigan and sneak back out. Meet me up the road by the park in ten minutes.'

'Why do *I* have to nick it? Why can't you?'

'Because I'm seven already, stupid. If I get caught, I'll go to jail. You're only five – you'll only have to go to juvy.'

'I don't wanna go to jooby.' Callum's eyes filled with hot tears.

'Then don't get caught,' Nicole said.

'Why we gotta steal, anyway? Mum gave us five quid.'

'If we nick it, we can keep some of the cash for ourselves, stupid.' Nicole slid off the wall. 'We'll go in separately. I'll go in first, you count to ten slowly then you go and get the stuff. Don't forget – spaghetti hoops, crisps and chocolate, right? That's three things.'

Callum nodded, unshed tears still brightening his eyes.

'And don't cock it up,' she added.

Nicole swaggered into the store, dizzy with the thought of free chocolate and cash. She made her way to the bakery aisle and soon located the store's own-brand white bread. She snatched a loaf off the shelf and made her way to the chiller cabinets and stared at the milk. Should she get a two-pint carton or a one-pint carton? She wasn't sure, and she didn't want to get in trouble for buying the wrong one. She opted for the two pints, gripping the condensation-covered handle in her free hand. She should've got a basket. Never mind.

Nicole marched over to the checkout, swinging the bread in one hand and the milk in the other. Callum had better not get caught. She'd kill him if he messed this up. An old woman smiled at her. Nicole was just about to stick the Vs up at the nosy old bag, but then she thought it wouldn't do any good to draw attention to herself – not with Callum nicking stuff – so she forced herself to smile back, dumping the milk and bread on the conveyor belt.

The queue wasn't too long. There was a man who'd almost finished packing his groceries, and there was a woman in front of her – the one who'd smiled at her a minute ago. The woman was chatting to the cashier about her grandchildren in Australia. Nicole huffed, keeping an eye on the main entrance, and pushing a ratty lock of hair out of her eyes. A security guard was standing by the doors, next to the newspaper stand. Why hadn't she noticed him before? If Cal walked out now, while that guard was there, he'd definitely get caught. What should she do?

Her hands grew clammy and her heart sped up. Mum would give them such a bollocking if they got caught stealing. And she'd know that it had been Nicole's idea. She'd know Callum had been put up to it. Nicole didn't even want to think about what Mum would do to her. She'd rather be sent to jail.

The old woman was still in front of her, yapping on to the cashier about her grandchildren. Nicole glanced around, made sure no one was looking and swiped a packet of sweets from the stand next to her. She dropped the packet into the old woman's open handbag.

Nicole turned her attention to the entrance doors. Where was Callum? Had he already finished and left the store? She didn't think so. It would take him a while to work out where to find each item. He'd probably be ages trying to find everything. It would be okay. She'd be able to distract the guard if she needed to.

The man in front had paid and was leaving. Now it was the old woman's turn. The scanner beeped as her groceries made their way along the conveyor belt and into the cashier's hands. The woman didn't stop talking. The cashier nodded and smiled, not really taking any notice. The guard by the door looked bored.

Finally, the woman's shopping was bagged up and she moved away from the checkout, towards the exit. Just at that moment, Nicole saw Callum head for the doors. Stupid bugger was clutching at the cardigan like he had a live kitten in there.

'Oi!' Nicole shouted across the store. Her gaze locked on the guard. 'That woman nicked something!' she cried.

Jolted from his boredom, the guard glanced from Nicole to where she was pointing at the old woman pushing her loaded trolley. Out the corner of her eye, Nicole saw her brother sidle past the guard and out to freedom. She smirked.

'What are you talking about, love,' the cashier said to Nicole. 'That lady just paid for her shopping.'

'Saw her stick a packet of Chewitts in her handbag without paying,' Nicole said.

The cashier pursed her lips. 'Dave,' she called out to the guard, 'Check her handbag – packet of Chewitts.'

Everyone was staring at the woman now, who was standing still, her mouth hanging open as the guard removed the offending sweets from her handbag. Nicole wanted to laugh at the old cow's expression.

'Can I pay for these?' Nicole said sweetly to the cashier. 'My mum'll kill me if I'm late back.'

'Course you can, sweetheart. And well done for spotting that thief. Honestly, she doesn't look like she's short of a few quid. What's she want to go and steal a packet of sweets for?'

Nicole shrugged and handed over the five-pound note. She put the bread and milk into a carrier bag and clutched her change. She'd sort out how much she could take out of the change once they were far enough away from the shop.

The woman was talking to the guard now, her face grey and creased . . . scared. She kept staring over at Nicole, a confused expression on her face. Nicole glanced down at the lino floor. She didn't like the look of things. She'd be happy when she was out of here.

Nicole walked past the woman and the guard, head down. Once she made it through the doors and out past the rows of shopping trolleys in the car park, she sprinted in the direction of home, making out the shape of her brother up ahead. He'd already reached the park by the look of things.

The shopping bag swung back and forth as she ran, bashing at her leg.

'I did it, Nic!' Callum's eyes shone as she reached him. 'I got the tin of spaghetti and Mum's crisps and I got us a couple of Mars bars.'

Nicole yanked him around the corner so they wouldn't be seen from the main road. She didn't trust that old bag back there not to wheedle her way out of things. Then, they might think Nicole had done something wrong. They might come after her. 'Stick that lot in here,' she said to her brother, opening up her carrier bag and waiting while he tipped his haul in with the bread and milk. 'We better eat the chocolate before we get home,' she said, suddenly not so hungry any more. 'And if you tell Mum we nicked stuff, I'll feed you rat poison and lock you in the wardrobe.'

Callum's eyes grew wide. 'I ain't a grass, Nic.'

'Better not be.'

Callum dug his hand into the carrier bag and pulled out one of the Mars bars, tearing off the wrapper. Nicole did the same. They leant against the side wall of someone's house while they crammed chocolate into their mouths.

'Look what we've got here.' A figure appeared around the corner and his hands shot out grabbing each of them by their school shirt collars. 'Got a receipt for that chocolate have you?'

It was the security guard, and he had them firmly in his grip. Nicole kicked him in the shin, but the man just laughed and held her further away from his body. 'You two can come back with me to the shop and wait while we call your parents. And you've got an apology to give to that lady you accused of stealing.'

'You can't prove anything,' Nicole cried through a mouthful of chocolate. 'We didn't do anything wrong.'

'We'll check the security cameras, shall we?' the man said. 'Then we'll see. Come on, back to the store.'

Nicole writhed and kicked, but the man had a firm grip on them. She wasn't going to get out of it. She pictured her mum's face when she got the news. A cold feeling settled in Nicole's stomach. Why had she let herself get caught? Next time, she'd have to be much smarter.

CHAPTER ELEVEN

2016

Flora's – a rustic artisan bakery-*slash*-café – is set on the corner of a small, exclusive row of cafés and restaurants just a short walk from school. Along with the various eateries, there's a designer florist, a winery, a deli and an overpriced gift shop. The obligatory Tesco Express looks somewhat out of place here.

I push open the door to *Flora's* and, as I weave my way past the other tables, I've already spotted various groups of yummy mummies and gym bunnies from our school. This must be the local hangout for ladies who lunch, workout and do coffee. Does that description apply to *me* now?

I spy Darcy seated at a table in the corner. Two other women stand chatting with her, laughing hysterically about something. They give me pursed-lipped, squinty-eyed smiles when I arrive. In my head, I dub them *the poison twins*. Darcy stands and introduces us and I treat them to my most charming smile, but I can tell I don't quite come up to scratch. My clothes aren't as well tailored, my handbag isn't genuine leather with the right name tag, my nails are bare of varnish and my curls are too . . . natural. I'm glad Darcy isn't snooty. Maybe it's the American influence – I'm sure they don't have such a blatant snobbism going on in the States.

The poison twins finally move away in a flurry of laughter and air kisses.

'Can I get you a coffee?' I ask Darcy.

'Come, sit. They'll take our order at the table.'

'Okay, great, I wasn't sure if it was waitress service or if you had to go up and . . .' I'm rambling like an idiot so I shut up, slide in opposite Darcy and dump my bag on the floor. We're meeting to finalise the details of the boys' party on Sunday. Not that there's that much to sort out – it all seems to be pretty much taken care of by Darcy.

She lays her small cream leather messenger bag on the table and slides out a notebook and jewel-encrusted silver pen. I curse myself for not being quite that organised, but I'm sure I'll be able to remember everything that's needed.

'Hi, Flora, I'll have a decaf Americano, please,' Darcy says.

I turn my head to see a stunning waitress standing behind me. She's tall and slim with coffee coloured skin and black, spiral corkscrew curls which tumble over her shoulders, 'Oh,' I say, momentarily distracted by her beauty. 'Hi. A double-shot cappuccino, please.'

'Flora, this is Louisa,' Darcy introduces us. 'Louisa, this is Flora's place – she set it up two years ago – it's won awards and everything.'

'You're embarrassing me now,' Flora says, dimpling.

'You have to try her pastries,' Darcy says. 'Can you bring us a plate, sweetie?'

'Sure,' Flora replies before sashaying away.

'So,' I say, turning back to Darcy. 'How are you? How're Mike and Tyler?'

'Everything's good,' she says. 'Tyler can't wait until Sunday.'

'Nor can Joe. It's like he has ants in his pants. He can't sit still, he's bouncing all over the place.'

'Tyler's the same. I think they might just explode when the big day actually arrives.'

I chuckle, picturing Joe's face, his eyes shining with excitement.

'So . . .' Darcy opens her notebook where she's written out some kind of schedule. 'The party starts at ten, but I thought you and I should get there at about nine thirty to check the place out, set up the birthday cakes on the table, that kind of thing, okay?'

'Sounds good,' I say. 'Do you want me to bring anything?'

'Maybe some balloons or streamers?' she says. 'To decorate the room where they'll be eating afterwards.'

'Great. And we're bringing our own cakes, right?'

'Yes.'

'And how about party bags,' I say. 'I know you said you had them covered, but do you want me to add anything to them?'

'No, honestly, they're done. All named and set out in boxes.'

'You're so organised,' I say as Flora returns with our coffees. She puts them on the table along with a plate of fresh pastries that smell heavenly.

'Wow,' I say. 'Those look great.'

'Freshly baked,' Flora says with a wink. 'Enjoy, ladies.' She leaves to take someone else's order.

'Try one of the maple and pecan twists,' Darcy says. 'They're to die for.'

I break a piece off. The pastry is warm, flaky and light. I put it in my mouth and sigh with pleasure. 'Oh my God, that is the best thing I've ever tasted.'

'Told you.' She pushes the plate towards me.

'Aren't you having any?' I ask.

'Gosh, no. I try not to eat sweet stuff – it's terrible for my weight.'

I wipe a few crumbs from my mouth. I really want to finish the pastry, but then Darcy will think I'm a gluttonous hog.

I see someone out of the corner of my eye. All other thoughts jolt out of my head. It's him. Again. I can't believe it. My nails press into my lips as my stomach clenches. He's pretending to study the menu in the window, but now he catches my eye, holding my gaze for a moment, making me gasp. He lowers his head once more. What should I do? I can't pass this off as a series of coincidences. Not any more. This man is everywhere. Wherever I go. I'll have to report him to the police, and I'll have to tell Jared.

'Louisa?' I realise Darcy is talking to me. Staring from my shocked face to the man standing outside.

'Hm?' I say. 'Sorry, I was miles away.' I drop my hand from my mouth and give myself a shake.

'You're white,' she says. 'What's wrong?'

'Uh, nothing, nothing. I'm fine.'

'You don't look fine.' She lays her pen on the table. 'Tell me what's wrong. Who's that man you're looking at?'

I wasn't planning on telling Darcy anything about my stalker – it sounds so dramatic. But now we're here, and the man is still there, my worries come spilling out. 'He's . . . I think he's been following me.'

'That man at the window's been following you?' she asks. 'The one in the corduroy coat? With the beard? Are you sure?'

I nod. 'Don't stare,' I say, my voice dropping to a whisper.

'How do you know? Maybe he just happens to be in the same place at the same time.' She looks sceptical and I can't blame her.

'That's what I thought, at first,' I say. 'But, Darcy, he's everywhere.' My voice is becoming shrill so I make an attempt to lower it again. 'I see him wherever I go – on the school run, when I'm shopping, near my house. He was even at Poole Quay yesterday when Jared and I were at the offices. It's really been freaking me out. What if he's dangerous?'

'What does Jared say?'

'I . . . I haven't told him.'

'What? Why not?' Darcy rises to her feet, a look of determination on her face.

'What are you doing?' I ask.

'I'm going to tell him to get lost,' she says, flicking her hair.

'No. No, it's okay,' I say. 'Look, he's leaving. You can't approach him. He might be dangerous. He could be violent.'

'He looks like a homeless person,' Darcy says. 'Don't worry, he'll leave you alone after *I* have a word with him.'

My pulse is racing. I can't allow Darcy to do this for me. What if he attacks her? But she's already left her seat. She's winding her way between the tables, heading for the door. I grab my bag and follow like a scared school child, while she's already out the door and striding up the hill after him.

'Hey!' Darcy calls out to the retreating man. 'Hey, you!'

My stalker throws a glance over his shoulder but he doesn't stop or even slow down. Darcy begins to jog after him. I have no choice but to follow. Eventually, she catches him up and puts a hand on his shoulder. I gasp – convinced he'll lash out. He stops and turns, his head down, his beard and cap obscuring his features.

'What do you think you're playing at!' she snaps. 'Who the hell do you think you are, following my friend around. You need to leave her alone.'

I come to a stop a short distance away from them, unable to draw any nearer. My hands are shaking, my heart is thumping, and there's a lump in my throat preventing me from speaking. Being in such close proximity to this man is freaking me out.

The guy mumbles something unintelligible.

'Do you understand what I'm saying?' Darcy continues as if speaking to a child. 'You need to stop following this person.' She points to me and I cringe as the man stares up at me. 'If you don't leave her alone, I'll call the police and report you.' Darcy's voice suddenly becomes steel-tipped: 'and I can do much worse than that – believe me. I know people who can fuck you up.'

I inhale sharply at her words, and the man flinches, averting his gaze from mine, staring instead at his own worn boots.

'Do you understand what I'm saying?' Darcy says.

He nods quickly.

'If I hear that my friend has caught so much as a glimpse of you again, you'll wish you'd never been born.'

The man shakes his head and mutters something under his breath.

'What did you say?' Darcy takes a step closer, putting her face near his. I don't know how she has the courage to confront a complete stranger like this. How she can be so . . . dauntless.

'Darcy,' I squeak.

She holds her hand up to silence me.

The man shakes his head again.

'Tell me you understood what I just said,' Darcy says to him.

He nods.

'Say it,' she demands.

'I understand.' It's not the loud, gruff voice I was expecting. It's calm and quiet.

'Good,' Darcy says. 'Now piss off.' She grins up at me as if what she just said was wildly funny.

Her levity shocks me more than her previous cold anger. How is she not trembling right now? She turns her back on him, takes my arm and we head back to the café. My coat is still inside, and the autumn wind slices straight through my shirt to my shivering skin.

'That was mad,' I say. 'Weren't you scared?'

'He won't bother you again,' she replies.

'Thank you, but how do you know that?' I say, worried she might actually have made things worse. 'What if he gets angry and tries to get some kind of revenge?'

'If you see him again, tell me,' she says. 'I know people

who could dangle him off the top of the multi-story parking garage in town. I think he understood that I know those types of people.'

'Do you?' I ask.

'What?'

'Know those types of people.'

She laughs. 'Oh, Louisa, you're so funny. Come on, let's not let that weirdo ruin our day. We need to get back to planning our boys' party.'

'Okay.' I nod, relieved to be returning to normality, although my heart is still pounding, my brain still whirring, unsettled by my stalker and by Darcy's behaviour back there.

She pushes open the door to *Flora's* and we walk back inside, the comforting aroma of baked bread and coffee enveloping us in its warmth.

'So,' Darcy says as we settle back in our seats like nothing just happened. 'What did you and Jared think of the offices? Nice huh?'

'They're beautiful,' I reply. 'And that view . . .' I'm trying to make small talk like everything's normal, but I hear the tremor in my voice. Darcy doesn't appear to have noticed, or maybe she's too polite to mention it.

'Yeah, I know, right,' she says. 'We bought the premises purely for that view. If the office space doesn't yield what we want, they'll make gorgeous flats.'

My stomach lurches at her words. What if they kick Jared

out? I guess as long as he has a lease agreement, he'll be fine.

'Is Jared happy with it?' she asks. 'Will the space work for him?'

'He's over the moon. Thank you, Darcy. Honestly, you and Mike have really made a difference to our lives. We owe you.'

She smiles and blows on her coffee. 'Nonsense. It's all good business. Talking of owing people, I wanted to thank *you*.'

I can't think what I could have done. 'Me?' I reply.

'Yeah, you'll never guess what?'

I sip my lukewarm cappuccino, waiting for her to continue.

'Your editor,' she says, 'Kathryn, she contacted me a couple of weeks ago. Turns out, she loved the guest post I wrote for you.'

I put my coffee cup back down on the table. I'm getting a bad feeling about where this conversation is heading.

'We got chatting,' Darcy continues, 'and actually we got on like a house on fire. She's so great, and . . . well . . . she asked me to write a weekly column for the paper. Nothing to do with yours – mine is more to do with style and fashion, but with a humorous angle. Isn't that cool! You and I, we'll be stable mates at the paper.' Her bright hair swings forward, and she flicks it back over her shoulder.

My head swims with humiliation. I don't have the

strength to tell Darcy that I think she's actually been offered *my* column. If I said the words out loud, I think I'd end up crying, and I can't do that. Not here. Not in front of Darcy and all these people.

'Congratulations,' I say, swallowing down bile. 'That's amazing news. I told you your piece was great, didn't I.'

'You did,' she says. 'I can't believe I'm a writer for an actual national newspaper. And it's all because of you.'

I smile and nod, but my chest feels hollow and empty. Like I've lost a part of myself. Like I might be shrinking.

CHAPTER TWELVE

I wake early. Before Jared. Even before the birthday boy himself. I could barely sleep last night, finally drifting off just before dawn. My heart wouldn't stop racing, my brain churning around like a piece of chewing gum in someone's mouth. So I give up trying to get back to sleep. Instead, easing back the covers and sliding out of bed. I throw on a tracksuit and tiptoe down the stairs, slipping my feet into trainers. The heating hasn't come on yet. At least the chill air inside makes it easier to step out into the dank, grey morning.

I'm not normally the first up on a Sunday. I prefer to light a fire and curl up on the sofa with a cup of tea, rather than leave the house. But I can't wait. I need to get to the corner shop. It's drizzling, a fine mist turning my hair to frizz. I don't have a hood so I step up my pace, my trainers hardly making a sound on the wet, leaf-strewn pavement. No one else is around. It's just me.

After a brisk five-minute walk, the shop comes into view – a splash of tatty, garish colour in an otherwise grey street. The news stand on the pavement proclaims that a pensioner was attacked in her home and the perpetrator is still loose. A man is untying his Labrador from the bike railings outside. He nods good morning to me and I give him a brief smile in return.

Pushing open the wire-lined glass door, I enter the brightly lit shop. A bell jangles above me and the young woman behind the counter looks up and smiles. I mumble a croaky *good morning* and shift my gaze to the neatly stacked Sunday papers. Feeling slightly nauseous, I lift a copy of my paper. Only, it isn't *my* paper any more. Slotting the heavy weekend edition under my arm, I make my way to the back of the store – may as well pick up some more milk while I'm here. A family-sized bar of Dairy Milk calls out to me, so I grab it on my way back to the counter. Maybe a thick slab of chocolate will help dull the pain of reading Darcy's new column.

The woman puts my purchases in a bag and I hand over a fiver. I probably shouldn't even have bought the damn paper. And yet I can't very well tell Darcy I haven't read it. She'd think it was sour grapes. She'd be right, but I can't let her know that. Maybe these things happen for a reason I tell myself as the woman hands me my change. Maybe this disappointment will spur me to finish my novel and I'll land a big, fat publishing deal.

I step back outside to see the rain is clearing, revealing a faint patch of blue sky. I'm keen to get home before Joe wakes up. It's his big day today. I stride back home, less despondent and anxious than earlier. I have a lot to be grateful for. My son is eight today and he's got a wonderful party planned. Looks like the weather might turn out okay, too.

The front door is stiff, swollen with rain. Finally, I manage to shove it open and step inside. I tip my head to the side and listen for any noises but the house is silent apart from the hum of the boiler. Jared and Joe must still be asleep. I check my watch – it's still only 6.40 am. My stomach rumbles, demanding breakfast. I'll wait until the others are awake. For now, I just need a moment of peace to read.

I slide the paper from the bag, along with the bar of chocolate. I'll put the milk away afterwards. For now, I leave it on the floor in the hall. The door to the lounge creaks as I ease it open and settle myself on the sofa, opening up the Lifestyle supplement. My page has always been about one-third in, a three-column spread with my photo at the top – a picture I've always secretly liked as I look young and slightly edgy. Today, for the first Sunday in three years, my photo has been replaced with the model-like image of Darcy Lane staring down the lens. It's a tongue-in-cheek photo, with a nod to the early sixties. Think *Bewitched* meets *Audrey Hepburn*.

I reach for the Dairy Milk, run my nail across the wrapper and break off a line. No one's here to see me so I shove all four squares into my mouth at once, letting the creamy sweetness soothe my hurt. Darcy Lane has been given a full page spread.

I skim the headline, Darcy's short bio, and then the first few paragraphs, but there's no mention of me or my old column. It's as though I never was. I force myself to read the whole thing, beginning to end. It's brilliant, interesting and funny. Uncharitably, I wish that it had been a pile of absolute shit. That the guest post she originally wrote for me had been a fluke. But, of course, it wasn't. I have to face the fact that Darcy Lane is a better writer than me – even if she isn't necessarily a better person. She did effectively eject me from my job, after all. Surely, after reading today's paper, and seeing my column's missing, she'll realise that.

* * *

'Party time!' Jared says an hour later, shimmying into the kitchen doing a seventies-style Travolta dance.

'You're so embarrassing, Dad,' Joe says covering his face.

'Sit down, both of you,' I say. 'One special birthday breakfast coming up.'

'With bacon and fried bread?' Joe asks.

'Of course,' I reply. 'And scrambled egg, mushrooms and asparagus.'

'I hate asparagus,' Joe says, screwing up his face.

'But we made you an asparagus birthday cake,' Jared

says.

Joe rolls his eyes, already wise to his father's teasing.

Jared starts pretend-boxing with Joe. 'Let's see how strong you are, now you're eight. Can you take me down yet? Come on, Joe Bo, gimme your best shot.'

The smile on Joe's face fills my chest with an ache of love. Jared catches my eye and we grin at one another, shared adoration of our son binding us together. He's wearing his birthday present – a brand new AFC Bournemouth kit. His sturdy legs clad in black and red socks, and a pair of brand new football boots on his feet.

'Sit down, guys,' I say again. 'Before it gets cold.'

They do as I ask, picking up their knives and forks and tucking in. I sit and join them.

'Reckon you're going to score today, buddy?' Jared asks.

'Yeah,' Joe says through a mouthful of toast. 'Course.'

'Think you can manage a hat trick?'

'Definitely.'

They polish off their plates in record time.

'Have you had enough?' I ask.

'Erm . . .' they both reply in unison.

We all dissolve into laughter.

'I'll make some more toast, shall I?'

'Yes please,' Joe says.

I glance at the kitchen clock. It's 8.30 am. It shouldn't take more than half an hour to get there at this time on a

Sunday morning. Darcy said to get there by 9.30, so as long as we leave by nine, we should be fine. I slice up some more bread and stick it in the toaster.

* * *

At 9.25 am, we pull up outside the football stadium.

'Mummy, my tummy feels a bit funny,' Joe says.

'It's probably just butterflies,' I say, hoping that's all it is. 'Does it feel a bit fluttery and worried?'

'Yes.'

Jared turns around to face Joe, who's in the back seat, his face creased and a little pale. 'You'll be fine, buddy,' Jared says. 'It's just the excitement. Even the top players get butterflies before a match.'

'Really?' Joe says, his voice brightening a little.

'Just have fun,' I say. 'All your friends will be here soon. Once you see them, you'll be fine.'

Jared gets out of the car and comes around to the passenger side so he can take Joe's cake off my lap before I get out. I didn't dare put it in the boot of the car in case it slid around and got squashed.

'Have you got Tyler's present?' I ask Joe as he steps out of the car.

He turns, reaches into the back seat and grabs the parcel. I pick up my handbag and the bag of decorations – balloons, streamers and party poppers – and Jared locks the car.

We walk across the car park to the main building. This morning's grey murk has disappeared, and now it's bright and clear with a wintery nip in the air, perfect weather for a football party. Jared is still carrying the cake and pushes open the glass door with his elbow as we all traipse inside.

The foyer is empty apart from an A-frame chalkboard which squats in the middle of the space with helium balloons tied to it. On it is written: "Tyler Lane's Birthday Party" and an arrow which points towards a corridor.

Where's Joe's name? I mouth to Jared over our son's head.

Jared raises his eyebrows and shrugs his shoulders. Luckily, Joe doesn't pick up on the error. I scan the foyer, looking for places where I might find a piece of chalk. If I can add Joe's name before his friends arrive . . .

I dump my bags on the floor and scoot behind the reception desk, rifling through the drawers and shelves.

'What are you doing, Mummy?' Joe asks, his forehead wrinkling. 'I don't think you're supposed to—'

'Don't worry,' I say. 'I'm just looking for something. I won't be long.'

'Leave it, Lou,' Jared hisses. 'It doesn't matter. No one else will notice.'

'I'm sure there must be some chalk here somewh—'

'Mummy, come on,' Joe says. 'I want to find Tyler.'

Reluctantly I stop my search, and leave the desk,

retrieving my bags. I feel like wiping Tyler's name off the chalkboard so that it simply says: "Birthday Party". If Joe's name isn't on there, Tyler's name shouldn't be on there either. But that would be petty and out of order. So I grit my teeth and leave the board how it is, inhaling deeply, trying to regain my good mood.

We follow more signs – thankfully these just say "Party this way". After a couple of minutes weaving our way through corridors and up staircases, we find ourselves in a plush bar overlooking the pitch. This must be the VIP spectator area. Joe runs over to the glass wall at the far end, pressing his hands and face against the window. Below, the whole Bournemouth team are kitted out and going through some kind of training exercise.

Joe is pointing and yelling out players' names. Jared joins him at the window and I forget my earlier annoyance about the board, enjoying watching Joe's delight at seeing his heroes in the flesh.

'Guys, you're here!'

I turn toward the voice. Darcy is standing in a doorway at the far end of the bar. She looks incredible, dressed in a designer tracksuit, her blonde hair in two plaits which make her look like a fifteen-year-old Swedish schoolgirl. I see Jared's eyes widen as he turns to greet her. In contrast, I'm wearing a knee-length, flowery dress, boots and a smart jacket. I thought I looked chic before we left the house, but now I feel like a frumpy mum.

'Through here!' Darcy beckons us over.

Jared peels a reluctant Joe away from the viewing gallery and heads over towards her. She bends down to kiss Joe, then she puts her hand on Jared's arm and kisses him on both cheeks. They're smiling at one other as I approach.

'Louisa, you look gorgeous,' she says. 'Love the dress. And how did you get such heavenly curls? Lucky you!'

'Thanks,' I say, kissing a perfumed cheek. 'You look gorgeous, too.'

'Oh, God, no. I didn't dress up. Just threw on a tracksuit. I really should've made more of an effort, like you.'

Somehow, this doesn't feel like a compliment.

Darcy leads us into a small function room, lavishly decorated with streamers, and balloons sporting the caption: "Happy Birthday Tyler!" And, just in case we still can't guess whose birthday it is, an enormous professionally made vinyl banner hangs from the ceiling proclaiming: "Happy 8th Birthday, Tyler!"

The Lanes must have been here since about eight o'clock this morning decorating the room. The table is laid with divine mini cupcakes, tiny triangle sandwiches, crisps and individual soda bottles. The *piece de resistance* is a giant 3D cake in the shape of a white leather football, which appears to have been signed by the whole of the Bournemouth football team in icing – How the hell did Darcy manage that?

Again, Tyler's name is emblazoned across the top. My Marks and Spencer pre-bought football cake is going to look absolutely pathetic sitting alongside that work of art.

'Did you want to hang out Joe's banner and balloons?' Darcy asks.

I turn to her, my face flushing red with embarrassment and anger that I'm desperately trying to keep in check. Jared is blithely unaware of my humiliation, already deep in conversation with his new best buddy, Mike. And Joe and Tyler are charging around the room, playing keepy-uppy with a few stray "Tyler" balloons.

'I have some balloons and streamers,' I say. 'But they don't have Joe's name on . . . I didn't think we were—'

'Oh.' Darcy pouts as if she's surprised. 'That's a shame. Do you need any help putting them up?'

'I didn't realise you were getting named decorations,' I say, 'or I would've—'

'Didn't we discuss all the decorations at *Flora's*?' she asks, frowning. 'I thought we went over all that?'

I know for a fact that she absolutely did not mention named decorations. My heart rate has doubled, and I feel a deep pull of disappointment in my gut. Is this woman trying to outmanoeuvre me? Is Darcy playing some subtle game of one-upmanship? But there's a niggle of doubt in my chest. Why would she do that? What would be the point? She's the woman with everything. I can't even begin to compete with her. I must be mistaken. Maybe it's me. Maybe I'm overreacting. Seeing things where there's nothing to see. Imagining malice where there is none. I need to snap out of it.

CHAPTER THIRTEEN

I can't let any of these trivial things get to me. Whether Darcy is playing some kind of game with me, or not, I won't let it ruin Joe's day. As long as my boy is happy, that's all that matters.

'You know what?' I say brightly. 'You've made such a good job of decorating the room, I don't think I need to add anything else. It'll just be overkill. Why don't we have a coffee while we're waiting for everyone to arrive.'

'Good idea,' Darcy replies, relaxing her face.

'Let me just put Joe's cake out,' I say, determined not to let its puny size make me feel like an inadequate mother. It's a normal-sized cake, for goodness sake.

I stroll over to Jared and take the box from his hands. 'Hi Mike,' I say. We kiss on the cheek and I walk back over to the table.

'I thought Tyler could sit at this end and Joe could sit at the other,' Darcy says.

'Perfect,' I reply, extricating Joe's small, circular football cake and placing it on the table opposite Tyler's monstrous creation. 'Amazing cake,' I say, trying to be nice about it.

'Thanks. We got Ty a signed Bournemouth kit for his

birthday, so we decided it would be cool if the pastry chef copied out the players' signatures in icing.'

'Great idea,' I say. Honestly, I never knew smiling could be this hard.

As Joe and Tyler's friends begin to arrive, and we make our way over to greet them, it becomes abundantly clear that no one else realises that it's Joe's birthday party either. So, I can safely assume that Darcy didn't email the other parents to let them know it would be a joint party. They all bring presents for Tyler. Only one other boy has a present for Joe, too.

Darcy has started talking to an official-looking woman by the door so I make my way over to see what's happening.

'If you could introduce me to Tyler,' the woman is saying to Darcy, 'then we can make sure the players and the coach know that he's the birthday boy. Here's a birthday rosette to pin on his shirt.'

'Hi,' I say to the woman. 'I'm Louisa Sullivan, Joe's mum.'

She smiles blankly at me.

'It's Joe and Tyler's birthday today. I'm Joe's mum.'

'Oh.' Her face drops. 'A joint party?'

'Yes, Darcy will have told you last month about it.'

Darcy doesn't speak.

'I . . . uh.' The woman pulls at the ends of her hair and bites her bottom lip. I take pity on her as I'm pretty sure Darcy must have forgotten to mention it.

'It was a last-minute change,' I say. 'So can we get a rosette for Joe?'

The woman's shoulders drop with the relief that she hasn't messed up. 'Yes, of course. Give me a minute. I'll be back with one for your son, too.'

I don't even look at Darcy. If I do, I'm afraid she'll see how much all this has upset me. I'm also mindful that Jared's new business is dependent on her and Mike's goodwill.

'Mummy.'

I turn to see my son behind me. He takes my hand and pulls me away from Darcy.

'What is it?' I say.

'Are you sure it's my party, too? No one else got me a present, apart from Lucas.'

'Of course it's your party,' I say with a big smile. 'There was just a bit of a mix-up. But the lady has gone to get you a special birthday rosette so everyone will know, okay?'

'Tyler got all those.' He points to a table piled high with brightly coloured wrapped presents.

'Yes, but you're going to be getting one great big present, instead of all those silly little ones.'

His eyes grow wide. 'Really?'

'Really.'

'What is it?'

'Well, I can't tell you that, can I. It's a surprise.'

'Wow!'

I bend down to kiss his round cheek. I have no idea what the big present will be, but I'm sure Jared and I will think of something fun and non-expensive.

'Is Joe okay?' Darcy calls out.

I don't turn around. 'Yes, absolutely fine,' I say, biting back several retorts. I decide to let it go. There's already a bitter knot of resentment hardening in my stomach, and I don't want Joe to see how upset I really am.

A fierce protectiveness of my family sweeps over me – I want to leave this excessive party with its self-satisfied adults and spoilt children, and escape back to our little house, away from all this showy crap. At this moment in time, I'd give anything to have Joe back in his old school, and throw him a normal party with his old school friends, without all this extravagance. To have Jared back in his old job, and me with my column – my little piece of self-esteem.

Yet there's no going back. I realise that, for good or bad, this is the course Jared and I have set ourselves on, and I'm going to have to accept it and deal with it.

* * *

In the car on the way home Joe is high on excitement and birthday cake, chattering non-stop about the game and the coach and how everyone played. He's had a great day, thank goodness. He scored two goals and won lots of praise from the Bournemouth players. Now he's finally silent. I nudge Jared to look at him in the rear-view mirror. Joe has fallen asleep in the back seat. His eyes closed, mouth open. Jared and I share a smile.

'Great day, wasn't it, Lou. Joe played so well. I wouldn't be surprised if he got scouted.'

'Yeah,' I reply. But my mind is instantly dragged back to whether or not Darcy has been playing subtle games. To use a child's party to score points is . . .

'I had a really great chat with Mike, too,' Jared says, interrupting my thoughts.

'Cool. What did you talk about?'

'Everything really. Business, football, kids, you know. I'm going to pick up the lease contract tomorrow.' He rests his hand on my leg for a moment before changing gear.

My stomach lurches. 'Do you think it's a good idea?' I say.

'Do I think what's a good idea?'

'You know. This whole free for a year thing. I thought you always said it wasn't a good idea to go into business with friends.'

'We're not really going into business. I'm just leasing a property from him. And anyway, they're not proper friends. We only just met them.'

'I just think . . . It could get awkward, with Joe and Tyler at the same school. If something goes wrong . . .'

'What can go wrong? It's free for a year and then I start

paying rent, by which time we'll be raking it in, anyway.'

'I have a bad feeling,' I say. 'Not necessarily about Mike, but about Darcy.'

Jared puts the heel of his hand on the car horn. 'Tosser just tried to cut me up. Watch where you're going! Dickhead.'

While Jared mutters under his breath at the other driver, I turn to check Joe's still asleep. 'I think Darcy might have left Joe's name off the invitation on purpose.'

'What?' Jared shoots a confused glance at me. 'Why would she do that? Wasn't it her idea to have the joint party?'

'Yes, but after the mistake with the invitations, she said she'd email everyone to let them know it was Joe's party, too. And she didn't do that either. Plus, she didn't tell the venue. And did you see all the banners and balloons with Tyler's name on? And the size of that cake!'

'Hey, hey, calm down.'

I realise I'm trembling, on the verge of tears. I don't want to cry. It's just, I can't think straight. And listening to myself air my worries to my husband, it all sounds so trivial and pathetic.

'Why would she do any of that on purpose?' Jared says. 'There'd be no point. Anyway, the main thing is that Joe had a fantastic time.'

'I know. I know you're right,' I say. 'But I feel bad for him that no one bought him a present.'

'He's got a couple of presents in the boot,' Jared says. 'One huge one from Tyler, so they must like him. How can anyone not love Joe?' He grins at me. I don't return the smile.

'I don't think it's Joe she wants to hurt,' I say. 'I think it might be me. And I don't think she cares if Joe gets caught up in it.'

'Caught up in what?' Jared's brow creases. 'Louisa, I really think you're making too much out of this. You're tired, and you're probably still a bit upset about your job.'

Jared's been so busy with his business this week, I realise I never told him about Darcy taking over my column. 'Do you know why I lost my job?' I say.

'No. Did you find out? Did Kathryn give you a reason?'

'Remember Darcy offered to write it when I was ill, and I stupidly accepted?'

'Yeah, I remember. But it wasn't stupid to accept her help.'

'She was helping herself, more like.'

'I don't know what you mean,' he says.

'Kathryn gave my column to Darcy. And Darcy took it. Her piece is in the paper today. I didn't tell you because I didn't want to ruin Joe's birthday.'

'God, are you sure?'

I can't tell if Jared is worried for me or if he thinks I'm

making it up. 'I'll show you the paper when we get home. She got a full-page spread in my magazine.'

'Surely she wouldn't have done it on purpose, Lou. If she knew she'd done you out of a job, I'm sure she'd be—'

'Take her side why don't you,' I snap. I know I shouldn't take it out on Jared, but why can't he support me in this?

'Easy. I'm only saying that—'

'That all these things are just coincidence? That she's really a sweet person who wouldn't dream of flushing my career down the toilet while she takes it all for herself? Never mind that she's already a multi-gazillionaire who doesn't even need a job.' I realise I'm sounding bitter and horrible now. And I'm probably being unfair to Darcy. I think the events of the past few days must have put a strain on my nerves.

Jared doesn't reply. I glance across to see his face is stony.

'Maybe I'm wrong,' I say. 'I'm just not sure that she's the lovely, generous person she appears to be.' I suddenly remember how she spoke to the stalker guy earlier this week. How she threatened him. How her voice changed. It scared me. But I can't mention that to Jared – he'll be cross that I never told him about it. He'll worry and make me go to the police.

'So, what?' Jared says. 'You want me to throw away this business opportunity because you've fallen out with Darcy? You seemed to be getting on okay, today. I saw you laughing and hugging each other before you left.'

He doesn't understand what's going on. And I appear to be hopeless at explaining it. I even agree that it does sound like I'm being more than a little paranoid. Perhaps I'm wrong about this. About *her*. I hope so. I try again: 'I just think things would be simpler if we didn't get too involved with the Lanes. Maybe if you found a cheaper office somewhere else . . .'

'Lou, I'm setting up a new advertising agency, not a telesales business. It's all about perception. We need those quay-front offices – it'll make us look premium. And what about Mike's contacts? I won't be able to get things moving without clients. I just can't do it. We can't afford to piss these people off. You'll just have to keep being nice to Darcy. I'm really sorry about your column. I truly am. It sucks. But the opportunity I've got will make up for it, I promise. I'll make this work, and then, who knows, maybe you can even set up your own magazine.'

His words trickle over me like cold water. I stare straight ahead. The roads are empty. We pull up to a set of traffic lights and stop as the lights change from amber to red. No other cars cross the junction. We sit in silence. Clouds are gathering and the gloom swallows me up. It's like I'm disappearing into the void.

CHAPTER FOURTEEN

The day after the party, I drop Joe at school and drive straight over to Beth's. I called her last night, needing to talk. To get her opinion on everything that's happening. To unpick the tangle of worries in my head. She has a spare hour this morning before she has to meet a client. It's not enough time to speak properly, but she's busy the rest of the week and I can't wait any longer.

As I drive, I squint into the piercing, morning sun. It's dangerously bright. Too bright for my mood. I pull up outside Beth's block and take a deep breath as the engine cools. I mustn't get myself into a state, she'll only worry about me and I can't put that on her. She has a busy enough life as it is – working full time, with a young daughter. I just need some advice, that's all. Her opinion on what to do for the best.

My seatbelt catches in the door as I try to close it. I swear, loop it back inside the car, and close the door with a clunk. Beth and Carys live in an unlovely seventies block, built from garish yellow brick. But the location is a fabulous five minutes from the sea, and the interior is high-ceilinged, light-and-airy beach chic. I climb the steps and press the buzzer. Beth lets me in and I make my way up to the third floor.

'Hey, Lou.' She's already at the door, her head tilted to the side, dressed in a skirt suit and towering heels.

'Wow,' I say. 'You look amazing, sis.'

'What, this old thing?'

We hug and laugh.

'Sorry, Beth,' I say. 'You could probably do without your flaky sister dropping in on you right before work.'

'Don't be daft. You're not flaky, and it's not a problem.'

I follow her through the hall to the kitchen, the aroma of fresh coffee setting my caffeine-craving taste buds off.

'I've already whipped you up a nice, strong cappuccino,' she says. 'Sounds like you need one.'

'Got any whisky to splash in that?' I ask, only semi-joking.

Beth raises one perfectly plucked eyebrow. 'Sit. Talk.'

I perch myself on a stool next to the granite island. Beth sits next to me cradling a tall glass of green tea.

'You're going to think I'm paranoid, or mad,' I say, taking a tentative sip of my drink. It's way too hot so I set it back down on the counter top.

'I already know you're mad,' she replies with a smirk.

I try and fail to smirk back. 'It's all to do with this mum from school,' I begin. 'Her name's Darcy.'

'The one we met at the beach? With her husband?'

'That's the one.' I proceed to tell Beth everything that's

happened between then and now. About the subtle little games I think she's been playing. About Joe's party. About Jared's plan to lease one of their offices. I also consider telling her about my stalker, but I haven't seen him since Darcy told him to piss off, so I decide to leave him out of it. That news will only detract from the stuff about Darcy.

Beth doesn't interrupt me as I speak. She lets me get everything off my chest. Her patience and listening skills are more than I could ever manage. If it were me listening, I'd be interrupting left, right, and centre. It must be her lawyer training or something. Whatever. I'm grateful. Now I've started, it all comes spewing out in a torrent.

Once it's out there, she sets her drink down and steeples her fingers together. 'Well,' she finally says. 'If Darcy's as bad as you say she is, then you need to steer clear of her . . .'

'But?' I say. 'I can sense a "but".'

She gives a wry smile, wrinkling her nose. It's something she always does before telling me something I don't want to hear. 'It's just . . .' she begins. 'Do you think there's any way you might have misinterpreted things? By the sound of it, Darcy is one busy lady. She could genuinely have forgotten to include Joe's name. It's not something *you* would ever conceive of doing because you're far too sweet and considerate to ignore a child's feelings. But, you don't really know this woman, Lou. She sounds like a flighty, self-obsessed socialite. Thinking about how other people feel is probably way down her list of priorities. I don't think she would have done it on purpose. What would have been the point?'

Hearing Beth talk about Darcy like this makes me doubt myself even more. But my sister hasn't spent time with Darcy. 'What about my column?' I say. 'How do you explain that?'

Beth takes a sip of her tea. 'You were ill, right?'

I nod.

'And she brought you soup and offered to help you out with your work?'

I twist my lip.

'And then, your editor offered the column to her. Darcy didn't go after it, did she?'

'I don't think so. I'm not really sure. I don't know how the conversation went between them.'

'Lou, I'm worried about you,' Beth says. 'You've been looking really thin and pale these past few weeks.'

'I'm always pale,' I say with an attempt at a smile.

'I'm serious, sis. I think . . . Well, Carys and I think you might be a little depressed.'

'You've been talking to Carys about me?' A spark of anger ignites in my gullet.

'I talk to Carys about everything,' she says. 'We both love you.'

'You think I'm overreacting,' I say, sliding off the stool,

ready to leave.

Beth takes my hand and squeezes. 'No. Sit back down. I don't think you're overreacting. I just think you might be seeing bad things when they're just coincidences or bad luck.'

I stay on my feet. Part of me wants to slam out of her apartment, but I know that wouldn't be fair. I know Beth is only trying to make me feel better. Trying to make me see the other side of the story. I want to believe that what she's saying is true. To shake the constant dread rolling around in my stomach. I realise my thumbnail is digging into the side of my forefinger so hard it hurts.

'And as for Jared's new agency,' Beth continues, 'you need to support him. Be excited for him. It's a big deal. He must be feeling nervous about it, too. The fact that Darcy and her husband are willing to give him a year's free rent is incredible. I actually think they must like you guys, a lot.'

My heart rate slows at Beth's words. I sit back down and gulp down a few mouthfuls of coffee. Could she be right? Could I be seeing bad things where there's nothing? 'Could there be some kind of catch, though?' I ask. 'With the free office thing.'

'Bring me the contract before you sign,' she says. 'I'll look it over for you.'

'Would you?'

'Of course. I can't believe you didn't talk to me or Carys

about it before.'

'I didn't want to bother you. I feel bad moaning to you now.'

'You're my sister, you're allowed to moan – as long as you don't do it too often.'

I roll my eyes and she pulls a stupid face. I feel better already. I knew talking to Beth would help ease my anxiety.

The chorus to *Mr Brightside* by *The Killers* emanates from my handbag on the floor. It's my ringtone – the song that reminds me of when Jared and I first met. 'I better get that' I say. 'Could be Joe's school, or Jared.'

'Sure, go ahead. I've got to get ready to leave in a minute, anyway.' Beth puts her glass in the sink and leaves the kitchen while I fumble in my bag and hook out my phone.

It's Darcy. Her ears must've been burning.

I take a deep breath and answer. 'Hello?'

Instead of her overly confident drawl, her voice is quiet – almost a squeak. 'Louisa?'

'Yes.'

'I didn't know who else to call,' she says. 'Can you come over?'

'What? Now? Are you okay, Darcy?'

'No,' she gulps. 'No, I'm not. Please, can you come over now?'

I wonder what can possibly have happened to make Darcy sound so upset. 'Yes, sure. I can be there in about ten, maybe fifteen minutes, okay?'

'Thank you,' she says.

'Okay.'

Beth comes back into the kitchen. 'Everything okay?'

'I don't know,' I reply. 'That was Darcy, of all people. She sounded really upset, like she's been crying. She wants me to go over there now.'

'Oh dear. Poor thing. I wonder what's happened.'

'I don't know. It's weird that she called me. She must have closer friends than *me*, surely.'

'People *like* you, Lou. You're easy to talk to – sympathetic. You should have more faith in yourself.'

'Well, you're family, you have to say that.'

She shakes her head. 'Let me know what happens. And I think this shows Darcy isn't out to get you. Enemies don't usually cry on your shoulder.'

'We'll see,' I say, putting my phone back in my bag. 'Anyway, I better go. Thanks for this morning. You're the best sister ever.'

'Aw, shucks.'

She sees me to the door and we hug before I leave.

I jog down the stairs wondering what could have made Darcy so upset, and what on earth she could want with me.

CHAPTER FIFTEEN
Summer 1993

'Why the fuck are you blubbing, Cal. I told you to stop being such a wuss.' Nicole gritted her teeth and pulled him around into the dirty alley. It stank of piss in the heat and was littered with fag butts and dog turds, but Nicole hardly noticed. Why couldn't her brother be less of a cry baby? Why was she the one who always had to look after him?

Snot trailed down his nose and he tried to wipe it away with his sleeve, but just ended up smearing it across his cheek.

'God, that's vile, Cal. You're making me wanna vom.'

'Sorry, Nic.' He hiccuped and took a deep, shuddering breath, trying not to cry.

Nicole clenched her fists. He was so pathetic. He needed to grow a pair. He was eight already but still acted like he was three. What was he going to do when she went to senior school and wasn't around to look out for him? She grabbed a handful of his hair and yanked his head back.

'Stop. Fucking. Crying,' she hissed, shoving her face right up close to his. 'Or I'll give you something to cry about.'

She'd copied that line off one of the other care kids. The older ones were always saying stuff like that. And they meant it, too.

'I'm trying, Nic,' he blubbered.

She and Cal had been in care for over two years now. A couple of different foster parents had tried them out, but no one had wanted to keep them permanently. It all started back when she and Cal had been done for shoplifting. Social services got involved and said their mum wasn't well enough to look after them properly – too pissed, more like.

'What happened?' she asked, loosening her grip on Callum's hair.

'Derek Mullins.'

'Becky's brother? The one with freckles?'

Callum nodded.

'What did he do to you?'

Callum shook his head and started scuffing the pavement with the toe of his shoe.

'Tell me or I'll bash you.'

Callum murmured something, but it was so quiet Nicole couldn't hear.

'What?'

'He told everyone I wet the bed.'

Nicole let go of his head and straightened up. Derek was a skinny little wanker who had no right to talk to her brother like that.

'Everyone was laughing at me, Nic,' Callum wailed. 'And then he kicked me. Look.' Callum hoiked up his trouser leg and pointed to a gash on his shin.

'That little shit did that to you?' Nicole spat.

Callum nodded, his lower lip trembling again. 'And now everyone in my class knows I wet the bed.'

'They don't know, you idiot. Derek just said that to wind you up.'

Callum's eyes grew wider.

'You should've called him a liar,' Nicole said. 'You should've kicked him in the balls. Where is he? Where's Derek now?'

'In the park, probably. He always goes there after school.'

'His sister lives up Howton Road. I know what we're gonna do.'

'What do you mean?'

'He's not getting away with it.' Nicole took her brother by the hand and dragged him down the alley.

'Where we going?'

'The shop.'

'You got some money?'

'No. What's your favourite drink?'

'Coke,' he replied. 'No, I mean Fanta – the orange one.'

They emerged from the dim alley into warm afternoon sunshine and walked back past school, past the rows of terraced council houses with their scrubby patches of front lawn, past the gypsy house with the brown and white horse in the driveway, past the man who sat on his sofa in the garden smoking B&H fags and drinking Bulmer's cider, and past the squat which always had house music blaring out whatever time of day or night.

The corner shop sat smack bang between school and the park. Outside the shop, a group of older kids hung out on their bikes, spitting and swearing, chewing gum and eating sweets and chocolate bars.

'Wait here,' Nicole told her brother, before crossing the road to get to the shop.

'Can I come with you?' Callum asked, eyeing the older boys nervously.

'No. I said to stay here, didn't I.' She let go of his sweaty hand, wiping her palm on her skirt, and she crossed the road. She didn't care about the older boys. If they said anything to her, she'd tell them to piss off. But they weren't bothered anyway – not by a frizzy-haired nobody like her.

A queue snaked back from the till – kids with sweets in their hands standing next to mums with tatty purses, blokes with cans of lager, and pensioners with loaves of bread and pints of milk. Nicole marched past them all until she saw what she was looking for at the rear of the shop. She angled her back to the security camera, reached across the open chiller unit and grabbed a can of Fanta, sliding it into her school bag. It made a bit of a bulge, but it could just as easily be a pencil case as a stolen drink. Then she straightened up pretended to look at the drinks a while longer, before turning and walking back out of the shop. No one looked her way or called out to her to stop. She wouldn't have cared if they had.

Callum was waiting on the other side of the road like she'd told him. She thought he'd be crying again. Instead, he was throwing bits of loose gravel into the road, even when cars were going by. He'd get his head kicked in if he wasn't careful.

'Oi,' she called.

He looked up and she beckoned him across the road. He skimmed one more stone and then ran towards her without looking left or right. Lucky no cars were coming.

'Did you get me a Fanta? he asked, breathless with excitement.

'Shut up, idiot,' she said, hauling him past the shop. 'Do you want to get me arrested?'

Callum shut his mouth and frowned.

After they'd left the shop behind, Nicole drew the drink out of her bag. 'Drink that,' she said, yanking the metal ring off and dropping it on the dusty pavement.

'All of it?' he asked. 'Don't you want some?'

'I'll have a bit, and you can have the rest.'

Nicole took a tiny sip, letting the bubbles fizz on her tongue before swallowing the chilled, sickly-sweet liquid.

'Here.' She passed him the almost-full can and he snatched it greedily from her, glugging the drink, only pausing to let out a loud belch, and then draining the rest. He stuffed the empty can in someone's hedge and burped once again.

'What we doing now?' he asked.

'You'll see.'

CHAPTER SIXTEEN

2016

The electric gates are open, so I drive straight through and on down the driveway, all the while wondering what could have made Darcy so upset. I pull up right outside the house. Darcy's there, in the doorway, her face red and tear-streaked, her hair uncombed. She's still wearing the same tracksuit she had on yesterday at the boys' party.

I undo my seatbelt, grab my bag, and slide out of the car. 'What's happened?'

'I sent all the staff home,' she says. 'I couldn't bear anyone nosing into my business. I didn't want them to see me like this.' She blows her nose into a soggy tissue.

I reach into my bag and pass her a fresh one. 'What happened, Darcy? Is it Tyler? Is he okay? Where's Mike?' I put my arm around her and lead her inside, pulling the door closed behind us. I spy a cosy looking sitting room off the entrance hall and guide her in there. It's some kind of snug, with a squashy u-shaped sofa and a deep-pile rug. We sit side-by-side on the sofa.

'Ty's fine,' she says. 'No. It's Mike.'

I wait for her to continue. She stares at me, her blue eyes pooling with more tears.

'We got in a fight last night.'

'A fight?'

'What about?'

'Oh, it's been building for a while. We . . . We haven't been getting on.'

'I'm so sorry.'

'We barely spoke to one another at the party, and then . . . when we got home. He said . . .'

I take one of her hands in mine. It's cold and damp. I give it a squeeze, to try to comfort her. To let her know I'm here for her.

She sniffs and continues. 'He said he was leaving me.'

My mouth hangs open for a second. 'Oh no. Darcy, I'm so sorry,' I say, meaning it. 'Is there anything I can do?' I really thought they were a close-knit couple. But, now I come to think about it, they're friendly with everyone else, yet I've hardly ever seen them talking to each another.

She shakes her head. 'He's gone. He's left me,' she whispers. 'He stormed out last night. Said he was going to stay at one of his apartments and he didn't know if he was going to come back. What am I going to do, Louisa? I love my husband.' She grabs one of the scatter cushions and clutches it to her chest.

'I really am sorry. I'm sure he'll come back, though. After

a night's sleep, he'll realise he's—'

'He won't. You should have seen him. He was so detached. So cold. He doesn't care about me . . . He doesn't love me any more.' Now, she dissolves into tears. Silently sobbing.

I can't believe that Mike would want to leave his beautiful, vivacious wife. He always gazed at her with such affection. But I must have misinterpreted things. 'What can I do?' I say. 'If there's anything I can—'

'Nothing,' she says. 'There's nothing you can do. I'm just so glad you came. I'm so glad I can count on you as a friend. I feel like I can trust you. I just . . . I didn't know who else to call. Everyone else I know would take pleasure in my misfortune. They'd gossip and the news would be all round school by lunchtime. I know you won't go blabbing to any of the other moms.'

Heat burns my cheeks as she gazes at me. Only thirty minutes ago I was slagging this woman off to my sister. I was so way off the mark. It would seem that Darcy really does like me. And the fact she trusts me more than her other friends – I didn't realise.

'Of course I won't say anything to anyone,' I reply. 'And I'm totally here for you. Whatever you need, just say the word.'

She hugs me, her tears smudging against my jacket. 'It's funny, but you're the only person I feel truly comfortable with. You know that, right?'

I do now. I give her a squeeze and pull away from her embrace. 'Would you like me to pick Tyler up from school this afternoon?'

'Would you? I don't think I could face everyone today. I just want to hide away.'

'Yes, of course. I'll drop him back straight after. Unless he wants a sleepover at ours?'

'No, no, that's okay. I'd rather have him here with me.'

'Sure,' I say.

'Also,' she says. 'When you drop him back, would you, maybe want to go for a run with me? Running helps me calm down and relax, but I hate doing it alone. Mike . . . he always used to come with . . .' Darcy breaks down again and I take her hand.

'I'm sorry,' I say. 'I can't run. It's my knee . . . How about I ask Jared if he'll go with you? He runs most evenings, anyway.' I regret the offer as soon as it's out of my mouth. I know Darcy's going through an awful time, but I don't like the idea of her and Jared out together, even though I trust him implicitly. We've never had a jealous type of relationship. We've been together too long, and we still have that spark. Still, the idea of the two of them as running partners . . .

'That would be amazing,' Darcy says. 'If you're sure he wouldn't mind?'

'No, Jared won't mind. If he's not too busy, I'll get him to text you later.' Bad though it is, I already know I won't tell him about it. I would worry too much. I would see things where there was nothing to see. I've already shown how bad my judgement is where Darcy's involved. I won't put myself in that situation again.

'You're an absolute angel,' she says, dabbing at her tears with the tissue I gave her. 'I don't feel quite as awful now. Now I know I have you and Jared on my side.'

* * *

As soon as he's through the front door, I can tell Jared's in a good mood. The way he holds himself, the fire in his eyes. I tramp down the stairs with a basket of laundry in my arms, trying to blow a stray strand of hair out of my eyes.

'Here, let me.' Jared takes the basket out of my arms and kisses me. I follow him through to the kitchen, where he puts the basket down by the washing machine.

'Where's Joe?' he asks.

'Zonked. He fell asleep as soon as his head hit the pillow.'

'I'll go up and give him a kiss goodnight in a minute.'

'You look chirpy,' I say.

He puts his record bag on the table and slides out a sheaf of papers. 'Tada!'

'The contract?' I say.

'Yup.'

'Congratulations,' I say with a smile. I half-wondered if he'd manage to get it, what with Mike and Darcy splitting up.

'Thanks,' he says, grinning back.

'I saw Beth today,' I say, opening the washing machine door and shoving in the dirty laundry. 'She said she'd look over the contract for you.'

'Great, I'll drop it over to her tomorrow.'

'Did you see Mike today?' I ask.

'No, apparently he was busy. I picked up the contract from his solicitor.' Jared grabs a pizza crust from Joe's discarded dinner plate and folds the whole thing into his mouth. 'God, starving. Shall we get a takeaway tonight? Chinese?'

'Takeaway sounds good,' I say. 'So, you didn't see Mike at all, today?'

'No, I just said so. Why?'

I tell Jared about Mike and Darcy. About how upset Darcy was earlier.

Jared's face falls. 'God, that's awful. I wonder why he left her. They seemed happy, don't you think?'

'I guess you never know what's really going on,' I reply. 'She was so upset. I really felt bad for her.'

Jared's phone shrills, making me jump. I close the washing machine door, press the start button and straighten up.

'Who's that?' I ask as Jared answers his mobile.

'Darcy,' Jared mouths.

I hear her voice, tinny and far away, but I can't make out the words. I know why she's ringing.

'Hang on,' Jared says to her. He covers the phone with his hand and turns to me. 'Darcy said you mentioned I could go running with her tonight?'

Shit. I can't back out of my offer now. 'Um, yeah, she asked *me* to go with her, but . . . my knee. So I said you might go. Sorry, I know how busy you are so don't worry if _'

'No, that's cool. I don't mind.'

My heart sinks.

He puts the phone to his ear again. 'No problem,' he says. 'Half an hour? Yeah, I guess I can . . .' He laughs. 'Okay, see you in a bit, Darce.' He ends the call.

'What about the takeaway?' I ask, 'Shall I order it for when you get home?'

'Nah, I'll grab a quick snack now and have cheese on toast or something when I get back.'

Disappointment tugs at me. I was looking forward to spending the evening with my husband, eating delicious food and maybe watching a movie. I know I shouldn't be so selfish. Darcy's going through hell. The least Jared and I can do is be there for her while she's so upset.

'I still can't believe Mike left her,' Jared says, opening the fridge and pulling out a tub of hummus. 'I hope this won't affect the contract.'

'Shouldn't think so,' I reply, sitting down at the table. 'Business is business, I guess.'

Jared dollops a lump of hummus onto a cracker and plants a kiss on my forehead. 'Right, going to get changed and then I'll be off. See you later, Lou. Love you.'

'Love you, too.'

* * *

I hear the squeak of the dial turning, the hiss of the water coming on, the clatter and bang of the rickety shower door. Jared didn't get home until after eleven. He texted me earlier to say that Darcy begged him to stay for a drink after their run. That she was really upset. What could I say to him? It would have been mean of me to say no. Now he's back home having a shower. I'm in bed attempting to read, but I can't concentrate on the words. I've read the same paragraph about a dozen times already, and I still don't know what it says. I give up, and set my Kindle down on the night stand.

I've never experienced this type of jealousy before. I don't like the way it makes my heart race, my head hot, and my guts churn. The way my fingers shake as I pull the quilt up to my chin. I draw in a deep breath and let it out again, slowly, trying to calm myself and stop the rush of unwelcome thoughts crowding my brain. I trust my husband so there's nothing to worry about. Darcy needs friends right now, and that's what we are – friends.

'Hey.' Jared comes into the bedroom, naked, drying his hair with a hand towel.

'Hi,' I say, my voice tight.

'You okay? Sorry I'm so late. It was hard to get away. She's really upset.'

'I know,' I say. 'Poor woman.' I sit up. 'Did she tell you why Mike left?'

'No. She just said they hadn't been getting on.'

'How did you leave things? Was she still upset when you left?'

'Pretty upset, yeah. I don't think she wanted me to go but it was getting late so I told her to get some sleep. I offered for you to go over tomorrow, but she said she had too much to do. She did ask if I could go running with her again tomorrow evening . . .'

'Really? Again. Do you think she wants to make a regular thing of it?' I have visions of Jared spending all his evenings over there while I wait here, alone. No matter how upset Darcy is over Mike, I'm not sure I could cope with that.

'I said I wasn't sure about my work schedule,' Jared says. 'Thought I better talk it over with you first.' Jared slides into bed next to me and kisses me on the lips, his breath minty clean.

'I don't mind you running together,' I lie. 'But . . . I'd rather you didn't spend the whole evening over there. It's lonely here without you.'

Jared scooches up close to me. 'I missed you, too,' he says, kissing my earlobe and my neck.

'Your hair's still damp,' I say, getting a waft of citrus shower gel. 'You're making the pillow all wet.'

Jared slides a hand down over my bare skin. I mould my body to his, briefly forgetting all about damp pillows and needy friends.

CHAPTER SEVENTEEN

'Cheers!' We raise our fizzing glasses towards Jared. He's standing by the window staring at us, the blue of the harbour and the sky behind him, the midday, winter sun casting a halo around his smiling face.

'I just want to say a huge thank you to all of you for joining me in *Create*, my new venture,' he says. 'Sorry, *our* new venture. I hope we'll be a successful and happy agency, and that we'll be here for many years to come.' He raises his glass again. 'To success and happiness at *Create*.'

'Success and happiness at *Create*!' we echo, sipping at our champagne.

We had Beth look over Mike's contract for the offices, and she declared it all legitimate and above board. *Generous*, she said, only tweaking a couple of minor clauses. So, here we are a few weeks later having a celebratory lunchtime launch party.

'I'd also like to thank my beautiful wife, Louisa,' Jared adds, 'for supporting me in this wild and crazy dream. I'm doing this for her and for our son. To the beautiful Louisa!'

'The beautiful Louisa!' I redden as everyone turns to face me, glasses aloft, feeling something of an imposter. I didn't exactly support Jared in his dreams of starting his own business. But, now that it's here, of course I want him to succeed. I nod awkwardly, unsure about whether you're supposed to drink to your own health or just stand there letting others do the drinking. I take a sip anyway, needing another slug of alcohol to calm my turbulent thoughts.

'Lastly,' Jared continues. 'I want to thank our landlady and great family friend, Darcy. Please raise your glasses to the fabulous Darcy Lane.'

'To the fabulous Darcy Lane!' we cry.

My eyes swivel from Jared to Darcy. She's standing off to the side, a shaft of sunlight illuminating her like a spotlight on the star of the show. Dressed immaculately in a cream trouser suit, her blonde hair gleams, and her features dimple prettily as we toast her generosity and friendship. She steps out of the spotlight and into Jared's embrace. They kiss on the cheek and she whispers something to him that makes him throw his head back and roar with laughter.

My heart twists with a familiar pain. One I've tried to swallow down for several weeks now. Ever since my husband started spending most of his evenings running with her, consoling her, laughing with her. But I only have myself to blame. Wasn't it I who suggested it in the first place? I have nothing to be jealous of, I tell myself. My husband still loves me. He still comes home to me each night. Nothing has happened with Darcy, and there's no hint that Jared is bored with me. So why then does my heart beat erratically and my insides turn over every time I see them together or think of them being together?

Mike isn't here. In fact, we haven't seen him since he left Darcy. Initially, Mike's absence worried Jared, but Darcy has managed to handle all his business queries, so far.

The toasts are over and someone cranks the music up. I introduce myself to a couple of Jared's new employees and we make polite conversation about the stunning location of the offices and how wonderful it will be to work here overlooking the quay and the harbour beyond. All the while, I have my eye on Jared and Darcy who are laughing with a cluster of young guys in suits. They look like the perfect couple. Him, tall and dark, ambition oozing from every pore. Her, fair and slender, expensively sleek. I feel dowdy by comparison.

Back when I was in my twenties, my wild auburn curls used to make me the cool, quirky one who everyone wanted to hang out with. Smart and edgy. Boho chic personified. I was a journalist with things to say. Now, I'm old-fashioned and irrelevant. I don't belong to this glamorous world of ad campaigns and designer offices. I'm simply Jared's wife. The mother of his son. I'm not . . . good enough.

I glug down the rest of my champagne and cast about for a waitress to top me up. A wooden tray floats past, laden with warm, bite-sized fish canapés. I grab two and shove them both into my mouth at the same time, chewing but not tasting, flaky pastry sticking to my lower lip and chin. I wipe it off with the back of my free hand just as Darcy approaches.

'Hey, sweetie,' she says, her air kisses hovering metres from my pastry-flaked, salmon-breath face.

I swallow my mouthful too quickly and plaster on a smile. 'Hi.'

'You look so pretty in that dress,' she says.

I dip my head in thanks, even though I know for a fact I look awful. That my dress is too tight. That my arse looks like a shelf you could rest your drink on, and my stomach is only semi-flattish because I'm wearing a pair of Spanx two sizes too small to suck everything in.

'You look stunning as always,' I reply. 'Thanks again for the opportunity with the offices and everything. Jared really loves this place.'

'Good,' she says. 'I'm sure he'll be really successful.'

'How are *you* doing?' I ask, lowering my voice. 'Any news with Mike?'

A cloud passes across her face and she shakes her head. 'He's saying he wants a divorce.'

'I'm so sorry.' I feel stupid for envying her style and looks earlier. She's losing her husband – her family is breaking apart and I'm worrying about my dress being too tight.

'I'm not accepting it,' she says. 'I'm going to do everything I can to get him back, Louisa.'

'Good,' I say. 'I really hope you two work it out. Mike's an idiot for leaving you.'

She smiles. 'You're sweet to say so.'

'Can I get you a top up?' I ask.

'What? Oh, no thanks. I don't normally drink during the day. I just had this for the toasts.' She places her almost-full glass down on a table behind me.

'Oh, sure, okay.' I set my own empty glass down next to hers. I'd better not have any more either; I remember I have to pick Joe up from school later this afternoon. In fact, I'd better have some more canapés to soak up the alcohol I've just had.

'I have had a bit of good news,' she says, leaning closer. 'But it's nothing to do with Mike, unfortunately.'

'Oh?' I wait for her to tell me.

She bites the inside of her lip and tries to suppress a smile.

'Well?'

'I got emails last week from two different literary agents.'

'Wow,' I say. 'That's amazing.'

'I know. I can hardly believe it. They've read my column and one of them said they know of at least three big publishers who would want to offer me a book deal.'

'I'm really pleased for you, Darcy. You always wanted to write. Well, now it's happening.' I reach for my empty glass and nod at one of the waiting staff to top me up. I'll get a taxi home.

'I know. I keep having to pinch myself. It kind of makes up for all the crap I'm going through with Mike.'

I nod. 'It always seems to work like that,' I say. 'You can never have it all, can you? When one area of your life is going well, another area has to go down the toilet. It's like a law or something.'

'I notice you haven't written much lately,' Darcy says. 'Are you taking a break from *Louisa's Life's a Beach*?'

'Kathryn gave me the boot,' I say, taking another swig of champagne, feeling my anxiety and self-control detach from my brain.

'Oh, no!' Darcy says, placing a hand on my arm. 'I hope I didn't have anything to do with that.'

'Shouldn't think so,' I reply. 'Your writing's much better than mine anyway. Wouldn't blame Kathryn for giving my column to you instead.'

'You're sweet to say so, but I feel terrible now. Like I'm responsible.' Her brow creases.

Did she really not realise? It's hard to believe. Maybe it's like my sister said, maybe Darcy is so self-absorbed she doesn't think about how her actions impact on other people.

'Forget it,' I say. 'I wasn't enjoying the column any more anyway. I'm glad I've got more free time. I'm actually writing a book, too. This way, I get to spend more time on it.' That's a lie – I miss writing for the paper terribly, but I can't guilt trip Darcy when she's obviously going through such a rough patch with Mike.

'Oh! You must let me have your manuscript when it's finished. I could pass it on to my agent – once I decide who to go with.'

I neglect to mention that I haven't looked at my novel in at least three years and I have a horrible feeling that it's total crap. 'Thanks,' I say. 'I may take you up on that.'

She kisses my cheek and stares over my shoulder. 'Sweetie, I've just spotted an old friend, will you excuse me for just a—'

'Sure,' I say, draining my glass. 'Go ahead.' I have an urge to laugh, or maybe to cry. I'm not sure which. The music and the chatter, the heat and the laughter in the room are all crowding in on me. I stare from the account handlers in their suits to the designers and techies in their jeans and trainers. Everyone here is in charge of their own life. They know what they're doing. They're on a course, focused and going places. It's only me – Louisa Sullivan – who doesn't have a clue what she's doing. I smile at a couple of Jared's employees, but I don't feel in the mood to make conversation. Instead, I wander over to one of the huge windows and stare down at the quay. At two young women in suits walking past, at the boats on the water waiting for their owners to take them out.

Back when I was at uni, studying Journalism, my career was the most important thing in my life. I was driven and sharp. Excited about all the things I was going to achieve. When did I lose that drive and energy? I keep in touch with a few of my college friends, and they're all still working in the industry. My best friend from back then, Corinne, she writes investigative pieces for one of the broadsheets. Another good friend works for a music magazine, others freelance for popular online magazines and websites. Too late, I realise I took my writing gig for granted. Now it's gone, I miss it terribly. Sure, I'm a wife and mother now, and I love being those things, but I also needed something that was just mine. My writing gave me that. I had it, and I gave it away.

'Louisa? Louisa!'

His voice cuts through my self-pity and I'm suddenly back at the launch party once more, away from my maudlin thoughts.

'Hey, Jared,' I say, running a hand down his cheek. 'Looks like it's all going great. I think your agency is going to be brilliant.'

'Do you really think so?' he asks, a momentary flash of doubt in his eyes.

'Of course,' I say. 'Look at you. Look at this place, these people. You're going to be mega-successful, Jared Sullivan. I'm surprised *Hello* magazine aren't here.'

'No, but we've got *Compass* magazine and *Dorset Life*. You ready to pose for the camera?'

'What? Now?'

'Yep, come on.' He pauses and stares at me. 'Are you drunk, Lou?'

'I might be . . . just a little bit. Gonna have to get a taxi home.'

'Honestly, what are you like.' He rolls his eyes and wipes his thumb across my lower lip. I thought he was being sexy, but he holds out his thumb, to show me a bit of pastry that was stuck to my lip.

'Can't take you anywhere.' He leans down to kiss me, and I grin up at him, feeling happier. Sod it. Who cares if Darcy Lane has my column. Who cares if she's getting an agent and a book deal. I have my gorgeous husband. And I'm going to write my own damn book.

* * *

By the time the taxi dropped me home I was sober again, if a little fuzzy-headed, so I decided to walk to school to pick Joe up. Now, we're home again and Joe's in bed waiting for Jared to come home and read him a story while I pick up random pieces of dirty laundry from Joe's bedroom floor – a pair of blue pants, a grey sock, a school shirt – and toss them into the linen basket.

'I think Daddy might be a little late tonight, Joe Bo.'

'Ugh, why is he always late?'

'He's building his new business.'

'Why?'

'You know how you like building stuff with Lego? Making cool things. And when you get into it you don't want to stop?'

'Yeah.'

'Well, grown-ups like making stuff, too. This is like Daddy's grown-up Lego, and sometimes he gets . . . caught up in what he's doing.'

'Can I see what he built?'

'I'm sure Daddy will take you to see his offices, yes.'

'Cool!' He yawns and flings his head back on the pillow. 'I'm bored of waiting. Can *you* read my story tonight?'

'Of course.' I drop an inside-out grey sock into the basket before sitting on the edge of Joe's bed. As I kiss his forehead, I hear the key in the lock.

'Daddy!' Joe nudges me out of the way, flings his duvet off and races out of the door and down the stairs.

The front door slams. 'He-e-ey, buddy!'

I stand and make my way downstairs. Jared smiles up at me as he grapples with our son in a play fight. So much for getting Joe calm before bed.

'How was the rest of the afternoon?' I ask.

'Great. The staff are really excited. Fired up, you know. I'm looking forward to really getting stuck in tomorrow.'

'Can we have a proper play fight, Dad? In the lounge.'

'Sure, sure, little man. Let me get my coat off.'

'It's a bit late for fights now,' I say. 'You've got school tomorrow. Daddy will read you a story instead.' I catch

Jared's eye and he nods.

'Your mother's right.'

'O-oh, plee-ase.' Joe stares up at me, and Jared looks at me with the exact same pleading expression.

'Fine,' I say. 'You go fight. I'll go and cook.'

'I'll eat later,' Jared says, shrugging off his coat and hanging it over the bannister. 'Gonna go for a run first.'

'With Darcy?' I ask.

'Yeah. Apparently, Mike's being a d-i-c-k.'

'Does that spell dick?' Joe says. 'Isn't that a rude word?'

'Daddy can't spell,' I say, rolling my eyes at Jared. 'He meant to say *duck*.'

'Why is Mike a duck?'

'I won't be gone long,' Jared says. 'Just an hour or so.'

My blood pressure is rising and I suddenly want to scream. Why do all our conversations these days revolve around Mike and Darcy Lane? And why have Darcy's needs suddenly become more important to my husband than mine? 'Fine,' I say. 'Do what you want, Jared.'

I march past him and into the kitchen.

'Hey!' Jared calls out to me, but I ignore him. I hear him speak to Joe: 'Your mum's right – it's too late for play fighting tonight. Hop upstairs into bed and I'll come and read you a story in a minute.'

'Oh, but—'

'*Now*, buddy. No arguing.'

I hear the mournful stomp of Joe's feet up the stairs, each step a clang of disappointment – my fault, of course.

'Lou.' Jared follows me into the kitchen. 'Why are you so cross? Did I do something?'

I shake my head, not trusting myself to speak. I don't want to cry. I don't want to shout. And I don't want an argument. But how else is all this going to get resolved? I have my back to him, my hands gripping the counter top, my shoulders hunched. He comes up behind me and places a hand on my shoulder.

'Lou, talk to me. What's going on?'

'I . . .' I snap my mouth shut. I can't tell him about my fears. He'll think I'm being irrational. I already told Beth, and she seemed to think I was blowing things out of proportion.

'Louisa?'

'I just . . . I just wanted us to spend a bit of time together this evening.' I turn to face him, folding my arms tight across my chest. 'I wanted you all to myself. If you go running, you won't be back till after nine and—'

'Okay,' he replies. 'How about if I promise to be home by eight thirty?'

I stare at him. This husband of mine who is bargaining with me so he can go out running with another woman.

'Tell you what,' I say. 'Why don't you stay out all night? I'd hate to think I was keeping you away from Darcy for longer than necessary.'

'Lou!' His brow furrows, his jaw clenches.

'What?' I say. 'You'd obviously prefer to be out running with her, than in here with me. So I'm saying, go. You should be happy now, right? Why aren't you smiling?'

'You know that's not true. I would much rather stay here with you, but I already told Darcy I would go, and she's so down at the moment.'

'She didn't look down at the launch today. She looked . . . *radiant* is a word that springs to mind. You and she were having a wonderfully hilarious conversation together.'

'Don't be ridiculous.' Jared scowls. 'It was a business launch. She's hardly going to cry in a roomful of strangers.'

'No, she'll save that for your shoulder.' I hate the words that are spitting from my mouth, yet I can't stop them.

'For God's sake! It was your suggestion I go out with her in the first place.' He runs a hand over the top of his head.

'Yes, but not every frigging night,' I hiss, suddenly mindful that our voices are becoming too loud, and Joe's still awake upstairs.

'It's not every night. And you know Darcy's going through hell with Mike. But if you want me to stay home then, of course, I—'

'Don't do me any favours, Jared.'

'Why are you being like this?'

'Actually,' I say, '*you* can stay here with Joe. *I'm* going out for a change. And you can do the school run tomorrow, too.'

'I have client meetings tomorrow, Lou. I can't—'

'Tough. You'll have to reschedule. He's your son, too. It won't hurt to drop him off and pick him up for one day.' My body is trembling as I speak. I have to get out of the house before I say more things I'll regret. I barge past him, grabbing my handbag from the table and swiping at a tear on my cheek.

'Don't go, Lou,' Jared says. 'We need to talk about this.'

'I'll be at Beth's if you need me,' I say.

I briefly consider packing an overnight bag, but I'm not calm enough to do it and I can't let Joe see me like this. Beth will have a spare toothbrush I can borrow. I grab my coat and keys and leave, feeling sick when I realise I didn't kiss Joe goodnight.

CHAPTER EIGHTEEN

Sunshine filters in through the blinds as I lie in bed in Beth and Carys' spare bedroom. The flat is quiet; quieter than our house. It's 9 am already, so I guess everyone already left for work and school. When I showed up on her doorstep last night, Beth was great. I didn't feel like talking, so she brought tea and toast into the spare room and left me alone, telling me she was there if I wanted to talk.

I didn't.

Now, I'm checking my phone. There are three voicemails, two texts, and seven missed calls, all from Jared, and all along the same lines of *I'm sorry, I miss you, Come home.* I guess I should reply, but I don't know what to say. Should I forgive my husband? Sweep it all under the carpet? What if he still wants to go running with Darcy? I can't face another argument. So, instead of replying, I set my phone back on the night stand, roll over and close my eyes once more, letting sleep take me again.

* * *

Eight hours later, I'm in the car heading home in the dark

through slow-moving, rush-hour traffic, headlights shining in my rear-view mirror, nerves clawing at my stomach, dreading another fight with Jared. I didn't wake again until midday, and spent the afternoon pottering about the place, reading old magazines, flicking through daytime TV and tidying Beth and Carys' kitchen. Not that it particularly needed tidying, but I had to keep myself busy. I wanted to make sense of the jumble of thoughts crowding my mind. Thoughts about Darcy and Mike, about Jared, and my lost or stolen career. I couldn't get any sense of perspective. I couldn't work out whether I was worrying over nothing.

I toyed with picking Joe up from school, but then I'd have had to call Jared to let him know, and I wasn't ready to speak to him yet. Anyway, I figured it wouldn't hurt for Jared to pick Joe up today. I still don't feel in the mood to speak to my husband, but I have to go home sometime, and I'm already missing Joe like crazy.

Finally, I make the turn into our road. Jared's car isn't outside the house. I hope he remembered to collect Joe. The school never called me, so I'm sure Jared must have picked Joe up. I notice someone else has parked in his spot, and then I recognise the sleek lines of Darcy's Bentley. What the hell is she doing here? I pull up opposite our house, outside Mrs Levinson's low front wall. She hates people parking outside her window – it means she can't be as nosy as usual. *Tough*. There are no other spaces close by.

Before I get out of the car, I pull down the mirror, switch on the interior light and check my make-up. If Darcy's in my house, I don't want to show up with smudged mascara and lipstick on my teeth.

My heart pounds as I let myself in through the front door, wondering if maybe Jared has confided to Darcy about our argument and she's here to try and talk me around. The hall lights are on, and a delicious smell of warm pastry wafts out of the kitchen. I walk straight through to see a vase of fresh flowers on the kitchen table, a basket of fresh bread, and various salad items laid out on the chopping board. Darcy is crouched down in front of the oven wearing a pair of oven mitts.

'Hi, Darcy,' I say, trying not to sound put out. 'What are you doing here? Is Jared with you?'

She turns and stands, closing the oven door. 'Louisa, you're back! Hi. I didn't realise you'd be home so soon.'

'Well, here I am,' I say attempting to sound light-hearted, and failing.

'You must be wondering why I'm in your kitchen,' she says, crossing the room to greet me.

'Well, yes, I thought Jared was picking Joe up. Is J—'

'Jared was working, so I offered to pick Joe up for him. It's no big deal. He said you were . . . busy?'

I bite down on my rising anger. 'You didn't have to do that. Jared was supposed to—'

'I was passing by the office and he seemed a little flustered. It's no biggie, honestly. I had to get Tyler anyway.'

I could kill Jared, but I don't want Darcy to know how I feel so I plaster on a smile and try to appear grateful. 'Thank you. You really shouldn't have.'

'I wanted to. You guys have been so supportive. It's the least I could do. I offered to take the boys back to mine, but Jared said he'd be home by seven – and he wasn't sure if you'd be back – so I said I may as well bring Joe here, save him schlepping all the way over to mine after work. I tidied up the kitchen a little and made a pie – hope you don't mind.'

I bite back the retort that he's happy to "schlep" over to hers most other nights.

'Now you're here,' she says, 'do you fancy slicing up some veggies for the salad?' She slides the chopping board in my direction.

Bloody cheek, I think. But I nod, sit at the table, pick up the knife and start slicing the cucumber. 'Where's Joe?' I ask.

'Upstairs with Tyler. They're watching the new Batman movie on Ty's iPad.'

'The new Batman movie? I thought that movie was rated 15?'

'Yes,' she says, shaking her head, 'but they love those superhero movies, don't they. You know what boys are like. It's probably just a bit of swearing – nothing they don't already hear at school.'

I have a feeling there's more in that film than just the odd swear word. I seem to remember the last Batman contained torture scenes. Joe really shouldn't be watching it, I should march upstairs and turn it off. But if I make a scene, I'll embarrass Joe in front of his friend. I decide to leave it for a few minutes. Hopefully, Darcy and Tyler will leave soon.

'I hope you don't mind me asking,' Darcy says, sitting next to me,' but is everything okay between you and Jared? It's just . . . he seemed a little—'

'What? Yes, everything's fine,' I say. 'I just had some stuff to do today, that's all.' Suddenly warm, I realise I'm still wearing my coat. I set down the knife, shrug off my coat and let it slide down the back of the chair in a screwed-up heap.

'Okay, good,' she replies. 'I was worried you two might have had an argument. Jared seemed . . . tense. The last thing I want is for you two to start going through the same crap as me and Mike.'

I give a sympathetic smile and a small laugh to dismiss her worries. 'It's probably just stress over the business launch. He wants everything to be perfect.' I should be polite and offer Darcy a cup of tea, but I need her to go. I don't want her to be here when Jared gets home, which will probably be any minute. 'Well,' I say. 'Thanks so much again. If you ever need me to get Tyler from school for you—'

'Oh, yeah, sure. My pleasure.' She takes the hint and gets

to her feet. 'The pie should be done in about fifteen more minutes. I set the timer so it should beep when it's done. And Jared's front door keys are on the hall table.'

'Thank you,' I say, faking gratitude. What I really want to do is take the pie out of the oven and sling it into the rubbish bin. My anger is irrational, yet I can't get rid of it. It's bubbling up from my gut and if Darcy doesn't leave in the next few minutes I'm likely to confront her over everything. I'm sure there's something "off" about her, but I can't risk voicing my fears yet. Not without sounding like a total lunatic.

I tramp halfway up the stairs to call Tyler down and finally they leave. Once I hear their car pull away, I stand in the hall, my heart pounding like I've just run a marathon. Leaning against the front door, I close my eyes, trying to get my breathing back under control.

'What are you doing, Mummy?'

'Come here, Joe.' I open my eyes and hold out my arms. 'I missed you, baby boy.'

'I missed you, too,' he says, allowing me to give him a great big squeeze. 'Why weren't you here this morning and after school? I had to play with *Tyler*.' Joe wrinkles his nose and wriggles out of my embrace, staring up at me. He's still in his uniform and his hair's all mussed.

'I thought you liked Tyler?'

'No. He's not nice to me now. He says mean stuff. And he

sometimes tries to hurt me.'

'He hurts you?' My fists clench.

'Only pinching and stuff, but it's annoying.'

'Pinching?'

'Yes, and he does this other thing where if I go anywhere near him, he falls over and pretends I've pushed him. The teacher told me off, but I didn't even do anything.'

'Oh, Joe!' I have to restrain myself from calling Tyler something I shouldn't. 'Do you want me to speak to your teacher about it?'

'No.'

'You sure?'

He shakes his head, and I make a mental note to talk to Darcy about her son's behaviour.

Behind me, I hear footsteps coming up the front path. The doorbell chimes. Joe and I move away from the door so I can open it.

It's my husband. He's standing on the doorstep wearing a sheepish expression. But I'm not in a forgiving mood.

CHAPTER NINETEEN

'Hi,' Jared says, stepping into the hall and closing the front door behind him. 'I just saw Darcy driving off.'

I turn away from my husband and walk into the kitchen as Joe starts chattering away to him.

'Hang on, buddy. I just need to talk to Mummy for a minute.'

'You're always doing boring talking,' Joe says.

'I know, I know. Just give me a few minutes and then we'll play, okay?'

'O-ka-a-ay.'

I hear our son thunder up the stairs. My stomach swoops and churns as Jared comes into the kitchen.

'Something smells good,' he says.

I grit my teeth and restrain myself from taking the pie out of the oven and throwing it at him.

'So, you got Darcy to pick Joe up from school?' I say.

'I couldn't get away, Lou. I'm sorry.' He rubs at his temple. 'She stopped by the office and she offered. I was so busy I said yes without thinking.'

'After everything we talked about last night. You thought it would be okay for her to help you out. What was she doing at the office, anyway? Is she going to be there every day?' As I speak I can hear how the words sound. I know how much of a cliché this is. The jealous wife accusing her husband. But I want him to see how his thoughtlessness makes me feel.

'She was just dropping off some paperwork – something to do with the fire regs. I didn't think you were coming home. You didn't return any of my calls or messages—'

'But, hey, it didn't matter if I came home or not, did it. Because you could just ask Darcy to fill in and look after your son and cook your supper.'

'That's not fair. You know how important this week is for me at work. It's our first proper working day at *Create*. I should still be there now, but I came home early because I wanted to sort things out with us.'

'I thought you said you didn't think I was coming home?'

'You know what I mean, Louisa.'

'Do I?'

He shakes his head and scowls. 'What do you want me to do?'

I sit down at the table and cover my face with my hands. I'm sick of all this anxiety and arguing. 'You better go and see Joe. He's waiting to play with you.'

'Right,' Jared says. 'But then I'm coming back down and we're going to sort this out. Whatever it is that's making you upset, okay?' I feel his hand on my shoulder.

'Fine,' I reply.

* * *

Half an hour later, I hear Jared coming back down the stairs. While he was playing with Joe, I tipped Darcy's pie in the bin and made us both an omelette.

'This looks great, Lou,' he says, coming into the kitchen. 'Shall I open a bottle of white? I think there's one in the fridge.'

I nod and take out a couple of wine glasses from the cupboard, setting them next to our plates. 'Is Joe in bed?' I ask, sitting down at the table, my throat tight with anger and nerves.

'Yep. All tucked up. I read him a chapter of *The Faraway Tree.*' Jared pours the wine and puts the bottle back in the fridge. Then he sits opposite me and tries to catch my eye, but I won't look at him. I chew my lip and cut into my omelette, even though I'm not at all hungry.

'Are you going to tell me why you're so upset?' he asks. 'You've been acting strange for weeks, Lou. I'm worried about you.'

I suppose this is where I should tell him everything, but I don't know where to start.

'We can't sort this out if you won't talk to me,' he says.

He's right, I guess. I set my knife and fork down and take a sip of wine. 'You're going to think I'm crazy.'

He doesn't reply.

I sigh and look up at him. His forehead is creased and he has dark circles under his eyes. He isn't touching his omelette or his wine. Guilt pricks at me. I shouldn't be angry with him. He's launching a new business and now he has a messed-up wife to contend with. 'Okay,' I say. 'Well . . . I'm worried about Darcy. About her involvement in our lives.'

'Go on.'

I tell him all my fears. Listing them out, one after another, like I did with Beth. This time, I also mention the fact that not only has Darcy taken my career, but now she's also muscling in on my family.

'I came home today to see Darcy in *my* kitchen, looking after *my* son, baking a pie for *my* family, while waiting for *my* husband to get home from work. Now tell me if that's not just a little bit weird.'

He shakes his head. 'I don't know, Louisa. When you put it like that, yes, it does sound weird, but—'

'Creepy,' I interrupt. 'It's creepy.'

'Can't you talk to her about it?'

'And say what, exactly? That I think she's unhinged?' I push my hair back off my face.

'Of course not. I don't know . . . Maybe it's all to do with Mike leaving. Maybe she's just screwed up because of it.'

'Maybe. But she was like it before. Remember Joe's party, and how she left his name off the invitations? And what about my column? That all happened before Mike left.'

'You should have told me you were worried, before,' Jared says.

'I have been telling you!'

'You've mentioned the odd thing, but you've never put it all together like this before.'

'Well, I'm telling you now, aren't I.'

'And why on earth did you say I'd go running with her if you felt this way?'

I watch him cut into his omelette and take his first bite.

'She was crying,' I say, remembering back to how upset she'd been. 'Mike had only just left her. But this is what happens. She does something dodgy, like taking my column, then she acts all vulnerable so people end up feeling sorry for her.'

'So, shall I not go running with her any more?' Jared asks.

God, he still doesn't get it. It's like déjà vu from last night. I can tell Jared's trying to please me, but I'm still pretty sure he thinks I'm worrying over nothing. My blood is heating up and I feel like either screaming or walking out. I can't do that again.

'Do you think I'm overreacting?' I ask through gritted teeth.

'No, not overreacting. But you've got to admit, it does sound a bit strange. Why would she want to hurt you? She doesn't even know us that well. You haven't done anything to offend her, have you?'

'No, I bloody have not.'

'Sorry, I didn't mean to—'

'I don't know why she's doing what she's doing, but she is.'

'Why would she purposely want to take your job? It's not like she needs the money.'

'I didn't say I knew *why* she was doing it.'

'Maybe she acts that way with everyone,' he says. 'Maybe it's not personal. It's just how she is.'

'So, does that make it alright?'

'No, of course not. I'm just saying that she might not have a personal thing against you.'

'Hm,' I say, not buying it.

'Thing is,' Jared says, 'we need to keep her on side with the business and everything. Mike's gone AWOL so Darcy is basically my landlady. If we piss her off, I could lose everything.'

'You've signed a lease for the offices. They can't just kick you out.'

'Yeah, but the Lanes gave me all my contacts. If they wanted to, they could take all my business from me. Blacklist me in the area.'

My shoulders drop as I realise the precarious position we're in. 'Shit. I didn't think of that.'

'Look,' Jared says. 'I'll tell her I'm too busy to run with her at the moment, okay? But I can't stop her from showing up at the office. I still have to be nice to her.'

I nod.

'But, Lou . . . me being nice to Darcy – it means nothing, okay? Don't start getting paranoid. I love you.'

I bite my lip and nod again.

'Does that make you feel any better?' he asks. 'Am I forgiven for being an insensitive git?'

I don't reply.

'Am I forgiven just a tiny bit?' He puts on his puppy-dog expression and I can't stop my mouth from curling into a reluctant smile.

'Mummy!' Joe calls out from upstairs. He sounds upset.

'I'll go,' Jared says, rising to his feet.

'It's okay,' I say. 'Sit and eat your dinner. I'm not hungry anyway.'

'Sure?'

I nod. Jared sits back down and I jog up the stairs to see what's wrong with Joe. He's in bed with the covers pulled up to his chin. The night light casts a cosy glow around his room, but his face is white and tear-streaked.

'Baby, what's the matter?'

'I can't sleep,' he sobs. 'I keep seeing horrible faces every time I close my eyes.'

'Is it because of the film you were watching with Tyler?' I sit next to him on the bed and smooth his fringe out of his eyes.

Joe nods. 'Some bits were good, but then it got really scary and Tyler was making fun of me because I didn't want to look.'

Bloody Darcy again, messing up my family life. 'It's not real, Joe. Don't think about it. They're just actors wearing funny costumes. Think about football instead. Think about all your favourite players, okay?'

'What if I can't stop thinking about the faces,' he says. 'They feel like they're real.'

'How about if I read to you until you fall asleep? Something lovely and friendly like *Old Bear*?'

'That's babyish.' He pouts.

'No, it's funny and lovely and it will help you get to sleep. Okay?'

Joe relaxes his expression and nods.

'I walk over to Joe's bookshelf and pull out the large hardback book. I haven't read this to him since he was about five. But I know it will help him calm down and forget his fears.

'Mummy,' he says as I sit back down next to him.

'Mm?'

'I don't think I like Tyler's mummy any more. I didn't like it when she was here instead of you and Daddy.'

'Why? What did she do? Did she say anything to you?'

'No,' he says, his brow creasing. 'She says nice things and she smiles at me, but it's not a real smile. It makes my tummy feel scared.'

His words chill me. That's exactly how I feel about Darcy. Maybe it's not just my paranoia, after all. My throat is tight and I realise my hands are shaking. I need to get that woman out of our lives.

CHAPTER TWENTY

Summer 1993

Callum and Nicole ran towards the park, a fizz of excitement building in Nicole's chest that wasn't anything to do with the few sips of Fanta she'd just had. They'd get that Derek Mullins, and he'd be sorry he'd messed with her brother.

'Down here,' she cried.

Callum followed her into the narrow alleyway that led to the playing field.

'You wait here,' she said.

'Can't I wait in the park?'

'I told you to wait here, didn't I.' Nicole stuck her hands on her hips and glared at him. 'God's sake.'

Callum thrust out his bottom lip but did as he was told.

Nicole walked along the rest of the alleyway on her own, glancing back to check her brother had stayed put. Then, she jogged across the playing field towards the swing park. Pretty soon, she had to slow to a walk, her lungs burning with the exertion, her face hot. Through the railings, she saw the swing park was busy. Full of school kids of all ages, some from her year. Then, she spied some of the lads from Cal's year group. They were spinning each other on the wooden roundabout, so fast it made her dizzy to watch. She stopped for a moment to get her breath back, suddenly a little nervous about approaching them. Nicole was older, but Derek was with about five others – all boys. Then, she remembered why she was here and so she stuck out her chin and pushed her way through the metal gate.

'Oi, Derek!' she called, shoving her hands in her pockets.

A couple of his mates looked over. They nudged Derek who was gleefully pushing the roundabout, delighting in the cries of the other boys yelling at him to *stop* and *slow down*. He stopped spinning his friends, straightened up and looked over in her direction, frowning.

His mates started elbowing him, teasing him; no doubt saying stupid stuff like she was his girlfriend. Nicole swaggered over, trying to appear friendly.

'I need to talk to you,' she said to Derek.

His pathetic friends all laughed.

'Why?' Derek replied, scratching his mousey-brown hair and folding his arms across his skinny chest.

'Come here and you'll find out.'

'Wooooooh!' the other boys jeered, making out she fancied him or something.

As if.

His cheeks reddened. They pushed him in her direction and she gave him an encouraging smile.

'You ever had a smoke?' she asked when he was close enough to reach out and touch.

'Yeah,' he replied.

Nicole bet he was lying. 'You want one now?'

'You got cigarettes?'

'Yeah. Wanna come and have a smoke with me?' Nicole could see him weighing it up in his mind. 'Come and have a smoke, then I'll give you some ciggies to share with your mates.'

'Really?'

She nodded. Nicole knew that would get him. The thought of showing off.

'They in your bag?' He tipped his head towards the school bag slung across her body.

'Yeah.'

'Let's see.'

'We'll go over there.' Nicole pointed across the playing field, back to where Cal was hidden in the alleyway.

'Why can't we have one here?' Derek said.

'Cos the older kids will nick them off us, stupid.'

Derek flushed. 'Oh, yeah, right.'

'Come on. We'll have a quick puff, then you can share the rest with your mates.'

'Okay.' Derek stuck his hands in his pockets and made his way out of the swing park with Nicole, his friends jeering as they walked away together.

They trudged across the field in silence. Nicole loosened her school tie, her heart pounding ferociously. She'd get this cocky little shit back for picking on her brother. He'd be sorry.

Once they neared the alleyway, Derek hesitated. 'Where's these ciggies, then?' he asked.

'Let's go in there,' Nicole replied, pointing to the entrance up ahead. 'No one can see us, then.'

It looked like he was about to object, so she linked arms with him and led him into the shady, grey alleyway. As soon as she saw it was clear of people, apart from Callum up the other end, Nicole let go of Derek's arm and shoved him hard in the back so he went sprawling face down on the concrete. Next, she slid off her tie, jumped on top of him and yanked his arms behind his back, tying them together. He'd been stunned for a few seconds but now he was trying to wriggle out from under her, swearing and cursing, yelling and kicking out at her.

'Get over here, Cal!' she yelled, sitting on Derek's legs.

'What you doing?' Derek cried. 'Get off me, you mad cow!'

Callum's footsteps slapped the concrete as he ran towards her.

'Gimme your tie!' Nicole cried to her brother. 'And help me pin him down.'

Callum slipped his tie over his head and thrust it at Nicole. She snatched it off him, and yanked Derek's legs together, slipping the ready-made loop over both of Derek's feet, and tightening it around his ankles so he could no longer kick out at her.

'Gotcha!' she said triumphantly, rolling Derek onto his back and standing over him so he was now staring up at her, shock in his eyes.

'Let me go,' he said. 'My arms . . . you tied them too tight. They're hurting.'

'Tough,' Nicole snarled. 'Say sorry to my brother for kicking him, and for saying he wets the bed.'

Derek's eyes wandered over to Callum. 'That weirdo's your brother?'

Nicole planted a savage kick on Derek's calf.

'Owww! Okay, okay, I'm sorry. Now let me go.'

'Not yet,' Nicole said. 'First, Callum's got a present for you.'

'I don't want a present,' Derek said, his bravado wavering. 'I wanna go home.'

'Callum,' Nicole said, turning to her brother. 'Remember I gave you that can of Fanta to drink?'

Callum nodded.

'Well, you probably need a wee now, don't you?' She grinned and then turned to look at Derek.

Derek's eyes flicked from Nicole to Callum and back again. She saw the confusion in his eyes, and then the disbelief as he began to realise what was about to happen.

Her stupid brother still didn't get it, though, his puzzled frown beginning to annoy her.

'Oh, for God's sake, Cal. Wee on him.'

'Eurgh. That's gross, Nic.'

'I know.' She smiled.

Derek was shaking his head, trying to wriggle out of his bonds, but he was tied too securely. 'Help!' he yelled.

'You shout out one more time and I'll get Callum to piss in your mouth.'

Derek clamped his mouth shut and squeezed his eyes closed, his whole body tensed, waiting.

Nicole shoved her brother and nodded towards his trouser area, her eyes wide and expectant. Cal knew better than to disobey her. He'd be in for it if he said no. Nicole's smile widened as Callum positioned himself over Derek's body and peed for all he was worth. A yellow arc spattered Derek's school uniform. Callum got creative, gyrating and making swirling patterns.

'Get his head, too,' Nicole said, giggling.

Callum moved around and let the last few drips soak into Derek's mousy hair. The boy was crying now. Served him right. He wouldn't mess with her brother again, that was for sure.

'Now kick him,' Nicole said.

'What?' Cal said.

'Go on. He kicked you. So you can kick him back. It's fair.'

Callum gave Derek a gentle kick on his thigh.

'Not like that, like this.' Nicole aimed a vicious kick on Derek's side, making him howl in pain.

Callum stared up at her and shook his head. 'I don't wanna, Nic.'

'Do it,' she hissed.

Callum kicked Derek in exactly the same spot. Derek sobbed.

'Again,' Nicole said.

Callum kicked him again.

'No one messes with me or my brother,' Nicole hissed. 'No one.'

CHAPTER TWENTY ONE

2016

The sky is a sheet of grey hanging thick and heavy with unshed raindrops. It meets the darker sea in a blurred line out on the horizon. Seagulls drop and rise, buffeted and thrown about by the gusting wind. My hair whips around my face and I tug my woollen hat down more firmly, protecting my ears from the piercing cold as I walk along the empty beach.

Now that I've aired my fears with Jared, I don't feel quite so alone. And, while I still think he's sceptical, at least now he understands why I've been so upset these past few days. At least he won't be going out running with her any more. That's something.

I love being on the beach out of season. Having it all to myself as the waves break over soft sand and broken shells. Like I'm the last person on earth. It's not very often I get to have this feeling of space. Yet the sense of freedom is fleeting. I check my watch. It will soon be time to pick up Joe from school. My stomach clenches as I realise Darcy will be there.

'Louisa!'

It sounds like someone's calling my name. It's hard to tell over the crash of the waves and the roar of the wind. I turn to see a dark figure waving in the distance. Squinting, I make out a man heading my way. Fear grips me for a moment as I flash back to memories of my stalker. But I see now that it's a more familiar figure. He breaks into a jog and I walk to meet him.

'Louisa, I thought it was you.'

'Hi, Mike.' He looks awful, his face gaunt, stubble grazing his chin and upper lip. I'm not sure what to say to him.

'How are you?' he asks.

'Fine. Just blowing the cobwebs away before I go and pick Joe up from school.'

He glances at his watch. 'Oh, yes, I guess it's that time. Are you going there now?'

I nod.

'Shame,' he says. 'I was going to suggest a coffee.'

'That would've been lovely,' I say. 'But I really have to go.'

'How's Darcy?' he blurts out, his face taut, distressed.

'Darcy?' I let out a breath. 'Still pretty upset I think. She misses you, Mike.'

'Really?' His eyes light up, which I find pretty odd considering he walked out on her.

'Do you think . . .' he begins. 'Do you think she might . . . take me back?'

I frown, confused. 'I thought you wanted a divorce?'

'What! A divorce? No. Why on earth would you think that?'

'Darcy said you asked for a divorce. I'm sure she did.'

'You must have got that wrong. I'm losing my mind here, Louisa. She kicked me out of the house with no explanation. She won't see me. She won't even let me see Tyler.' His voice cracks and I can see how much it's costing him to not break down in front of me.

I put a hand on his arm. 'Mike, she told me you walked out on her. She was devastated.'

His eyes cloud with confusion. 'But—'

'Mike, I'm really sorry, I have to go and get Joe. I can't be late for pick up.'

'Of course, of course. But you must be mistaken. I would never leave Darcy. She's the one who wanted me to go.'

I don't know what to say. This is a completely different version of events to the one Darcy told me. So one of them must be lying, and I know who I'm inclined to believe.

'Can we meet later?' he asks. 'Will you come over to my place?'

I open my mouth to think of an excuse. I really don't want to get in the middle of this.

'Please,' he says, sensing my reluctance. 'I'm desperate here. Just for half-an-hour or so.'

I nod. 'Okay.'

Mike takes a business card out of his wallet and scribbles an address on the back. 'I'll be in all evening. Here's where I'm staying. My mobile's on the front.' He presses it into my hand with a squeeze. 'Thank you.'

'Okay. See you later,' I say with a tight-lipped smile, wishing I'd never agreed to it.

I head back to the beach car park at a brisk pace, knowing I'm going to be late for Joe. Even so, I have to call Jared to let him know what's happened. I stop for a moment to rummage through my bag for my phone. My bag swings back in the wind, tipping my purse, keys and hand gel into the sand. I scrabble about, picking them back up and end up dumping half the beach back into my bag. Finally, I locate my phone in my coat pocket and call my husband.

He picks up his mobile after one ring.

'Hey,' he says. 'Everything okay?'

'You'll never guess who I just bumped into?' I say as I jog up the sandy steps onto the promenade.

'Who?'

'Mike.'

'Darcy's Mike? Did he say anything about the lease?'

'No, but he did say something pretty weird.' I tell him what Mike said about Darcy kicking him out, and not the other way around.

'That's odd,' he says. 'Why would Mike lie about something like that?'

'That's if he *is* lying,' I say. 'Maybe she's the one who lied.'

'But Darcy was so upset when he left,' Jared says. 'You saw her. No one can fake that kind of hurt.'

'Mike was shocked when I suggested he'd left Darcy. You didn't see him. And when I said Darcy was devastated when he left, he looked so hopeful, like he really wanted to get back with her.'

'So, maybe it was all some massive misunderstanding,' Jared says. 'Look, Lou, sorry, but I can't talk about this now. I'm about to go into a meeting.'

'Sure, okay, I've got to get Joe anyway. I just wanted to let you know tha—'

'I've really got to go. We'll talk later, okay? Love you.'

'Okay, love you, too.' I end the call with an uneasy feeling. This whole situation is weird. Why would Darcy lie about Mike leaving her? It makes no sense.

* * *

School is only a ten-minute drive from the beach, but there are absolutely no parking spaces anywhere in the vicinity of the gates, so I drive round and round the block, my hands clenching the steering wheel, my breaths coming short and fast. Reproaching myself for not getting here sooner. By the time I eventually find a space, it takes me five attempts to parallel park, and I'm sure the workmen across the road are sniggering at my poor attempts to shoehorn myself into the tiny space. Finally, with sweat gathering at my neck and my heart pumping, I exit the car and race the two and a half blocks to school, my knee groaning in agony.

Turns out I needn't have worried – Mrs Landry and several of the other teachers are late out today, and the playground is still crowded with parents. I stand at the edge getting my breath back, trying not to catch anyone's eye. I don't feel like talking. But luck isn't on my side.

'Hey.'

It's Darcy. I manage a limp smile.

'Your face is really red,' she says. 'You okay?'

'I thought I was late for pick up. I had to run.'

'They'll be a while yet. Wasn't it lovely. Joe was so funny.'

I'm not sure what she's talking about. 'Sorry? What?'

'The Year 3 assembly this afternoon. Just now. Oh, but you just got here so you mustn't have watched it.'

'The assembly was today?' My heart sinks. 'I thought it was next week.'

'Oh,' she sticks out her bottom lip. 'Did you get the wrong date? Personally, I can't live without a wall planner. If I don't write it on there, it doesn't happen. You should really get one.'

I grit my teeth, gutted that I missed Joe's assembly. With everything going on, I totally forgot. And yet, I still had time for a walk on the beach. I feel like a totally shit mother. At least there's one thing I can do to help Joe.

'Actually, Darcy, while you're here, I wanted a quick word with you about Joe and Tyler.'

She raises an eyebrow.

'It's a bit awkward, but Joe says Tyler's been pinching him, and also getting him into trouble with the teacher. Would you mind having a little chat with him? And of course, if Joe's done anything to—'

'Actually,' she says, her eyes narrowing, 'I wasn't going to mention it, but Tyler has been saying the exact same thing about Joe. So maybe you might want to have a little word with *him*.'

I'm taken aback by her sudden and barely concealed rage. 'Oh, sorry, I didn't realise. Of course—'

'It's okay,' she says, smoothing away her anger, 'boys will be boys. I would certainly appreciate you speaking to Joe about it. Tyler's not usually one to tell tales, so this must really have upset him.'

I don't believe for a minute that Joe's been hurting Tyler. It's just not in his nature. But I'll pretend to take her concerns seriously if it means she'll also speak to her son.

'Great,' I say. 'So if we both have a word with them, hopefully, they can go back to being friends again.'

Darcy gives me a perfunctory smile, which makes me doubt she's going to mention anything to Tyler. Fine. If he hurts Joe again, I'll just have to go direct to his teacher.

'I bumped into Mike this afternoon,' I say, hoping what he

said might put her in a better mood.

Darcy's face leaches of colour for a moment. 'You saw Mike?'

I nod. 'I think you might have got things wrong, Darcy. He said he wants you back.' Maybe this is the news she's been waiting for. The news that will make her happier.

'Mike said that? To you?'

I nod. 'He asked me to pop over to his place this evening – just for a quick chat. If you want me to pass on a message, or put in a good word for you?'

'You're going to see my husband?' she says, her voice icy.

'He seemed so upset, Darcy. I think he really wants to get back with you. That's good news isn't it?'

'You don't know what you're talking about, Louisa,' she hisses. 'And if you don't mind, I'd rather you stayed out of my business.'

I can't believe *she's* telling me to stay out of *her* business.

'Oh,' she adds, tilting her head, 'and I take it you're the one behind Jared telling me he's "too busy" to run any more. I thought you were my friend. After everything I've done for you. I didn't realise you could be such a bitch.'

'What!' My mouth falls open and I shake my head. 'I'm not . . . I'm only trying to—'

'Just leave my husband alone, Louisa!' Her voice is so loud that some of the other parents and teachers turn to look from Darcy to me. Darcy now has tears in her eyes and I don't believe for one minute that they're genuine. This display is purely to make me look bad in front of everyone.

'Darcy,' I say, through gritted teeth. 'I'm just trying to help—'

'Like hell. First, your son starts bullying Tyler,' she cries, 'and now you're sneaking around with my husband. I don't know what game you're playing, but I need you to leave me and my family alone!'

Heat floods my cheeks and I glance about for a friendly face. All I'm met with is embarrassed glances, confusion and open hostility.

'Darce, are you okay?' A petite lady with a designer puppy in her arms steps over to Darcy with concern in her eyes.

Darcy chokes back a sob and nods. 'I'll be fine,' she says, bringing her hands up to her face.

Yet more people approach her, and she's soon swept away in a secure cocoon of sympathetic parents, leaving me standing alone in the fading light on the edge of the playground. My mouth hangs open, confusion and anger clouding my mind. Her bright hair swings as she lurches away from me, gradually surrounded by a gaggle of reassuring mums. They shoot dark looks my way, throwing their arms around Darcy's hunched shoulders as they lean in with comforting words.

What the hell just happened?

CHAPTER TWENTY TWO

I'm sitting on the sofa in the lounge hugging my knees to my chest. The curtains are drawn. A moth hurls itself at the table lamp which is doing its best to cast a comforting glow, but I'm too shaken up to feel anywhere near comfortable. There's a hard knot in my stomach and a lump in my throat as I mentally play back the events of this afternoon.

After standing awkwardly in the playground for what seemed like forever, enduring the stares and whispers of the other parents, Joe's class finally came out. I collected him in a shocked daze, barely able to focus on any of his excited chatter about his class assembly. Thankfully, Joe didn't seem to be upset that I hadn't been in the audience. Somehow, I got him home. I remember very little about the journey back, my emotions wildly swinging between distress and anger. I'm only thankful I didn't crash the car.

I managed to get him into bed early tonight. Now, I'm waiting for Jared to get home so I can tell him about my awful experience with Darcy today. At least I know it's not me being paranoid any more. She's unhinged. She's a liar. And she's been trying to destroy my life for weeks. I should have listened to my gut right from the start. The question is, *why?* Why has she been gunning for me all this time? Did I do something wrong? Did I offend her in some way? Is she a deranged person who behaves like this with everyone? Or, am I missing something?

I'm really not sure I should go over to Mike's this evening. I think it would probably be better if I just stayed the hell away from all the Lanes. I'm seriously considering pulling Joe out of Cerne Manor and putting him back in his old school. How can I walk back into that playground when all the mums think I'm some kind of husband-stealer? The looks on their faces this afternoon . . . it was awful.

The radiators hiss and the pipes gurgle. The house is warm, yet my hands and feet are icy cold. I cross my arms and slot my hands under my armpits to try to defrost them. Jared's key turns in the lock but I don't move from the sofa. I don't want our evening to be marred by another conversation about Darcy. And yet I have to tell my husband what happened. I need his support in this.

'Hey?' Jared calls. The front door bangs and his keys land with a clatter on the hall table.

'In here!' I call, hearing the listless tone in my voice.

His head pops around the door. 'Hey.'

'Hi.'

'How you doing?'

'Not great.'

His face falls. 'Why? What's the matter?'

'Give you three guesses.'

'Not something to do with Darcy.' He gives the slightest of eye rolls, and I guess I can't blame him. Everything these days seems to be about that woman.

'Sorry, yes it is,' I reply.

'I'm starving. Let me grab something to eat,' he says, 'and then you can tell me.'

With some difficulty, I peel myself off the sofa and follow him into the kitchen. 'There are jacket potatoes in the oven,' I say, 'but they won't be ready for another twenty minutes.'

'I'll just have a cheese cracker or something in the meantime,' he says, his brow creased, his mouth a hard line. He's obviously pissed off that he's come home to another Darcy drama, but what am I supposed to do? It's not my fault I have a psycho friend trying to hack apart my life.

I sit at the table as Jared pulls a beer from the fridge, and loads a plate with crackers, sliced cheese and salad. He pops the bottle cap and takes a long swig.

'How was work today?' I ask.

'Good,' he replies.

'Everything going as planned? Are you getting the business in?'

He nods and leans back against the fridge for a moment, eyes closed. Then, he slides into the chair opposite me.

Okay, this isn't going well. He's not happy. What should I

do? Should I not tell him what happened today? Ignore it and pretend everything's fine.

'So?' he finally says, his eyes open again. 'What's happened?'

I tell him about the playground incident. About Darcy making out that I'm going after her husband, and about her accusing Joe of bullying Tyler when it's clearly the other way around. I tell him about Darcy raising her voice so that all the other mums now hate me.

Jared shakes his head, and I can't tell whether he's annoyed with Darcy's behaviour, or annoyed that I'm talking about her, yet again.

'Are you pissed off or something?' I ask. 'I could really do with some support about now.'

'Just tired, Lou.'

'Sorry,' I say, not sounding sorry at all. 'I hate loading all this on you, but don't you think she's totally out of order?'

'Yes,' he says wearily. 'Yes. It sounds like you had a horrible afternoon. What made her say those things, anyway? Did you say anything? Something that could have provoked her?'

'No,' I reply. 'Well, I told her about bumping into Mike, and that he asked me to go over there —'

'Well, there you go,' he says. 'She's going through a breakup, Louisa. You telling her that you're going to see her husband probably isn't going to make her feel great.'

'I was tactful and nice. I didn't say anything to provoke her. And anyway, I'm pretty sure she lied about him leaving her. I told you on the phone, Mike says *she* kicked *him* out.'

'Maybe she lashed out without thinking. I'm sure she'll apologise.'

'You weren't there,' I say, trying to keep my voice under control. 'She's not right in the head, Jared. She's trying to wreck my life.'

He nods and takes another swig of beer. 'So, what do you want to do about it? What can we do? Because this is getting beyond crazy. Every day there's something else with Darcy. I don't think I can deal with it for much longer.'

'Me neither,' I say.

'No, Lou,' he says through gritted teeth, 'I mean, I don't think I can deal with your obsession for much longer.'

'My what!'

He stares across at me. 'Every day, Lou. Every day. It's Darcy's done this, or Darcy's done that. I want to be supportive, but I think it would be better for everyone if you just stayed away from her. Don't go to her house, or organise joint parties, or go for coffee with the woman. Just stay the hell away, and then we won't have all this constant drama.' He rakes his fingers through his hair and takes another swig of beer. His plate of cheese and crackers still sits untouched on the table.

I scrape my chair back and stand up, my whole body

shaking with hurt and rage. Then, I turn my back on my husband and leave the kitchen.

'Where are you going?' he calls.

'Out.'

'Louisa!'

I ignore him, fumble on the floor for my handbag and snatch at my coat from the coat rack. My hands are shaking so badly I can barely get my arms through the sleeves. Jared comes out of the kitchen.

'Lou, I'm sorry,' he says. 'I'm just tired.'

'No,' I say. 'It's fine, you've made it perfectly clear that I'm a demented woman who's making a mountain out of a molehill. So, I'll leave you in peace. Joe's in bed. It's Saturday tomorrow, so you can have a nice boys' weekend together.' I glance around for my car keys. They're not in my bag, or on the hall table. I pat my coat pockets and hear the metal jingle.

'Where are you going?' he says, putting a hand on my coat sleeve. 'Stay. Please. I'm sorry. I'm just cranky, that's all.'

I glare at him, open the front door and walk out into the cold night, closing the front door behind me with a soft click. My hurt over Darcy's behaviour is bubbling up into a cold, determined fury. I'm sick of being a victim. Sick of being treated like I'm behaving unreasonably. That woman has been undermining my confidence since the day I met her. Manipulating me, fooling my family, and I'm not going to stand for it any more.

I'm shivering, my hands are clammy and my head doesn't feel right, but the best thing now is to get this over and done with. I draw the keys from my pocket and unlock the car.

I'm going to go to Mike's place and I'm going to get him to tell me all about his wife. I'm going to ask him exactly what Darcy's problem is with me and why she told me *he* left *her* when it was quite clearly the other way around. I'm going to tell Mike exactly what she's been saying and doing, and I'm going to get answers. And if Mike doesn't know, or if he won't talk, then I'll drive round to Darcy's and demand that she tell me exactly what the hell is going on.

I slide into the car. It's cold enough in here to see my breath. There'll probably be a frost tonight. I take my wallet out of my bag and draw out the business card Mike gave me earlier. It's too dark to see, so I switch on the car's interior light and check the address – Chaddesley Glen – I know where that is, so I start the engine and pull away with a judder and screech.

Disappointment pulls at my gut, reminding me that Jared didn't follow me out of the house. That he didn't try to persuade me back in. I might have let him if he'd at least tried. Maybe it's better this way. I need to find out what's really behind Darcy's passive-aggressive behaviour. If I can end her subtle attacks on me, then I can go back to having a normal life with my family.

The apartment isn't far away – only about ten minutes by car, yet it might as well be on the other side of the world. Jared and I couldn't afford a garden shed on this road. Mike's place is situated on the top of a hill, minutes from the harbour. I pull up outside a new block of blue and glass apartments. I don't give myself time to stop and think about anything. Determined, I turn off the engine and exit the car, the chill air making me catch my breath.

The street is silent. Next door to the apartments, a beautiful 1920's arts-and-crafts house sits on its own, alone amid all the shiny new blocks, its garden wild and untended. I have a sad feeling its days are numbered. I wonder how long it will remain there. How long until developers like Mike and Darcy seize the land and dump another multi-million-pound concrete and glass apartment block on it.

I make my way up the stone steps and through the automatic doors into the spacious lobby. A man comes out and holds the inner door open for me. I murmur a thank you, go straight through and call the lift. Flat 9 – Mike's flat – is on the top floor. It's the penthouse, of course. After a short wait, the lift doors slide open and I step inside. The unforgiving lights and the gleaming mirror inside declare me a mess. My face is pale, my mascara smudged, my hair greasy and my clothes crumpled. I don't even try to repair the damage. Instead, I turn away from the mirror and face the doors, trying not to inhale the cloying scent of pine air freshener.

The lift whooshes up and the doors open with a loud ding. Stepping out, I find myself in a small lobby with a leather armchair and a tall, leafy pot plant.

There's only one door. He must have the whole top floor to himself. I'm curious to see what it's like inside. I press the buzzer and wait. No answer. I check my watch – almost nine o'clock. He said he would be in all evening. I press the buzzer again.

Nothing.

I was all geared up to get this sorted out. I'll be gutted and annoyed if he's not at home. Maybe he's got the TV turned up too loud to hear the buzzer. I'll call his mobile. I sit in the leather armchair and root around in my bag for my phone and Mike's card. I punch in the number. It goes straight to voicemail.

'Hey, Mike,' I say. 'It's me, Louisa. I'm at your apartment. You asked me to pop by this evening. No worries if you're out. Anyway, give me a call if you need to talk. Bye.'

Maybe he forgot, or maybe he changed his mind. Maybe Darcy didn't want me to come over here, so she invited him to hers. Whatever. I'm done with it. Done with the Lanes and their crazy lives. What am I even doing here? I need to go back home, make up with my husband and stay the hell away from all three of them. I'll talk to Jared about moving Joe back to his old school. Everything will be fine. Relief sweeps across me and I suddenly feel lighter.

I slip my phone and Mike's business card back into my bag and stand up. As I do so, I notice that Mike's front door isn't closed properly. I push with my fingertips and it swings open, revealing a large hallway with polished wooden floorboards, a geometric-patterned rug and Scandi-style hallway furniture. The hall light is on but the rooms beyond appear to be in darkness.

'Hello!' I call out.

There's no reply. I tilt my head, listening for any sounds within, hesitant to step over the threshold.

'Mike?' My voice sounds loud. The back of my neck prickles. Everything suddenly seems too quiet. Maybe he had to go somewhere in a hurry and forgot to lock up properly. I hope he hasn't had a break in. The hall looks untouched. I should probably go in and double-check that he's not here, then I can lock up and leave him a message that his door was open.

I step inside. All my senses on heightened alert, telling me to get out. To leave and call the police. But I can't stop myself moving forward into the silent hallway. I push open one of the inner doors and press the light switch. A bedroom. Empty. I move to the next two rooms, one is another bedroom, the other an office. Nothing looks as though it's been disturbed. I enter the living room, next. It's a vast space opening out onto a glass balcony, the harbour lights twinkling below. The TV is on with the sound down, bright images of some American city flickering across the screen. I can't imagine Mike would have left without turning the television off. Unless there was some kind of emergency . . .

I leave the lounge and open the next door along the hallway. It's dark, so I fumble for the light switch. And now I see him. Mike is here. In the kitchen diner. On the floor. Eyes wide and staring. The tang of blood and fear in my nostrils.

He's dead.

His shirt is torn. There's blood everywhere. Staining his pale blue shirt, darkening his jeans.

I want to scream or run, but I don't. Instead, I stay rooted to the spot as I hear myself whisper *Oh my God, oh my God, oh my God*, over and over again. It's like I'm in some TV drama. It doesn't feel real. I tell myself to keep it together, not to faint or panic. I have to do something. Should I call an ambulance? Maybe they can do something. Save him . . . No. He's dead. He's not coming back. He's actually dead. I've never seen a dead person before.

Call the police, Louisa, call the police. I'm muttering. I think I must be in shock. I want to call Jared. Instead, with shaking hands, I pull out my phone and call 999.

CHAPTER TWENTY THREE

I can't get the image of Mike's face out of my head. Of his open eyes and slack mouth. Of the blood. I wait outside his apartment in the hall, sitting in the chair next to the pot plant. I don't want to be here. I want to go home but the police told me to stay put. Who killed him? Why? A robbery gone wrong? A business deal gone bad? Something more . . . personal? Poor Darcy. What's she going to do now? Unless . . . No. That's just crazy. She's certainly got a screw loose, but would she really go so far as to kill her own husband?

The strains of *Mr Brightside* startle me. I stare at my phone screen, my vision hazy, and see it's Jared calling. I answer.

'Hello,' I say shakily.

'Louisa, I'm sorry about before. I was being a knob. Come home.'

'Jared, something's happened.' My voice cracks.

'Are you okay?'

'No. No I'm not.'

'Where are you? Are you hurt?'

'No. It's Mike. He . . .' I look up as the lift door opens, disgorging two male uniformed police officers. 'I've got to go,' I say, rising to my feet. 'The police are here.'

'The police! Lou, tell me where you are. What the hell's going on?'

'I'm at Mike's. Look, I'll call you back.' I'm well aware that Jared is probably freaked out by now. But one of the officers is asking me to end the call.

'Louisa, don't hang up.'

'I'll call you back,' I repeat and end our conversation.

'Are you Louisa Sullivan?' the older officer asks.

'Yes.'

'Was it you who made the 999 call just now?'

I nod.

'My name is Sergeant Merton, and this is my colleague Constable Santani. Are you hurt at all?'

I shake my head. 'No.'

'Can you tell me where you saw—'

'In there,' I interrupt. 'In the kitchen.' I point through the semi-open door to the flat. 'I don't want to go back inside.'

'No, that's fine,' he says. 'You can stay out here. We'll be out in a minute.' He nods to the other officer and they stride into Mike's flat.

My phone rings again. It's Jared. He keeps calling. The music from my ringtone is making my nerves even worse, so I set my phone to silent. I'll wait until I get a proper chance to talk to him before calling him back. A small, petty part of me is punishing him for how he spoke to me earlier. I want him to worry about me. The officers' voices float out of the apartment, deep and low, but I can't make out what they're saying. Then, I hear the louder static click of a police radio, and a woman's voice, asking questions about the body and the female witness. I guess they mean me. Only I didn't witness anything.

The officers come back out into the lobby.

'Did you touch anything inside the flat?' Sergeant Merton asks.

I shake my head. 'Only the door handles. Oh, and the light switches.'

'How about the deceased? Did you touch his clothing or the weapon?'

'No. He was . . . he was like that when I got here. I didn't touch anything.'

'You're sure?'

'Yes.' I nod.

'Good, okay. CID are on their way, and they'll want to talk to you when they get here.'

'Can I call my husband?' I ask.

'Sure, go ahead.'

They make no move to go back into the apartment, so I guess I'll have to speak to Jared while they're listening in.

I don't need to make the call. My phone buzzes and Jared's tanned face flashes up on my screen – a photo of him I took last year on holiday in Cornwall. I press reply.

'Hi. Sorry I had to hang up before. The police just got here and wanted to talk to me.'

'God, what's happened? You're at Mike's?'

'Yes, look, hang on and I'll tell you.' I run a hand through my hair and sit back down on the seat. The younger officer shakes his head and motions to me to get up, so I stand and walk over to the edge of the lobby where a window looks down into a car park full of expensive vehicles. 'I came over to see Mike,' I say in a low voice. 'I wanted to hear his side of things. And then I changed my mind. I was about to come home and forget all about the Lanes. But Mike's apartment door was open, so I got worried. I went inside, and he was on the kitchen floor. Jared, he's dead.'

'Shit. No. Dead? What happened? An accident? Or . . .'

'It's awful. He's in there right now. There's blood. It looks like he was killed.'

'Fuck. Where are you?'

'In the hallway outside, with the police. They're waiting for CID to arrive. They want to talk to me. I'm freaking out, Jared. What if they think I'm something to do with it?'

'Did you touch anything? His body or . . .'

'No.'

'Okay, good. And you were the one who called the police, right?'

'Mm.'

'So, then that's fine. You're hardly going to call the police if you killed the man, are you?'

'No. No, I guess not. Unless it's like a double bluff or something.' My heart is suddenly loud in my ears, my whole body pulsing with fear.

'I don't think so,' he says. 'I'm coming over. Where's the flat?'

'No,' I say. 'You need to stay with Joe.'

'I'll get a babysitter.'

'No, it's too late, you'll never get anyone at this time.'

'What about your sister?'

I pause. Beth would do it . . . No. I don't want to call her out at this time of night. She'll be tired from work. 'I'll be fine, Jared.' I'm not fine – far from it, but it'll be too complicated for him to come here. 'Look, hopefully, they'll ask a few questions and then I can come straight home.'

'Okay,' Jared says, 'But, I'm not happy about it. I should be there with you. And anyway, I still think I should call your sister. It might to handy to have a lawyer, just in case.'

'Oh my God, Jared. Do you think I need a lawyer?' I take a breath and press my fingers to my forehead.

'Calm down. You'll be fine. I'll call Beth just as a precaution.' He pauses. 'What about Darcy? Should someone tell her about Mike?'

'Let the police do it,' I say. 'You need to stay with Joe, and it's not something you can tell her over the phone. She'll need to be with someone.'

'Okay. So, let me ring Beth and then I'll call you straight back.'

'I might not be able to answer. The police . . .'

'Well, okay, ring me as soon as you can. Give me five minutes to talk to your sister.'

'Okay.'

The lift door opens again and several people get out. I assume they must be police officers, even though they're not in uniform.

'They're here,' I say to Jared. 'The other officers. I better go.'

'Okay, speak soon.'

'Love you,' I say.

'You too.'

I notice Jared didn't say the actual words. He normally says he loves me, too. The window has steamed up. I run my finger across the glass, turn around and brace myself for more questions.

* * *

I've been "invited" to the police station for an interview to answer more questions. I already told them everything back at Mike's flat but apparently they want to clarify some things. So here I am, two-and-a-half hours later, in a tiny interview room with stained blue walls and no window. A musty smell permeates the small space – it's so bad, I'm not sure whether it's better to breathe through my mouth or my nose.

Sitting opposite me are the investigating officers DS Locke and DC Benson. They've both been studiously polite, offering me a sandwich and a cup of tea, but I'm not hungry. So I sit on my chair with a plastic cup of water, waiting for the interview to begin, a black video-recording device between us on the fake wooden table, a ceiling camera angled down at me.

When I first got here, they took my clothing as evidence, so now I'm wearing a borrowed navy tracksuit. It's clean, at least. I voluntarily gave them my fingerprints and DNA as a precaution to eliminate me from their enquiries. I've been told I'm not under caution and I don't need a solicitor. That this is purely a witness interview. Yet my heart still clatters like a guilty person. It's so loud, I'm sure the two officers can hear it. I wish Jared or Beth were here with me to tell me everything's going to be okay.

'Stick the air con on, will you,' DS Locke says to his colleague. 'It smells rank in here.'

I'm already freezing but at least the fresh air might get rid of the cheesy smell. Benson nods, stands and leaves the room. I'm left alone with Locke for a moment. Rather than look at him, I stare fixedly at the wonky blue carpet tiles. After a brief moment, a faint hum emanates from a vent high up on the wall. Benson re-enters the room and sits next to

Locke, their faces merging as my vision blurs with anxiety.

'Have you told Darcy yet?' I ask. 'Mike's wife.'

'We've informed Mrs Lane,' Locke replies, 'and she's currently helping us with our enquiries.'

I wonder if she's here, too, in a different interview room. I wonder whether she's taking the news calmly, or if she's hysterical with grief. God! I hope she doesn't spin any of her lies.

'Do you know who did it, yet?' I ask. 'Who killed Mike?'

'We're trying to establish that, Mrs Sullivan,' Locke replies.

'Do you think you could call me Louisa?' I ask.

'Sure. We'll be recording the interview now, and DC Benson will also take notes, okay?'

'Okay,' I reply.

Locke presses the record button. He states the date, time and place, and we all have to introduce ourselves. Then Locke asks me all the same questions they asked back at Mike's flat, and I answer in the same way, telling them how the apartment door was open and so I went inside, which was how I found Mike on the floor. That I never touched anything apart from the door handles and light switches, and then I called 999.

'And why were you at the apartment, Louisa?' Locke continues.

I tell him about Darcy and Mike's break up. How Mike

was upset and wanted me to come over.

'Have you visited Michael Lane's apartment on any previous occasion?' Locke asks.

'No.'

'Have you met with Mr Lane alone, on any previous occasion?'

'What? No.'

'You're certain about this?'

'Absolutely. I hardly know him. It's Darcy who's my . . . friend.'

Locke nods and smiles at me, but I don't feel reassured. I rub my eyes – they're raw and scratchy. The skin around them feels dry and greasy at the same time. The glands in my throat are swollen like I'm fighting off a virus.

'Would you say you have a good relationship with Mrs Lane?' Locke asks.

My heart rate speeds up and my hands begin to sweat. I wipe my palms on my jeans. If I tell them about my argument with Darcy, will they think I had something to do with Mike's murder? I wish Beth was here, but if I ask for a lawyer they're going to think I'm guilty for sure. No. I'll have to tell the truth and trust that they'll believe me.

'I've always had a good relationship with Darcy,' I say, stretching the truth a little, 'but we did have a little falling out today.'

'Oh?'

'Our kids haven't been getting along, and Darcy got upset when I asked her to speak to Tyler about it – Tyler's her son. Also, she didn't . . .' I pause, putting my hands to my cheeks

'Go on,' Locke prompts. His voice is deep and even, almost soothing, which is completely at odds with the panic his questions are stirring.

'Also, she wasn't happy about me going to see Mike this evening.' I swallow. My mouth is dry as dust, my throat rasping. I take a sip of water. 'The Lanes are separated at the moment,' I explain. 'I was only going to see him to see if I could help patch things up between them. Mike was really upset when I saw him on the beach earlier.'

'You met Mr Lane on the beach today?' Locke says.

Shit, that sounds bad. 'I was out walking on my own,' I explain. 'I bumped into him. That's when he asked me to come over to his place so he could ask me about getting back with Darcy.'

'And yet, you said a moment ago that you had never met Mr Lane alone on any previous occasion?'

'Before today, I meant.'

'So, other than today on the beach, you never met with Mr Lane alone?'

'Yes. I mean, no, I never met with him. I didn't even want to go there this evening, but he was upset.'

'Upset in what way?'

'He was sad. He wanted to get back with Darcy, and said

he didn't understand why she kicked him out.'

'Mrs Lane tells us you threatened and taunted her this afternoon in the school playground.'

'What! No. I . . .' I'm sweating now, my hands trembling. This interview isn't how I thought it would be. They're making me feel like I'm guilty of something.

'Mrs Lane says she has witnesses,' Locke continues. 'She says that you caused her considerable stress and upset.'

'No!' I can't believe she actually lied to the police about this. Actually . . . I *can* believe it. 'It was the other way around,' I say. 'I told my husband all about it earlier. Darcy made out that I was moving in on her husband, but it's not true.' The more I say, the worse it sounds. I hear the words as they fall from my lips, and even *I* wouldn't believe me.

'Okay,' Locke says, in his calm manner. 'Well, we'll be interviewing the witnesses. And I have to warn you that Mrs Lane is confident they'll back up her story. She says you threatened her and you threatened her husband.'

'That's a total lie!' I realise that of course all the other mums will take Darcy's side. As far as they're concerned, they saw Darcy get upset after talking to me. They'll have put two and two together and come up with twenty three. What can I say that will make the police believe me?

'Am I under arrest?' I ask. 'You said this was just a witness interview.' My brain has turned to mush. 'Look,' I say, my voice quavering, 'I'd really like to go home now. I'm exhausted. I can always come back tomorrow and—'

'Louisa Sullivan,' Locke says, interrupting my plea, 'I'm arresting you on suspicion of the murder of Michael Lane. You do not have to say anything. But it may harm your defence if you do not mention when questioned something which you later rely on in court. Anything you do say may be given in evidence.'

As he speaks, the room fades in and out of focus. His words sound as though they're being spoken from a long way away. How can this be happening to me? How can I be under arrest? Do they really think I have something to do with Mike's murder? I grip the edge of the table, my cold knuckles white as bone.

'I need Beth,' I cry. 'Get my sister – she's a lawyer. I won't say anything else without her here.'

CHAPTER TWENTY FOUR

'Louisa, look at me,' Beth says, trying to get me to concentrate. She's sitting where Locke was sitting only a few moments ago, her blue eyes concerned yet focused. 'You're white as a ghost. When did you last eat?'

'I don't know. I'm not hungry.'

'You need food, or you're going to keel over. Here.' She reaches into her bag and offers me a granola bar.

I screw up my nose and shake my head.

'Eat it,' she says in a tone that brooks no argument.

I take it from her, tear the wrapper and take a bite. It's like chewing sweet cement, but I force myself to swallow.

She pushes the cup of water towards me, and I take a swig. 'Now, tell me what happened,' she says. 'From the start. Don't leave anything out.'

'Even the Darcy stuff?' I ask. 'The things I told you before.'

'Tell me *everything*. Especially the Darcy stuff.'

I slide the unfinished granola bar onto the table and start to speak. My throat is already dry and swollen from too much talking, but I do my best to be rational and clear, to not become hysterical. When I've finished, I have to ask: 'Do you believe me, Beth?' Even to my own ears, my accusations make me sound delusional. I wipe away a tear, the first one I've cried tonight.

Beth leaves her chair and comes around the table, crouching in front of me. She puts her arms around my quivering body and whispers that everything's going to be okay. That she'll find out what's going on and get to the truth. My mind is closing down. I'm so tired and so confused by everything that I can't seem to latch onto any more coherent thoughts.

'Louisa!' My sister's voice cuts through my woolly brain. 'Louisa, snap out of it, and listen.'

I blink and try to refocus: I'm at the police station . . . they think I've killed Mike . . . Beth is here to help me. I almost want to laugh it's so absurd. Am I dreaming?

'Listen,' she says, taking my hand. 'I know you didn't do this. There are no witnesses. You have no motive. And you, yourself, called the police. Okay?'

I nod. Mute.

'It's all good,' she says. 'And unless they get more evidence, I don't think they'll charge you, in which case they'll have to release you today . . . or tomorrow at the latest.'

'More evidence?'

'Look, don't freak out,' she says, 'but they've gone to search your house.'

'What! Joe's asleep! Jared's going to go nuts.'

'Jared won't go nuts. He'll let them in. You've got nothing to hide.'

'But Joe—'

'They'll try their best not to disturb Joe. It's not a dawn raid, Lou. They'll be civilised. They'll go in with minimum disruption.'

My fists are clenched, my teeth grind together and the blood whooshes in my head. This is all Darcy's doing. She's behind it, I know she is. 'Don't they need a search warrant?' I say.

'Not in situations like this,' Beth replies.

'Murder, you mean?'

She nods.

'Jared will go mad, Beth. He's already pissed off with me over all the Darcy stuff. This will tip him over the edge.'

'Jared's your husband and he loves you,' Beth snaps. 'He'll support you, and if he doesn't, I'll cut his bollocks off.'

I smile despite myself.

Beth kisses my forehead, straightens up and returns to her seat. 'Now, are you ready to let them back in?'

I swallow and nod. 'No, but okay.'

* * *

After a gruelling two more hours of questioning with Beth by my side, and an uncomfortable night in a depressing cell, I'm released without charge at lunchtime on Saturday. Beth returns to the station to pick me up. Jared was going to come and get me, but I told him to stay with Joe. I don't want my son to know what's been going on. I don't want him to get even a hint of it.

It's strange to step outside into the daylight, after everything I've been through. The sunshine sears my retinas and the cold air stings my cheeks, burns my lungs. Yet it feels good to be outside, to be walking away from the station where I was made to feel like a criminal.

'I'm parked over the road,' Beth says, taking my arm and leading me through a lull in traffic like I'm a child incapable of crossing on my own. I gaze around at all these people driving their cars and vans, cycling, walking, getting on with their regular lives, while my own life is disintegrating. How does it happen that you're going along perfectly fine, and then, little-by-little, events twist and conspire to pull you down until you don't recognise anything from your life any more?

We walk along a quiet side street flanked with bland sixties office blocks until we reach Beth's car. She opens the passenger door for me and I climb in like an old person, easing myself into the seat, somehow astonished by its comfort, and by its warm, clean leathery smell. Beth gets in beside me, closes her door and starts up the engine. 'Let's get you home,' she says.

'I'm scared.' I fold my hands together to stop them shaking.

'It'll be okay.' She takes her hand off the gear stick and places it on my knee. 'They've released you, and they haven't charged you. I'm sure that will be the end of it. And whatever happens, we're all here for you.'

I nod, but the lump in my throat has returned.

'Come on,' she says, starting up the car again. 'Let's get you back home. The longer you dwell on things the more you'll worry.'

'Okay,' I say.

Yet her words provide no comfort.

* * *

Beth drops me off, offering to come into the house with me. I tell her I've taken up enough of her weekend. That I'm sorry for everything. That she must be exhausted. That she should go and spend the rest of the weekend with her family. She waves away my apologies, telling me to call her anytime I want, and gives me a warm hug before driving off.

'Mummy!' Joe hurls himself at me as I let myself into the house. I pull him in close and squeeze him so hard I worry about squashing him. He doesn't seem to mind – he squeezes me back equally tightly.

'Oh, Joe Bo!' I say, kissing the top of his head. 'I missed you like crazy.'

'Daddy said you went to your friend's house for a sleepover.'

'Yes,' I say. 'But I'm very happy to be home now.'

Jared comes out of the kitchen. I see his eyes widen as he takes in my dishevelled appearance.

'You okay?' he asks.

I nod. 'Joe, can you go and get me a glass of water, darling?'

Joe scampers off to the kitchen. Once he's out of earshot, I tell Jared: 'Beth thinks I'll be fine. She doesn't think they'll charge me. They have no evidence.'

He shakes his head. 'This is crazy.'

'Tell me about it.' Talking to my husband about being under arrest has to be ranked as one of the most surreal moments in my life.

'Are you hungry?' he asks. 'I got you some soup. Waitrose leek and potato. And I bought a French loaf.'

Suddenly, I'm starving. I nod. 'Give me ten minutes to jump in the shower.'

'Okay, I'll heat it up.' He steps forward and kisses me. A brief touch of lips and a squeeze of my shoulder. What does that mean? Is he pleased to see me? Does he still love me like he used to? Are we still good? Butterflies flit across my stomach. Or maybe it's just hunger.

* * *

Lunch was nice, if a little subdued. Just the three of us sitting around the kitchen table. Joe must have picked up on the vibe because he wasn't his usual chatty self. Now, he's upstairs playing with his Lego while Jared and I skirt around each other in the kitchen, clearing the lunch dishes. My hair is still damp from the shower, my skin clean and tingling. I feel more "normal" even though the atmosphere between me and Jared is still strained.

Finally, I can't stand it any more. 'Are you upset with me, Jared?' I ask, sitting down at the table and scoring the scrubbed wooden surface with my nail.

'Upset?' He turns and leans back against the kitchen units, arms folded across his chest.

'Because it seems weird to me that I was arrested under suspicion of murder last night, and you've hardly said a thing to me since I got home.'

'I'm giving you space,' he says. 'It must have been traumatic, so I'm trying to be . . . I dunno, quietly supportive, I suppose.'

'Okay, well can we talk about it now?'

He bites his lower lip and nods. I was expecting more from him – either a, *what the hell's going on* kind of thing or maybe an, *oh my God, Lou how are you? What happened?* This strange silence is unnerving.

'You do know that Mike's death is absolutely nothing to do with me, don't you?'

He nods, looking unconvinced.

'Jared . . .'

'Louisa, I don't know. You've been acting so differently lately. I'm wondering . . . if maybe you've been having some kind of breakdown. I know you'd never normally do anything to hurt anyone . . . Maybe you should go and see a doctor. I can come with you if you like.'

'You think I'm having a breakdown?' I press my palms flat on the table, splaying them wide like dead starfish.

'I think life is getting on top of you and it might be a good idea if you talk to someone about it.'

'A psychiatrist?'

'Or your GP.'

'Is this your idea?' I grit my teeth and raise an eyebrow.

He looks down at his feet. 'Okay, don't get mad, but Darcy said . . .'

'Fucking Darcy!' I interrupt. 'She thinks I should go and see a doctor? This just gets better and better. Can't you see what she's doing? How she's making me out to be this crazy person. But I'm not. And everything I do or say just makes things worse. I can't deal with this any more.'

'Louisa . . .'

'No! You know me, Jared. You know me. We've been together for years. Have I ever acted this way before?'

'No—'

'Exactly! It's her. It's all her.' I scrape my chair back and rise to my feet. 'She's done all this to split us up. It's some kind of vendetta or plan. I don't know why, but she's been trying to ruin my life all along, and she's succeeding. You're letting her succeed.'

'Louisa,' Jared says, his so voice quiet and sad that I stop talking and look at him. 'Louisa, I'm sorry but I can't do this any more. I think we need a break.'

'No. No, please.' Tears fall and I taste salt on my lips. 'She's winning,' I cry. 'She's ruining everything. I love you, Jared. Please.'

'I think it's best if you go to your sister's and Joe stays here with me. You need rest.'

'I don't want this to split us apart. Please.'

'I just need . . . I need a break from all this Darcy stuff,' he says. 'It's too much, Lou. You haven't talked about anything else for weeks. You're not interested in my new business. You don't want to go out or have fun. And now this thing with Mike . . . and the police coming here and searching our home. It's so screwed up. I want the old you back.'

'I am the old me,' I say. 'None of this is my fault. I had nothing to do with Mike's murder. It's—'

'Darcy.' Jared finishes my sentence. 'This is exactly what I'm talking about, Louisa, look, I didn't want to bring this up, but didn't your real mum have some kind of breakdown when she was your age? Wasn't that the reason you were adopted? Maybe . . .'

'What? You think I'm genetically programmed to go nuts? Thanks a lot, Jared. I can't believe you'd say that to me!' I move away from the table and start pacing the kitchen, chewing at the corner of my thumbnail.

He knows I don't like talking about my past, about the abuse I suffered at the hands of my birth parents. I've always made sure that Joe's had the gentlest of childhoods. I never so much as raise my voice to him. That Jared could accuse me of being anything like my mother makes my blood boil.

'I don't think you're nuts,' Jared says. 'I just think you're not thinking straight at the moment, and it would be good for us to have some time apart.'

I glower at him. I know bloody well what he meant. He was comparing me to my mother. He's worrying I'm going to lose the plot like she did.

'I'm serious, Lou. I want us to take a break. And I want Joe to stay with me, so you can rest and get back to normal.'

'You're working,' I point out. 'How can you look after Joe while you're at work?'

'It's okay, I've got it covered.'

'Not Darcy.' The ground feels like it's shifting beneath my feet. I place the flat of my hand on the wall to steady myself and bend forward to take a breath. There's no way that bloody woman is going to be looking after my child. And I'm certainly not having Joe forced to play with her bully of a son. 'Anyone but her, Jared. For God's sake, the woman's set me up for murder! And Tyler is a little bully – he's been pinching Joe and getting him into trouble. Ask him. Ask Joe. He'll tell you.'

'Calm down, Lou,' he says. 'It'll just be for a little while. Just till you get back on your feet again.'

'No,' I say. 'No way. Joe can stay with me at Beth's.'

'You need a break, Lou. You need peace and quiet.'

'Beth has a four-year-old, in case you'd forgotten. I'm hardly going to get peace and quiet with Megan in the house. Anyway, Beth and Carys will help me – not that I need helping. I'm perfectly capable of looking after my own son.' I glare at my husband for his insensitivity and lack of support. I thought we were stronger than this. That he would take my side, no matter what.

He's shaking his head, but I can tell he's going to relent. There's no way on earth I would allow Darcy to look after Joe, and I can't believe Jared's even suggesting it.

'Okay,' Jared says. 'But Joe stays with me at weekends.'

'Fine,' I snap. 'I'll pack a bag, shall I?'

CHAPTER TWENTY FIVE

Winter 2002

'You're a treasure,' he said, reaching up for the delicate china cup of tea with a wrinkled, liver-spotted hand.

'It's my pleasure, Arthur,' she replied in the overly loud voice she always had to use with the partially deaf octogenarian.

'Did you leave the teabag in?' he asked. 'You know I don't like it when it's weak as dishwater.'

'Yes. Teabag's in there, Arthur.'

'Lovely.' He brought the cup up to his lips and took a loud slurp. 'Nice and hot, too,' he said approvingly. 'You make a good cup of tea, Nicole.'

'Would you like a couple of biscuits with that?'

'Custard creams?' he asked hopefully.

'Let me go and check what you've got in the cupboard.' Nicole left the sitting room and made her way down the narrow hallway – with its flowered wallpaper and framed prints of the countryside – to the kitchen. This room was where you really felt like time had jumped back several decades, with its ugly brown wall tiles and sludge-green Formica kitchen units. The whole place was dingy. Probably hadn't been decorated since 1972.

She opened the larder door and shuddered as a family of silverfish scuttled beneath the floorboards to hide from the unexpected shaft of daylight. The biscuit tin sat on the third shelf up – a faded red and black metal box with a picture of a man in a kilt playing the bagpipes, which had once, long ago, contained Highland shortbread. Prising open the scratched lid, she saw that Arthur was in luck as the last carer had bought a selection of the old man's favourites – custard creams, jammy dodgers and bourbon biscuits.

Nicole scooped out a couple of the creams, replaced the lid and stuck the tin back on the shelf. Then she closed the larder door and opened one of the kitchen units, selecting a rose-patterned china plate. When she'd first started working here, six months ago, she hadn't known how particular Arthur was about having his tea and biscuits out of the right cup and plate. Apparently, his wife had always insisted on proper china, and now he did it to honour her memory. Nicole thought it was a load of sentimental crap. His wife was dead and couldn't give two shits whether he ate off bone china, or stuck his face directly into the biscuit tin.

'Here you go,' she said brightly, plastering a smile on her face as she returned to the sitting room. 'Custard creams.'

'Wonderful.' He smiled and patted her hand as she set the plate down next to him on the lace-doily which adorned the wooden side table. 'Sit down,' he said, pointing to the faded flowery armchair opposite him.

Nicole sat gingerly on the edge of the musty chair. Why were all old people obsessed with flowers? Flowered cups, plates, carpets, tiles, wallpaper, furniture – everything was covered in frigging flowers. It was depressing.

'Have you got yourself a cup of tea and some biscuits, too?' he asked. 'I don't want to sit here eating and drinking while you go without. You look like a skinny, young thing, what I can see of you. You could do with feeding up.'

'Thanks, but no. I had a late lunch, Arthur.' She patted her stomach to show how full up she was, momentarily forgetting that he was registered blind and probably couldn't see her anyway.

'Did I ever tell you about my Margaret's homemade biscuits?' he said.

Only about five thousand times. 'She liked to bake did she?'

'Best biscuits you ever tasted,' he said. 'Not like the shop-bought rubbish you get nowadays.'

Still, you don't mind shoving shop-bought custard creams in your fat gob, these days, do you, Arthur? 'Lovely. Sounds like you were lucky.'

'I was, I was, I don't mind telling you. And the smell of those biscuits when they came out of the oven – like heaven it was. She'd stand there, with her oven gloves on, slapping my hand away if I tried to pinch one before they'd cooled down. "You'll burn your mouth, Artie," she used to say. "It'll be worth it," I'd reply. And it wasn't just biscuits, either – She'd bake Victoria sponges, scones, rock cakes . . .'

Arthur had about five favourite memories of his wife that he liked to recount on a loop, over and over again like a stuck record. And Nicole was the mug who was expected to sit and listen and pretend to be interested. Honestly, his wife was the lucky one now – at least she didn't have to put up with his droning voice going on and on any more. Some days, Nicole thought, if he didn't shut up, she'd bash him on the head with one of his stupid dead wife's tacky china figurines. For Christ sake, she was nineteen, supposed to be out there having fun, not sitting in a decrepit old person's house trying to stop her ears bleeding with boredom.

To make matters worse, she still hadn't found anything of any value, and she'd looked everywhere, in all the usual places – under the mattress, in the larder, the wardrobe, chest of drawers, bathroom cabinet. But, so far, nada, zip, zilch. Just some pictures of his ugly, dead wife. He had to have some valuables stashed somewhere. He lived in a swanky house on a posh road – one day soon, she'd have a house like this, only it wouldn't smell of cabbage and farts.

Old fogies like him always kept cash at home, didn't they? They didn't trust the banks to look after it properly. Arthur had moaned about them enough times. But *where* did he keep it? That was the question. Where did he hide all his lovely money? It was the only reason she'd taken this crappy carer job – the pay was shit, so she had to make it worth her while somehow. And anyway, Arthur wasn't ever going to spend it. He'd pop his clogs soon enough. He had no kids – probably leave it all to some ridiculous cat charity.

She couldn't believe how many of these old gits and miserable old biddies were living out their lonely days, sitting on stacks of money, rattling around in their big, old houses all by themselves, pristine cars in the garage that they never drove, while she had sod all. Some well-meaning person had decided that it was better for them to stay in their massive houses – apparently, they'd live longer and feel more secure and comfortable. Sod that. Stick 'em all in care homes and let other people have their houses. People like Nicole who was living in a grotty bedsit that stank of fish. It wasn't right. It wasn't fair.

No, Arthur had had his life. Now, it was her turn.

He was still yammering away, but Nicole had perfected the art of saying yes and no, without actually listening. She stifled a yawn and checked the time on the gold carriage clock on the mantelpiece. That tacky piece of shit was probably worth at least a hundred quid, but it was too obvious. He'd notice if it went missing. She needed to be clever about things and not get herself in trouble with her employers, or with the law. She was smart. She'd figure it out.

'I'll let you into a secret,' Arthur said, deviating from his usual boring monologue.

Nicole made appropriate sounds of interest.

'You're my favourite,' he said. 'Out of all the people who come here and look after me, you're the only one who's interested in my stories. The only one who really listens, or who makes my tea just the way I like it. You're a good girl, Nicole. If I'd ever had a daughter or granddaughter, I'd have wanted her to be like you.'

Nicole wasn't used to hearing words like this spoken about her. *Sentimental old codger*, she thought. *Just shows what a crap judge of character you are.* 'Thank you, Arthur,' she said, taking his hand and giving it a squeeze, 'that means a lot. You know I haven't got a family of my own, so maybe we could pretend? You could be my fake grandad if you like.'

'I'd like that very much,' he said, wiping a tear from his rheumy eyes. 'And, also, I'd like you to know something important . . . I've changed my Will.'

Nicole's heartbeats sped up as she held her breath waiting for his next sentence.

'I'm going to leave you a little something. Not too much, don't get excited, but enough to maybe help you put a deposit down on your own house.'

Yesss! Nicole tried hard not to show her excitement.

'I know how difficult you youngsters find it today, what

with the house prices and the cost of living, so this little windfall will help you along. And then, maybe, when you're settled with a family of your own, you'll look back fondly on old Arthur, and I won't be completely forgotten about.'

'Arthur! I can't believe it. You really didn't have to—'

'Nonsense. It's my pleasure, dear. I wanted to tell you myself. I wanted you to know how much you're appreciated.'

'Thank you,' she said, leaning forward and kissing his cheek. 'You're a sweetheart, Arthur. A real gentleman.' She knew he loved to be called a gentleman. It was something he prided himself on. In Arthur's world, there were three types of men – layabouts, oafs and gentlemen.

Now . . . she just had to wait for the old fucker to die.

CHAPTER TWENTY SIX

2016

I sit on Beth and Carys' sofa flicking through the Sunday papers. I purposely haven't bought any newspapers since Joe's birthday – that awful morning when I first read the column Darcy stole from me. Beth and Carys buy a more serious, left-wing newspaper – one that doesn't have throwaway pieces like mine or Darcy's, so it doesn't hurt too much to read it.

'Please come,' Carys says, putting a cup of tea on the side table next to me. 'You'll love Tom and Sally. They've said the more the merrier.'

I appreciate Carys inviting me to their friends' house for Sunday lunch, but the last thing I want is to be sociable. I can barely string two sentences together today, let alone make small talk with total strangers.

'Yes, come,' Beth says coming into the lounge and sitting on the sofa opposite.

'Thanks, guys,' I say, meaning it, 'but I'm not good company.' I lay the newspapers back down on the table and pick up my tea.

'Want me to stay with you?' Beth offers. 'Carys and Megan

won't mind going without me. We can curl up and watch girly movies and eat cake.'

Carys smiles. 'Sure. That's cool with me.'

'You two are the best, but no, Beth. You go. You're already dressed up to go out. Anyway, I think I'll be better off on my own today.'

'You sure?' Beth asks with a frown. 'I'm worried about you. You've had a traumatic experience, and bloody Jared should've been more supportive.'

'I think the whole thing has freaked him out,' I say, not quite sure why I'm defending him, when what I actually want to do is punch him.

'Hmm,' Beth replies.

Carys remains tactfully silent on the subject of my husband.

Last night, when I arrived at Beth's, I broke down and told her what Jared had said. How he'd compared me to my birth mother. How he thought I was having some kind of mental breakdown. Beth wanted to march straight round there and give him a piece of her mind. She's my adopted parents' natural daughter, and when I went to live with them, at the age of ten, she took me under her wing and nurtured me. Made me feel so loved and welcome. She's always been there for me. She's my sister, but she's also my best friend.

'When are we going?' Megan pokes her head around the

lounge door.

'Any minute,' Carys replies. 'You need to go and have a wee before we leave.'

'I don't need a—'

Carys gives her a look, and Megan rolls her eyes and goes dutifully to the loo. Beth gets to her feet.

'Have a great time,' I say, trying to sound cheerful. 'Thanks so much for letting me crash here . . . again.'

'I feel bad leaving you alone after what you've just been through,' Beth says.

'Don't be daft. Go. Eat lunch. I'll be fine. I'm happy to relax here.'

'If you're sure,' Carys says.

I finally shoo them out of the house with further blandishments to ease their consciences.

As the front door closes, I heave a sigh of relief, even as the first brutal wave of melancholy hits me in the chest. I'm in no mood to hang out with strangers, yet the sense of abandonment knocks the breath from my body. Nothing and no one could make me feel okay today – well, maybe Jared could. He's the only one. I wish with all my heart that he would come over and apologise. That he would tell me he trusts me and believes in me and that he knows I'm right about Darcy. I know that's not going to happen. My accusations against Darcy have unnerved him, and the police allegations have confirmed his fears. He thinks I'm losing my mind. He doesn't know what to do.

I get up from the sofa, wishing I could pick something up and smash it. If this was my house I would hurl something heavy at the wall. But I don't think my sister would appreciate me vandalising their pristine flat. I need to do something to relieve my anger and hurt. My skin prickles, my brain races. I need to get out of here. I march into the spare room and throw on an extra jumper. Then I grab my coat, hat, gloves and the spare set of flat keys Beth gave me, and I leave the flat, slamming the door behind me.

* * *

I've walked and walked and walked, almost to Hengistbury Head and back again. Until the soles of my feet throb and my legs ache. Trying to tire myself out so that I'll sleep tonight. So that I won't think about what a mess my life has become. Now I'm back at Branksome Beach where all the benches have been taken by sickeningly happy families and loved-up couples, so I'm perched on the edge of the concrete promenade, my legs dangling above the sand. The damp seeps through my jeans, numbing my thighs and backside. I shift position a little, but that just makes it worse. The weak, winter sun throws out zero heat, and the lukewarm coffee in my gloved hands isn't comforting me like I hoped it might.

Sunday on the beach is not a great place for a sad, lonely person to come. Not when the sun is shining and the place is packed out with cheerful people. I had hoped to walk off my anger. Instead, it seems to be building to a crescendo. A hard, bitter lump sits in my chest and I can't shake it free.

I remember back to the summer when we all came down here for the day. When we gathered on rugs beneath sun umbrellas to shade us from the blistering sunshine. It was a perfect moment in time. Our happy, secure family. Even when Darcy and Mike happened upon us that evening, I welcomed them. Introduced them to my family. I had no idea the woman was my enemy. That she would pick apart the strands of my life like a poorly made jumper.

It seems the harder I try to hold onto everything, the more it's slipping away. I don't know what to do next. When I try to explain to my family and to the police about Darcy's subtle games, I end up sounding crazy. But if I do nothing, then my life falls apart anyway. It's a win-win for Darcy. And I still have no idea why she's got it in for me.

Tipping out the remnants of my coffee, I watch the foamy liquid splatter onto the sand. It's too weak, too cold to finish. The sun is already sinking. I suppose I'd better go back to Beth's before I freeze. I heave myself up, my cold joints protesting, my bad knee clicking. There's a blue bin to my right. I drop my empty coffee cup into it, tug my hat down over my ears and start walking.

The beach empties out as the sun dips behind the low cliffs. I think I'll head back along the top path to make the most of the last rays. Leaving the beach, I turn off into Branksome Chine – one of the narrow gullies that leads down to the sea. The muddy path has been paved over, flanked by steep, thickly wooded banks, dotted with ornate Victorian street lamps. As I huff my way up the steep incline, my breaths puff out into miniature clouds that hover and melt. No one else is around, but I'm too wrapped up in my thoughts to feel uneasy about the lack of people. Anyway, it's not far to the cliff top.

I reach the last few steps and turn left onto the narrow ridge path, the sky darkening over the sea, the citrus rays of the sun splaying out from behind a thin veil of cloud, like pale shooting stars. An elderly black Labrador trots past me, his equally elderly owner coming into view seconds later. He nods *good evening* and continues on his way. I pause for a moment to get my breath. At least I've warmed up now.

The sun dips still lower, so I start moving again. I hear soft footsteps behind me. My heart jolts, but this is a popular dog-walking route so I shouldn't be worried. Nevertheless, I pick up my pace. Not far until I reach the road.

The footsteps are closer now. I think I'll let whoever it is go past me. I stop and move to the side, glancing behind . . . and my heart freezes.

It's him.

It's my stalker.

After Darcy's interference, I thought he had left me alone

for good. To see him this close up is bone chilling, the sunlight catching his bearded face. He is tall, burly, strong-looking and his blue eyes have locked onto mine. He's wearing the same brown corduroy coat as last time, but he's not wearing his fisherman's hat today. Instead, a woollen beanie is pulled down over his ears, his longish hair curling out beneath it. He opens his mouth as if he's about to say something but I have no wish to hold a conversation with this man. I'm held in place by fear for a split second before my fight-or-flight reflex kicks in – and I'm no fighter – so I turn and I run.

I hear his footfalls behind me, gaining. I have no breath left to scream.

'Stop!' he growls.

Yeah, right. I put on an extra spurt of speed. I don't know where from. My lungs are squeezed tight, my thighs and calves already burning from my mammoth walk, and steep climb up the chine, my knee grinding in agony – I'm sure I'm going to need an operation on it soon – if I manage to live that long. If this guy catches me, I dread to think what he'll do – Murder? Rape? Worse?

I hear his breaths now, merging with my own. Oh God, no. I can't outrun this man. He's almost on me. I try to scream but my breath is taken, my lungs squeezed from the effort of running. His fingers close around my shoulder. I squeal and manage to jerk away and veer off the path into the woods. As soon as I do so, I realise this was a bad idea. There's no daylight in here, no chance of a passer-by to save me. Branches twist and bracken crunches underfoot. Twigs claw at my face and now I'm crying with terror. His fingers scrape the backs of my arms. 'Stop!' he snarls again, frustration and anger in his voice.

I scream thinly as his arms lock around my body and he tackles me to the ground. We crash into the undergrowth, his weight pinning me. Soggy leaves and mud slide into my mouth and up my nose. I cough and spit and choke. A bird screams out a warning. Too late for me.

'Help!' I try to yell, but my voice comes out weak and croaky. His hand slides under my face, smothering my mouth and nose. I can't breathe. *Shit. Is this it? Will I ever see Joe again? Am I going to die today?*

CHAPTER TWENTY SEVEN

His warm hand still covers my mouth and nose, my hands pinned below my chest where I tried to break my fall. He's half-sitting, half-lying on my back, his beard scratching my neck, his knees either side of me. Terror numbs my body, freezes my mind. If he doesn't remove his hand from my face soon, I'm going to suffocate. I try to wriggle free. He's too heavy. I kick out my legs, but I can't do anything other than bend them back impotently.

'Stop struggling,' he says, his voice soft and low in my ear. 'You'll hurt yourself.' His accent is local – a Dorset accent, probably Poole. 'Don't try to scream.'

I want to tell him to get off me, but it comes out as nothing more than a muffled whimper. If he takes his hand away from my mouth, the first thing I'll do is yell as loud as I can.

'Sorry I scared you,' he continues. 'I only wanted to talk, but you started running away.' He pauses. 'I have to tell you something. It's important.'

His words don't sound aggressive, and, despite my sweating, shaking terror, I'm curious to hear what he has to say. But why does he still have me pinned to the ground?

Why did he chase me in the first place?

'If I let you go, will you stay and listen?' he asks. 'I won't hurt you again.'

I want to yell at him to *get the fuck off me*. Again, my words are stifled by his thick fingers.

'Shh,' he says, easing his hand away from my mouth. I gulp in lungfuls of loamy air, too choked to scream straightaway. I feel him ease up off my body, his other hand still pressing down on my back. I draw in a steadying breath, tense my body and then, twist my body around on the ground, kicking out at him with my right leg. My foot doesn't connect, and he lunges across me, pinning both legs as I contort my body around and begin pummelling his back with my fists.

'Help!' I yell 'Someone, help! Over here! In the woods!' My voice sounds pathetically weak, but we're not too far from the path, someone could hear. Please, God, let someone hear.

'Shut up!' the man growls. 'I'm trying to help, you silly cow.'

He rolls me onto my back, straddles me, grabs both wrists in one of his massive hands and presses his free hand over my mouth again. If only I were stronger. No matter how much I writhe and jerk, I'm helpless to get free, pinned like a butterfly on a board.

'If you'd stop struggling and listen,' he grunts,' you'd

know I don't want to hurt you.'

My body is bruised and aching, but I can't give up. I have to get away from this man.

'For Christ's sake stop!' he shouts. 'Look, I know Darcy Lane.'

This gets my attention and I stop struggling against him for a moment.

'I know her,' he says. 'I know what she's really like.'

The fight escapes from my body, and my shoulders sag, sinking into the earth as I digest his words. He takes his hand from my mouth and springs to his feet. Then he reaches down a hand to pull me up. I hesitate for a second, but then accept, my battered body peeled from the muddy ground.

On my feet once more, my breath comes ragged and uneven, my heartbeats slowing to a clatter, rather than the echoing boom that filled my ears only moments ago. The light has almost disappeared from the woods and this man from my nightmares towers above me. Yet I don't run.

'You know her?' I ask.

He nods. 'Look, I'm sorry about just now. I just wanted to talk to you. I could tell you were scared. I shouldn't have chased after—'

'Tell me how you know Darcy,' I demand.

'Shall we go somewhere else?'

I shake my head. 'No, here's fine. I need to know. I need

to . . .' My legs wobble, and I sit back down heavily on the frigid ground. I straighten my legs out in front of me, my knee grinding painfully.

'You okay?' He crouches in front of me.

I flinch back instinctively.

He raises his hands as though I'm pointing a gun at him. 'I'm sorry,' he says.

I nod. 'I just have to sit for a minute. My legs, they're a bit shaky.'

In the gloom, I see him stand and shuffle off, looking around for something. He soon spots what he's been searching for, and heaves up a huge fallen log before placing it on the ground next to me with a rustle and a thud. 'Here, sit on that,' he says. 'The ground's cold.'

I do as he asks. This time, tentatively accepting his hand as he helps me off the ground. He squats opposite me and sighs.

'I've wanted to talk to you for ages,' he says, 'but I wasn't sure if she was doing it to you, too. I had to be sure. I had to wait and see.'

'Doing what?' I ask.

'Destroying your life,' he says. 'Like she destroyed mine.' His gaze lifts from the ground to my face. We stare at one another in the gathering darkness. Is he telling the truth?

I wipe my muddy, tear-streaked face with the sleeve of my coat. My feet are like ice blocks and my whole body throbs in pain, but I can't be side-tracked by encroaching thoughts of central heating and warm baths. I need to hear what this man knows about Darcy.

'Tell me,' I say.

'My name's Max Allerton,' he begins, 'and I used to be rich and successful, happily married with children.' He pauses and takes a breath. 'But I was stupid. Tempted.'

'By Darcy?'

'Yes.'

'When?'

'It was about ten years ago. Just before she met Michael Lane.'

'You had an affair with her?' I ask.

'A one-night-stand. Worst decision of my life,' he says. 'She knew I still loved my wife and kids. So she blackmailed me. Ripped me off for every penny I had.'

I find it hard to feel sorry for a man who cheated on his wife, but his voice is filled with so much pain, it's clear he knows he made a terrible mistake. And I know how Darcy can manipulate people into doing things – things they don't want to do. How she can get under your skin and make you question everything. She almost fooled me, and she's already fooled Jared, the school mums, the police . . .

'She worked for me,' he says. 'She was my book keeper – knew exactly how much money I made. She destroyed my business, which I guess some might say I deserved after what

I did. But she didn't stop there. She also made sure my wife knew what had happened between us. She taunted Maggie with our affair, even though she'd promised me she wouldn't. And then, the final blow – she set me up for tax evasion. Got me put away for eight years.'

I gasp, although I don't know why I'm so surprised. 'She did all that?'

'She did.'

'And you were actually sent to prison?'

'They released me last year. Let out early for good behaviour.'

Something occurs to me. 'That time outside Flora's café,' I say, 'when she told you to stay away from me. Surely, she must have recognised you. Is that why she warned you off?'

He shakes his head. 'No. She didn't recognise me. I look different now to how I looked back then. I was a rich young man with a beautiful family . . .' He breaks off and digs into his jeans' pocket, pulling out a mobile phone, its screen illuminating his worn face. He presses a few buttons and swipes the screen several times. 'Here.' He holds it out in front of me and I see a photograph of a handsome, clean-shaven, fair-haired man dressed in a suit – nothing like the man who's crouched before me now – with a pretty, dark-haired woman and three laughing children.

'Is that . . .?'

'Me. Yeah. I know, hard to believe isn't it?' He gives a dry laugh. 'Me, before Darcy shredded my life. Like she's trying to do with yours.'

I take his phone and stare hard at the photo, looking from it to Max and back again. I can see a faint resemblance – the same eyes and nose. I hand him back his phone.

'Why has she even made a move on me?' I say. 'I'm not rich.'

'You must have something she wants.'

'She's stolen my career . . . my husband's trust . . . my life. But I still don't understand *why*. I've done nothing to her, and she already had a perfect life before she met me. My career wasn't anything special. She could've picked on a much more successful writer.'

'I don't know why,' Max says. 'But I couldn't stand by and let her destroy another innocent person's life. I had to let you know she's done this sort of thing before.'

'I think you're too late,' I say, shaking my head. 'My life's already a mess. If you'd warned me about Darcy earlier, I could've avoided all—'

'I already told you, I had to be sure she was targeting you,' he says. 'To start with, I wasn't sure. And, honestly, would you have even believed me, back then? I mean, would you, really?'

'Probably not,' I say.

'Once I saw all those police go into Mike's place on Friday

night, and I saw you get taken off to the station, I knew things must have gotten to a really bad place. I knew I had to come and tell you about what she'd done to me.'

'You saw all that at Mike's apartment? You followed me there?'

He nods.

I give a shiver. 'How does that help me now? I take it no one believed you back then when you said the tax evasion was Darcy's doing? So why would they listen to you – a convicted criminal – now?'

'I just thought if we worked together, we might have a chance of stopping her going any further . . . maybe we could play her at her own game.'

I rest my chin in my hands and think. 'Will you come and talk to my husband, Jared, about it? Tell him what you told me?'

He doesn't reply, so I prompt him. 'Max?'

'I . . . I don't think that's a good idea,' he says. 'Not straight away. Darcy's got a restraining order against me. I'm not allowed to go anywhere near her. If we tell your husband and he doesn't believe us . . . if he tells Darcy, she'll make sure they put me back inside, and we won't be able to catch her out. And if we don't stop her, you'll be the next one to end up in jail.'

'The police let me go,' I say.

'For now. But Darcy won't leave it there. No way. She

likes to finish what she starts.'

Max's words chill me further. Cold dread flooding my body. My teeth have started chattering together and I can no longer feel my fingers. I finally have an ally, someone who believes me. So why do I feel more scared now, than I did before?

* * *

Thankfully, when I finally get back to the flat, the others aren't home yet. I couldn't deal with all the questions they'd fire at me if they saw the state I'm in. I catch sight of myself in the hall mirror – I look like I've been on an SAS assault course. My face is scratched, bruised and smeared with mud, my hair tangled, mud-caked, and infested with leaves and twigs. And as for my soaking clothes . . . they're completely ruined. If the stains weren't enough, the rips will consign them to the bin or the fire. I already left my boots outside – I should have dumped them straight in the recycling.

Bath then bed, I tell myself. My stomach growls. Okay, maybe some food should figure somewhere in the equation. The wall clock in the hall shows that it's only a few minutes to six. It feels like midnight already.

I head into the kitchen and rummage in the cupboard under the sink, finally finding a roll of black bin bags. I tear one off the roll and take it into the guest bathroom with me, switch on the light and avoid looking in the mirror again. I'll check myself over once I'm clean. I realise I'm going to have to have a shower before getting in the bath – otherwise I'll be sitting in a tub of muddy water.

I peel my clothes from my body, finally thawing out, but my whole body throbs. As I remove my jumper and t-shirt, I notice livid bruises have begun to appear on my torso and arms. I dump all my clothes in the bin bag. I'll wash them later and work out if anything can be salvaged once they're clean.

Beth's shower is way better than our one at home. As I step into the cubicle and turn the dial, the spray comes out hot and fast. Too fast. The jets are so powerful, they're hurting my battered body. I ease back the pressure and let the water cascade over me, wincing as my split, bruised skin is cleaned from head to toe, mud, leaves and pine needles swirling around my feet. I'll have to unclog the plug hole.

Over the sound of the shower, I hear the front door slam and Megan's running footsteps. I was lucky. I only just made it back before them.

'Aunty Lou!' Megan's fists bang on the bathroom door.

'I'm in the shower, Meggy. I'll be out in a minute!'

'We had sticky toffee pudding for afters!' she calls. 'And I brought you some back. Do you want it now?'

My heart melts at her sweetness. 'Lovely!' I shout back. 'I'll have some later with a cup of tea.'

'Sorry, Lou!' Carys' voice calls to me from outside the

bathroom. And then I hear her chastise Megan. 'Leave Aunty Louisa. She's in the shower.'

'See, I told you,' Megan replies. 'She *does* want the sticky toffee pudding.' Their voices fade as they move away from outside the bathroom door.

I'm not sure whether to tell my sister and Carys what happened today. But, I never told anyone about my stalker, and Beth will go mad that I never mentioned him before. They would want me to tell the police. I can't afford to tip Darcy off about Max. And I don't want to get him into trouble either. If Darcy has a restraining order against him, then he could get sent back to prison. I tip my head forward under the spray and work my fingers through the tangled mess that used to be my hair. Sharp twigs have embedded themselves into the curls. I even find a couple of small stones caught up near my scalp. I shudder as a squashed, drowned spider drops from my fingers into the shower tray, and wonder what other hideous creepy crawlies have found their way into my hair.

I've arranged to see Max again, tomorrow. We can't risk being spotted by anyone I know so we're going to meet back near the cliff-top path. There's a wooden bench in a clearing off the main track. There shouldn't be many people up there on a cold, November, Monday morning.

CHAPTER TWENTY EIGHT

I'm early for our 9 am meeting, but Max is already here as I arrive at the clearing. He's sitting on the damp, wooden bench and rises to his feet when he sees me, brushing imaginary dirt off his coat and trousers. He holds out his hand and I shake it. It's a gentle handshake, belying the man's strength. Maybe he doesn't want to do anything that could remind me of yesterday's violence. Either way, a polite handshake feels a strange way to greet one another after the shock and terror of yesterday's encounter.

I take my hand back and shove both hands into my coat pockets – actually, Beth's coat pockets; mine is wrecked beyond saving. Max and I perch next to each other – he sits in the middle of the bench and I've positioned myself on the edge, wary in his company. Despite everything he told me yesterday, I still can't help thinking of him as my creepy stalker. The cold has already begun to numb my feet and hands, and I'm starting to wish we'd chosen to meet in a warm, anonymous café. But we're here now so I'll just have to ignore the icy chill.

Max clears his throat. 'I wanted to say sorry again. About yesterday. I didn't plan on it going that way. I pictured a more . . . civilised meeting.'

'Thanks,' I say. 'Apology accepted. But, yes, you probably could have been a little less determined. I'm just glad you didn't turn out to be the nutter I thought you were.'

He raises an eyebrow and gives a hesitant smile before turning serious again. 'I've got a few ideas,' he says. 'About how we can catch Darcy out.'

'Good,' I reply. 'Because I've got nothing.'

'Well, I picked up some stuff . . . in prison. Ideas and skills that could help us expose her.'

'Nothing illegal,' I say, 'or dangerous.'

He waggles his head from side to side. 'Hmm, how about semi-illegal?'

'Like what?'

'We could bug her house and her car. Put some kind of hidden camera on her.'

'How would we do that?' I ask. 'You're not allowed within one hundred feet of her, and she hates my guts.'

'I can do it,' he says. 'I'll be careful not to get spotted. I managed to follow you, didn't I?'

'Well . . .' I begin.

'What?'

'As stalkers go, you weren't particularly good. I spotted you every time you came near.'

'Thanks.' He gives me a wry smile. 'Not every time, actually. Did you see me at all after Darcy warned me off?'

'No. I thought she'd managed to scare you away.'

He shakes his head and smiles.

'You mean you've been following me ever since?'

He nods.

'Well, that's not creepy at all.' I pull a face.

'Sorry, but like I said, I had to know if she was targeting you. If I hadn't followed you, I'd never have known what was going on.'

'True, I suppose.' I gaze down at the carpet of brown leaves beneath my feet and think about how strange my life has become. About how a few weeks ago I was merely a writer, wife and mother, and now I'm a murder suspect, sitting in the woods with an ex-convict, plotting to bug someone's house.

'The thing is,' he says. 'It's awkward to ask, but I would need some money for the surveillance equipment.'

Immediately, my senses go on full alert. Is this some kind of scam? Am I being taken for a gullible fool?

'It's humiliating,' he continues. 'I've got no savings from before. Like I said, Darcy took the lot. Now I have to work shifts stacking shelves in a supermarket and I live in a B&B. There's nothing left over after bills. She took everything.' He looks me in the eye, his soft gaze unwavering. I break eye-contact first.

'How much are we talking about?' I ask.

'For everything I'd need, we're looking at a little over eight grand.'

I inhale and bite my lower lip. 'That sounds an awful lot.'

'It's actually not that much, not for the type of gear we need,' he says. 'I've researched the cheapest options.'

I lean against the back of the bench and exhale, linking my hands behind my head. I don't have any spare money at all, let alone eight thousand pounds. 'Is there any way we could do it for less than that?' I ask. 'My credit card only has a four grand limit, and I'm already up to two. If I spend the rest, I'll have absolutely nothing left.' An arctic breeze sweeps through the almost-leafless trees; their branches creak and groan.

'If we want to do this properly, we need the right gear,' he insists.

'What if I told Jared, my husband? He'd be able to help us. He's got a couple of credit cards we could use.' I drop my hands back into my lap.

'No.' Max says. 'It's too risky to involve anyone else.

And anyway, I thought you two weren't getting on. You're staying at your sister's aren't you?'

I nod, uncomfortable that this man knows where I'm staying and what I'm doing. I know he says he's on my side, but still . . . 'You can stop following me now, you know.'

'Just looking out for you,' he replies.

'Well, it's not necessary. It's . . . creepy.'

He bows his head and pulls at his fingers.

'I don't mean *you're* creepy, I mean the situation is—'

'I know what you mean and it's fine,' he says. 'But that's beside the point. The fact remains that Darcy has already driven a wedge between you and Jared.'

His deduction gets my hackles up despite the fact he's absolutely right. 'It's only temporary.' I snap. 'Couples argue, you know.'

'Are you sure it's temporary? Darcy's a beautiful woman – if she's set her sights on him, it'll take a strong man to resist.'

'Stronger than you, you mean.' I instantly regret my sharp words. 'Sorry, that was uncalled for.'

He gives a rueful smile. 'No, you're absolutely right. I already admitted I was weak enough to fall for her.'

'I really don't think Jared will betray me like that.'

'I hope you're right.'

So do I. Max's words send shivers down my back. If Darcy wants Jared, will he really be able to say no? Will he stay true to me now he thinks I'm losing my mind? Will he turn her away if she flashes her eyes at him and flicks her silky hair? A wave of nausea sweeps over me, but I manage to fight it off, taking in a lungful of the frigid morning air.

'Okay, I'll extend my credit limit,' I say, exhaling. 'Or, I'll get another credit card. I'll figure something out. We need to trip her up. We need to stop her before she completely ruins my life.'

'Only if you're sure,' Max says.

'I'm not sure about anything,' I say. 'But I don't think I've got a choice.'

'Okay, well the sooner you get me the cash, the sooner I can get going with this.'

'Can you get me a list of all the equipment you need? Is it available online? I'd like to see what my money is buying.'

'Sure,' he says. 'Give me your email address and I'll send you a link to the store. You can buy the stuff yourself, if you prefer?'

I breathe a sigh of relief at his suggestion. If he's willing to let me buy the equipment . . . well, it gives me a greater sense of security that he's not after the money.

'Just make sure you get *next-day delivery*,' he says. 'Otherwise, we could be waiting around for days.'

'Do you think it will work?' I say. 'Can we really catch her out like this?'

'Truthfully? I don't know. She's a smart woman. Let's just say this will give us our best shot.'

I nod and chew my lip.

He gets to his feet. I guess this means our meeting is over, so I stand up, too. We shake hands again.

'Give me your email address and I'll message you in an hour or so,' he says, scratching at his beard.

'Okay. Thanks.' I rummage in my bag for a pen, and scribble my email on an old receipt.

He takes the address from me, nods and turns, fallen leaves crunching under his boots as he walks away.

* * *

I'm not going to worry and dwell on things like I normally would. I'm just going to do it. I close Beth's front door and stride through the hallway, shedding my shoes, coat, hat, scarf and gloves on my way through to the bedroom.

I sit on the bed and take my phone out of my bag. I search out the number for my credit-card company, then I call them, waiting interminably for a real person to speak to. When I'm finally put through to someone, I tell them I'd like to increase my spending limit for home improvements and a family holiday. To my surprise, they agree a further four thousand pounds on my limit without a fuss – madness if you ask me, seeing as I have no job and we're absolutely skint. Now I'm just two grand short of the eight thousand pounds we need.

Next, I call my bank and manage to extend my overdraft limit by two thousand pounds. My heart is pounding at the thought of borrowing such vast sums of money. But I can't dwell on it. It's worth it to get Darcy off my back, to expose her for who she really is. To get Jared to believe me. To reclaim my life.

Max's email already came through, so I open up the website and add all the gear he's listed to my basket, checking and double-checking that I've got it right. I pay extra for *next-day delivery* like he suggested, so I should receive the order tomorrow. Finally, I press the *checkout and pay* button, swallowing down my fear at spending such a vast sum of borrowed money. I text Max to let him know it's done.

Only moments ago, my account was showing a whole heap of zeros. Now, I barely have enough money left over for a weekly grocery shop. Jared and I have no savings, and my credit card is completely maxed out. I should've asked the bank to extend my overdraft by a bit more, so I at least had a little cushion to tide me over. I can't panic about it now. Just take one day at a time. Money is the least of my worries.

I leave the bedroom and pad down the hall into the kitchen. Maybe a spot of lunch will stop my head from swimming and my stomach from rolling. My gait is unsteady like I'm walking across the deck of a heaving ship. I put my hands out onto the walls to steady myself for a moment.

I take a breath and continue on. I need to stay strong for my son. Whatever else is going on, I still have Joe to think about.

* * *

Dusk softens the edges of the day as I walk down the hill towards school, excited to see my son, at last. It's only been two days, but it feels like forever since I last saw his sweet face.

Even though I'm skint, I've decided to take him out for a pizza. We could both do with a treat after all the upset of the past few days. There's a new trattoria at Penn Hill. I've heard good things about it. The alternative is to go back to Beth's and brood about everything.

I walk through the school gates, flexing my fingers in a futile attempt to warm my hands. It's bone-chillingly cold, the tang of snow and wood smoke in the air. As I enter the playground, my gaze remains firmly on the ground, I'm wary of catching anyone's eye after what happened here on Friday. And if Darcy approaches me, I've decided I'm not even going to engage with her. I'll simply back away and ignore anything she says. Luckily, the dark evenings mean I can stay relatively hidden, my hair tied back in a ponytail, a thick woollen hat wedged down low over my forehead.

I'm right on time. Mrs Landry is standing outside with her line of pupils. She's stamping her feet and blowing on her hands as she releases each child into the care of their parents.

I don't see Joe in the line, but it's quite a jumble of children, and it's almost dark so I'm sure he's there somewhere. Either that, or he's forgotten something and has run back in to get it. I'm loathe to step forward and draw any attention to myself, so I wait until the crowd of parents has thinned.

Joe is definitely not in the line of children. I hope Jared hasn't gone against our agreement and picked him up without telling me. I pull my phone out of my bag, pull one of my gloves off with my teeth, and check to see he hasn't called me. No. There are no missed calls or texts. I ring my voicemail, just in case. My phone has an annoying habit of being selective about which alerts it chooses to show me. But there's nothing there either.

There are just two children standing with Mrs Landry now, neither of which is Joe. I skirt around the edge of the playground, trying to make myself as invisible as possible.

'Hello.' I smile at Joe's teacher.

'Mrs Sullivan,' she says without smiling back.

'Just wondering where Joe is. Is he still inside?'

Mrs Landry holds her hand up to halt our conversation for a moment. She turns away to relinquish another child. 'Yes, goodbye, Eva.' They shake hands and the girl runs over to her dad who's just come into the playground.

'Joe?' I enquire again.

She frowns. 'He had a playdate with Tyler today. Did you forget?' She gives a brief wave to another parent who collects the last remaining child from her.

My pulse begins to race, partly in anger, partly in fear. 'Joe certainly did not have a playdate with Tyler,' I say. 'Aren't you supposed to have a note from the parents if someone else picks up your child from school?'

Mrs Landry's mouth drops open, and then she purses her lips. She reaches into her pocket and fumbles around for a moment, bringing out a crumpled tissue and a square of blue paper. She hands me the paper. 'Your note,' she says crisply.

I take it from her and hold it out so it's illuminated by the exterior wall light. It's handwritten in what looks to be almost exactly like my handwriting. The date at the top is today's date. The note itself says:

Hi Mrs Landry

Just to let you know, Joe is going back to Tyler
Lane's house today after school.

Thanks so much

Louisa Sullivan

My signature is on the note. It's exactly the kind of brief letter I would write if Joe was going on a playdate. Only, I didn't write this one, and I don't even have any notepaper like that.

'Where did you get this?' I say.

'It was in Joe's bag,' she replies. 'Mrs Lane came and picked them both up half an hour early today. I asked for a note and said she'd asked you to write one. So she checked in Joe's bag, and there it was.'

'So, Darcy produced the note from Joe's bag?' I ask, shaking my head in disbelief.

'Yes. Is something wrong? That is your note, right?'

'Yes something's wrong,' I snap. 'And no, that's not my note.' My hands are shaking. I stuff the note into my coat pocket. My mind races. That mad woman has my son. Could Jared have asked her to pick him up? No, no, he would have told me. And anyway, Darcy forged my bloody signature. Cold terror clutches at my heart.

'Are you okay?' Mrs Landry puts a hand on my shoulder. 'Would you like to come inside? Is there a problem. Should we talk to the headmaster about this?'

'No, no, it's fine,' I mutter. 'I need to go. I need to go and get Joe.'

'Mrs Sullivan!' Joe's teacher calls out to me as I turn away from her and jog across the playground. But I don't acknowledge her cries.

My heart thumps in rhythm with my footfalls. Oh God! Darcy's got Joe. What's she going to do with him?

CHAPTER TWENTY NINE

I jog up the hill to my car, trying not to cry. My whole body trembles. Darcy is a murderer, I know she is. And now she has my son. Should I call the police? What if it really is a misunderstanding and Jared arranged for Darcy to pick him up? I'll kill him if he did, but I'll also be relieved because then it won't mean that she's taken him without permission. If this is Jared's doing, the police will think I'm a deluded crazy person. They might arrest me again or lock me up in an institution like they did with my birth mum.

I slow down for a moment, trying to get my jumbled thoughts straight. This can't be Jared's doing – Darcy forged a note. My brain is racing, spinning. Am I crazy? Actually, it doesn't matter – not when Joe is involved. If there's the tiniest chance that he's in danger, I have to try to save him, even if I'm wrong and end up having everyone think I'm mad.

A thin skin of ice coats the car, glistening under the streetlights. I open the door and slide into the driver's seat, putting a call through to Jared at the same time. I growl in frustration as it goes to voicemail. I end the call and redial. Voicemail again. I end the call again and redial, praying for my husband to answer this time. Bloody voicemail again.

'Jared, please get back to me.' I sound shrill and wavery. Unhinged. But I can't make my voice any calmer. 'Did you arrange for Darcy to collect Joe from school tonight? I thought we agreed that I would pick him up. Call me back, urgently.'

I shove my phone into my bag, chuck my bag on the passenger seat and start up the engine. Then, I put the car into first gear and press down on the accelerator. I release the handbrake too quickly and roll backwards, almost smashing into the SUV parked a few feet behind me. Luckily, I stomp on the brake just in time.

I take a breath, pull on the handbrake and sit still for a minute, my hands gripping the cold wheel, desperately trying to calm down. It won't do Joe any good if I end up having a crash. I try again. This time easing out of the space without mishap. I'm going straight over to Darcy's. The bitch better be in and she better not have harmed a hair on Joe's head. I barely register the short drive over there. The roads, the lights, the cars – they're all just a blur through a haze of anxiety as I mutter to myself, head swimming, fingers shaking.

Almost there.

The automatic gates are open, thank goodness. I tear down the driveway, her fancy, contemporary garden lamps lighting my way. If I wasn't in such a hurry, I'd want to smash into each one, uprooting them, destroying her perfect driveway.

She's there, standing in the doorway under the porch light, the chill wind blowing her hair. As if she's expecting me. Dressed casually in jeans, boots and a white t-shirt, she must be freezing. No sign of Joe or Tyler.

The car skids on the driveway as I pull on the handbrake too soon, like a boy-racer in a deserted car park. I grab my bag and car keys, fling open the car door and almost fall out onto the driveway in my haste to get answers.

'Where's my son, Darcy?' I cry. 'If you've hurt him . . . if you've so much as harmed one hair on his head, I'll—'

'Calm down,' she says, raising her eyebrows as if I'm some minor inconvenience. 'Joe's fine. Come in.'

'How dare you take my son out of school without permission. How bloody dare you.' I'm shaking with anger while she is cool and composed, admiring her nails.

'I thought I was helping,' she says. 'Are you coming in, or not?'

'*Helping*? I don't think so.' I shoulder past her into the hallway lit by a huge crystal chandelier. 'Joe!' I yell. 'We're going now!' My heart pounds as I listen for a reply.

Darcy closes the front door and strolls past me into the kitchen.

'Where's Joe?' I call after her. 'Are they upstairs? In the garden? Get him now, Darcy. This isn't funny.' I dump my bag and keys on the hall table and follow her into the dimly lit kitchen, scanning for any sign of my son. But it's quiet. Still.

'Marianna's taken the boys out for ice cream and then to the movies,' Darcy says. 'So you don't need to worry. They'll be in heaven.'

'What! You mean they're not here?'

'That's what I just said.' She heads over to the black marble island in the centre of the room. It's dark, apart from a couple of central pendants illuminating her workspace. Two huge beef tomatoes sit on a chopping block next to a black-handled knife. She grasps the knife and slices into one of the tomatoes, the knife going in smoothly. 'I'm making a salad,' she says. 'Care to join me for supper while we wait for them to come home?'

'No I bloody don't want to join you for supper. I just want my son.' I clench and unclench my hands by my sides impotently. 'Darcy, why did you take my son out of school?' As I wait for her to answer my question, the blood whooshes in my ears and my heartbeats fill the pregnant silence.

'I needed to get you over here,' she finally replies. 'But I didn't think you'd be quite this keen. I think you might have left skid marks on the driveway.' She laughs at her little joke.

I don't find anything she says funny any more. '*You needed to get me over here?* What do you mean? Why didn't you just call me?'

'No, that wouldn't have worked. I couldn't risk my call being traced.'

A chill sweeps through my body. What's she talking about? 'Call Marianna!' I cry, hearing the shrillness in my voice. 'Get her to bring Joe home, right now.'

'Oh, they'll be in the movie theatre already. Her cell will be switched off. You're not allowed to have your phone on once the movie starts. Or are you one of those selfish types who keeps it switched on? It's very annoying, you know. You'll be in the middle of a tense scene, and then someone's phone starts ringing. Takes you right out of the moment.'

'What the hell are you on about? Try her phone,' I demand. 'Call the cinema and tell them it's an emergency.'

'No,' she says, her eyes glinting.

'Fine. Then tell me which cinema, and I'll go and collect him.'

'No.' She smirks and laughs, and I can tell there's something really wrong with her. Something rotten.

'Okay,' I say, my voice trembling. 'Then I'll go and find him myself. And if he's not at the cinema, I'll call the police and tell them you abducted my son.'

'No,' she says softly as she turns towards me with the knife in her hand. Tomato juice drips from the blade onto the white marble floor.

Surely she wouldn't try to . . . But I remember Mike's blank eyes, the blood everywhere, and I know without a doubt that she killed him. I glance to my right and see the bifold doors are closed tight. Probably locked, I can't get out that way. I'll have to go back through the front door. The same way I came in. I turn and run, fumbling with the front door, shoving it open. I head straight for my car, her laughter chasing me out onto the floodlit driveway.

Too late, I realise my keys are with my bag on her hall table. I swear under my breath. Darcy's footsteps are close behind me. I can't turn back now. Instead, I swerve and make a run for it, racing around the side of the house, my heart battering my ribcage. A security light flashes on.

'I can see-ee you!' she calls, enjoying my blatant fear.

The freezing night air takes my breath and chills my tears of terror. I make my way down the side path, past the white-rendered wall of her house, tall, dark pine trees on the other side, her steady footfalls behind me. I have no idea if this path leads anywhere, or if I will find myself at a dead-end, with a wall in front of me and a mad woman brandishing a knife behind me.

Luckily, it's not a dead-end. The path leads to the decking area behind the house. Through the closed bifold doors, I glimpse the half-lit kitchen. There's no time to look behind me. I have to find a way out of here. The wooden deck is slippery, a thin film of ice forming on its surface. I skid and slide across it, stumbling down the wooden steps and almost falling head first onto the grass below, the place where Tyler and Joe played their game of football all those weeks ago when I first got caught up in Darcy's web.

'You can run, but I'm gonna get you, Louisa,' she calls out from behind me.

The icy, brittle grass crunches underfoot as I race towards the gate, set into the white wall that leads onto the beach. Security lights click on, illuminating my progress, like moving spotlights on the star of the show. I crash into the wooden gate at the end of the garden, pushing and pulling at it in desperation. It won't budge.

'Don't strain yourself,' Darcy calls out, amusement in her voice. 'It's locked!'

I'm unfit. Un-athletic. Weak. And my knee is shot to pieces. But somehow I scramble up and over the high gate, tearing my nails in the process. I guess fear of death is a powerful motivator. I land on the hard sand with a thump, pausing for only a few seconds before struggling to my feet and limping away across the sand dunes.

She's behind me. I hear her laughter, her fragmented taunts whipped away by the wind. As I stumble across the dark sand, I picture the knife in Darcy's hand. The sharp edge of the steel, the glint of the blade. Again, I remember the sight of Mike's body covered in blood. Will that be me soon? Lifeless and bloody? My knee feels torn and ragged, the pain a throbbing precursor to what is about to come. It hurts so much, I don't know how I'm even still running. Will it hurt to die? To be stabbed in the chest? Or will the shock blot out the pain?

The swish of the waves merges with the thump of my heart. It's never beaten so loud before. Like a war drum, a death knell in my throat. I daren't look round. What if she's there, right behind me, ready to tackle me to the ground? She may be slim, but she's tall, strong, sinewy. She could beat me in a fight, I'm sure of it. Especially armed with a knife. In my mind, I see Darcy's mocking face. The glint of steel in her hand. Will she catch me any second and stab me in the back?

I have to run faster. My breath comes in wheezing gasps, my lungs bursting, thighs burning. The cold wind stinging my cheeks, boots thudding unsteadily across the hard sand. To my right, the rolling sea. To my left, the millionaire mansions shimmering as fear blurs my vision.

A shape looms up ahead. It's a man walking towards me.

'Help!' I cry, my voice half-strangled.

The man stops. Comes into focus, the three-quarter moon throwing his face into relief. *Thank God. Thank God.* It's Max. He must have ignored my request for him to stop following me. Sobbing with relief, I stagger straight into his arms and he gathers me into the safety of his solid body.

'She's coming!' I pant. 'Darcy. She's got a knife. We need to get out of here. Have you got a car?'

I try to step back out of his arms, but he's still cradling

me.

'Max, didn't you hear me? She's got a knife. Let's go. We need to run.'

His grip tightens. I try to lever my body away from him but it's like being held by warm stone. He's unmoving. Through my panic, I'm trying to make sense of it. Does he want to confront her? Another, more distressing thought cuts through. I push my hands against his chest, twist my body back, then kick him in the shins, but still he doesn't move.

'Shh,' he says, his soft voice merging with the crash of the waves. 'Don't struggle. You'll only hurt yourself.'

The sound of Darcy's laughter comes to me through the salty air. 'Oh, Louisa,' she says, her voice closing in, 'you are funny. Thinking you could ever outrun me with your gammy knee. And I see you're already acquainted with my brother. Actually, I think he's got a bit of a soft spot for you.'

Her brother? 'What? . . . I . . .' and then the penny drops. Max was working with Darcy the whole time. He's her *brother*. He's her bloody brother. My shoulders sag. So everything Max told me was a lie! I've been so stupid. So gullible. No wonder Darcy's laughing at me. I've been played so beautifully. She's been several steps ahead of me this whole time. And I thought I was actually making progress, getting her out of my life.

'Max is your brother,' I say, my shoulders sagging.

She tuts. 'That's what I just told you, isn't it. You're a little slow on the uptake today, Louisa. I needed him to keep an eye on you this week. To see what you were up to. Find out your plans. That's when I had the fabulous brainwave of promoting him from being your stalker, to being your friend. Clever huh?'

But she's American. And Max is English. How can they be related?

Max eases me around so I'm facing Darcy, his arms still circling my body like chains. The moon illuminates her face, eyes gleaming, hair shining. She's not even mildly out of breath, while I'm still wheezing like an elderly, asthmatic cat.

'I'm going to enjoy the next part of this evening,' she says, dropping her smile. 'Let's get you back into the warm, Louisa. Look at you, you're shivering.'

CHAPTER THIRTY

Spring 2003

She'd waited not so patiently all through the brutal winter, sure that eighty-seven-year-old Arthur would pop his clogs by March. But the old git was still going strong. Apart from his hearing and his sight, he was healthy as a horse, worse luck. Nicole had hoped the icy conditions would have weakened him, especially as she'd accidentally on purpose left the heating off one night. Arthur had said that it would take more than a bit of cold to see him off.

She realised with alarm that old people lived to be past one hundred these days. It was selfish. Make more room on the planet, she thought. Toddle off early for fuck's sake. But no, now it was spring, and Arthur was still hanging in there, sprightly as ever, holding on to *her* inheritance.

Nicole jiggled the key in the front door, the April rain had swollen the lock and it was a bugger to open. Finally, the key hit home and she turned it and pushed open the door, shaking her umbrella out over the front step and stepping into the hallway.

It was her turn to do earlies this week. She yawned, took off her raincoat and hung it over the bannister, tramping up the creaky stairs. She wondered who had been on nights. Nicole never minded doing the night shifts; the spare room here was a lot nicer than her grotty place, and she got paid more for the privilege.

'Morning, Arthur!' She rapped on his bedroom door and called out again. He was becoming deafer by the day.

'Morning,' she heard him reply.

Nicole eased open the bedroom door. Arthur was sitting up in bed wearing a pair of checked pyjamas.

'You just missed Natalie,' he said. 'She had to leave a few minutes early – her daughter had a doctor's appointment. I told her she needn't have bothered staying all night, I'd be fine on my own until you got here, but she's a conscientious girl. She's new. Have you met her?'

No, Nicole had not met her, and she didn't like the sound of her. Not at all. She hoped this Natalie person wouldn't become Arthur's new favourite. If Natalie was on nights, she'd get to soothe his nightmares and while away the evenings with him. Arthur might change his Will again, and Nicole couldn't have that. She'd have to be especially nice to the old git from now on. Nicer than she already was.

'Let's go and get you washed and shaved,' Nicole said, 'and then I'll lay some clothes out for you. How about your grey trousers? And then I thought a pale green shirt and dark green jumper - the one your Margaret always liked. Will that be all right?'

'Yes, that's fine. You know I'm not fussy about what I wear, dear.'

Did she detect a bit of impatience in his voice? She'd have to be careful not to irritate him. Nicole helped him out of bed and onto his feet, wondering just who this Natalie person thought she was, trying to move in on *her* Arthur. Nicole had been with him for months now, listening to his boring stories, cooking for him, picking up after him, having to be nice to him, and she wasn't about to let some jumped-up newbie take preferential place. No way.

Despite his blindness, Arthur always insisted he could find his way around his own house perfectly well, but Nicole took his arm anyway, and led him out onto the landing, suddenly wanting to make herself indispensable.

'How about I cook you a nice fry up this morning?' she asked. 'With all the trimmings?' That should get her into his good books. Arthur always loved a cooked breakfast.

'I'm not sure,' he said. 'Natalie was telling me about these people in California who are vegetarians and, according to her, they're the healthiest people in the world – just eat nuts and berries and raw vegetables, can you believe it?'

'You want nuts and berries for breakfast?' she asked, one eyebrow raised.

'Well,' he chuckled. 'Natalie was very persuasive. She wants me to try a new healthy diet – said she'd try some of her vegan recipes out on me. I was very impressed with her,

I don't mind telling you. Not sure she'd be happy with me eating a fry up.'

Nicole led Arthur over to the bathroom door, her blood boiling at the thought of this vegan bitch putting all these healthy-eating ideas into Arthur's head. It would ruin her plans. He'd live much longer if he stopped eating fry ups and stuff. Plus she would have to work twice as hard to keep him sweet with this new girl as competition.

Or . . .

'Are we going into the bathroom, dear?' Arthur asked. 'You've stopped.'

'Sorry, Arthur, miles away.' She eased his body around and led him away from the bathroom door.

'Just a couple more steps,' she crooned. 'There. Door's open. You go in first.'

'Aren't we going in the wrong direction?' he said, turning his head from left to right, trying to make sense of his surroundings. 'The bathroom's the other way. Are you sure this is the—'

'In you go,' she said brightly, giving him a little nudge.

Arthur took a step. Instead of the bathroom floor, he found nothing beneath his foot. He wobbled but somehow managed to stay upright.

'Careful, Arthur,' Nicole said, letting go of his arm. 'You don't want to slip.' With her toe, she nudged the back of his calf – the one that was still on firm ground. His slippered foot shot out from under him and he slipped backwards towards her. 'Don't worry, Arthur, I've got you,' she cried, giving his back a light shove so he ended up careering head first down the steep flight of stairs.

'Arthur!' she screamed, suppressing a smile. 'Oh my God, are you okay?'

There was a crunch and a thud, and then silence. The air seemed to thicken for a moment as if holding its breath.

Nicole stared at the crumpled shape of the old man at the bottom of the stairs, admiring her handy work. This would be easy. She'd say that when she arrived Natalie had already left, and she'd found the old man dead in the hallway.

Nicole couldn't believe that the new girl had left Arthur on his own this morning. What a slacker. And now look what had happened! Natalie – or whatever her name was – was supposed to have stayed with him until Nicole got here. You couldn't leave these old people on their own – that was how accidents happened. There were rules about that sort of thing. God, that girl was going to get into so much trouble.

CHAPTER THIRTY ONE

2016

The shock of discovering that Max is actually Darcy's brother freezes my brain for a moment. I stare open mouthed at her smug expression. My heart is still pounding and my legs are weak, yet I have to get away from them. Max's arms encircle me. I try squirming free but his grip only tightens. I take a breath and start to scream. His massive hand comes over my mouth, squeezing my cheeks.

'Make one more sound,' Darcy says, 'and I will cut you so bad your son won't recognise your face.' She holds the blade up to my nose as I stifle a whimper. Her words take the fight from my body. 'Understand?' she says.

I nod, and Max removes his hand from my mouth.

'Good,' she says. 'Now we've got that sorted, let's get back home. It's chilly out here.'

Max leads me across the beach, back towards the house, both hands clamped around my shoulders. I can barely feel the cold any longer. My body and my mind are numb. Defeated. Everything I tried to do was pointless. She had it all planned out. She's ruined me. But why? Why the hell did she do it? I need to know. I have to find out.

Somewhere during my bid for freedom, I lost my hat, and now my hair whips around my face. Max and Darcy are quiet. There's just the crash of the waves and the sound of my breath and heartbeats, of our soft footsteps out of time with one another.

'Just tell me one thing,' I ask, 'Is Joe okay?'

'Of course, he's okay,' Darcy says. 'I told you, he and Ty are at the cinema. Honestly, he's an eight-year-old child. What kind of person do you think I am?'

I don't answer.

The white boundary wall of Darcy's property comes into view, stark against the dark sand, and I instinctively slow down, knowing nothing good will come of going back inside. Max notices my hesitation and grips me tighter, urging me forward. I should fight, yell, try to escape, but Max is big and Darcy still has the knife in her hand. Please, God, don't let her use it on me. I'm not ready to die. I want to see my son again. I want to see Jared, despite the fact he lost faith in me.

The gate to her garden is still locked. Darcy must have climbed over it, too. Looking at it now, I can't believe I made it over. Max takes a bunch of keys from his pocket, slots one into the keyhole and unlocks the gate. Darcy walks in first. This is my last chance to try to escape before I'm taken back inside, but Darcy's threat has chilled my bones and turned my knees to jelly. I'm too scared. I'm no runner. I know they would catch me. Should I at least try?

'Don't even think about it,' Max says softly. 'You heard her. She'll make you suffer for it.'

His words do the trick. I step through the opening and onto the icy grass, with Max keeping hold of my elbow. Darcy is already striding back towards the house, knowing we'll be following close behind. She slides open the bifold doors. Seems I could've escaped out that way – too late now. It seems like days since I was in her kitchen, but it can't have been more than half an hour ago.

'Let's go,' Darcy says, heading to a door just off the kitchen. Max and I follow her into a long, narrow utility room. At the end, she opens another door and presses a light switch illuminating a flight of stairs which leads down into a basement.

I stop at the top, watching Darcy disappear down the narrow steps. Max prods me in the back and I'm forced downwards, our footsteps loud on the wooden treads. At the bottom, lies a vast white cube of a room. I glance around the immaculate space. It's clean down here, but there's still a musty smell of damp. Of decay.

At one end runs a floor-to-ceiling wine rack stuffed full of bottles. Next to the rack is a wooden table and six dining chairs. At the opposite end of the room, running along the top of the wall a thin strip of window is the only view of the outside world - a partial view of the floodlit driveway. Darcy presses another switch on the wall and, with a faint whirring sound, a Venetian blind drops down from the ceiling to cover the glass.

She nods to her brother, and he manoeuvres me forward while she sets out one of the heavy wooden dining chairs beneath the strip of window. I land heavily on my backside, banging my coccyx, my pulse racing, fingers burning as the circulation returns to my hands. Max pulls my arms behind the back of the chair and ties them with something that digs into my skin. When he's done, he comes around the front and takes a couple of black zip ties from his pocket. He crouches down and secures one of my ankles to the chair leg, and does the same with the other, the plastic biting through my jeans.

'What are you going to do?' I stare across at Darcy who now sits, legs crossed, on another of the dining chairs. My voice quavers, betraying my fear. If only I were stronger, braver. Max straightens up and stands by my side.

'Let's not worry about that right now,' Darcy replies.

'No, really,' I say, my tone sharpening. 'Let's worry about it *right* now. You can't keep me down here, tied up forever.'

'You're right about that,' she says.

I swallow.

'Go and move her car,' Darcy says to Max. 'Put it out of sight in one of the garages for now.'

'Are the keys—'

'How should I know.' Darcy turns to me. 'Car keys?'

With dismay, I remember my keys are on the hall table next to my bag and phone. I'm well and truly fucked.

'Don't make me hurt you,' she says.

'On the hall table,' I mutter.

Max nods and leaves.

'What's going on, Darcy?' I ask. 'Why do you want to destroy my life? Did you kill Mike? Did you set me up?' I hear a car engine outside and my heart lifts only to sink again as I realise it's probably just Max moving my Golf out of sight.

She stands and walks over to me. Instinctively I cringe back in my chair, my gaze flitting from her unsmiling face to the knife in her hand.

'If you hadn't come along, they'd have picked me,' she says bitterly.

'What are you talking about? What do you mean?'

'I mean . . .' She leans in close to me, her eyes flashing, glinting. 'You stole the life I was meant to have. Because of you, I lost my chance.'

I have absolutely no idea what she's on about. I need to know what it is she thinks I've done. Maybe she's confusing me with someone else. Maybe I can talk her round. 'Darcy, if I've done anything to upset you, I'm sorry. But doing this . . . keeping me here, a prisoner in your house isn't going to solve anything. It will only make things worse. Can't we talk about whatever it is that's troubling you?' I'm trying to sound sincere. To get her to be reasonable.

The front door slams and heavy footsteps cross the hallway above us. Seconds later, he reappears down the stairs. Damn. Max is back. I was hoping Darcy and I could have had the chance to talk alone for a moment longer.

'You see,' she says, ignoring Max who is now back by my side. 'You don't even know what you've done! That's how little my life has affected you. But I've been cursed by you my whole life.'

'So tell me,' I cry. 'Tell me what I'm supposed to have done.'

Max stands by my shoulder and Darcy sits back down on her chair, running her forefinger along the blade of the knife which lies on the table next to her. I try not to imagine it sticking out of my body.

'Do you remember your brief stay in Ashlands Residential Care Home, back when you were a kid?' she asks.

Her question wrong-foots me, setting my heart racing again. Why is she asking me about that? I do remember it. I was ten years old, and it was one of the most unsettling times of my life. I've tried to fold it away and keep it locked in my mind. It was such a brief period, and nothing really bad happened. The staff were nice enough. I remember them as kind and welcoming, motherly even. But I had just been removed from my family home, from my birth parents – a mother who was mentally unstable, and a father with anger issues. My whole stay at the care home was surreal, like it wasn't even happening to me.

'How do you know about that?' I ask. 'And what's it got to do with you? With what's happening now.'

'Did you know,' she said, 'from the age of eleven, I was fostered by six different families. Six. None of them loved me. None of them wanted me, and I hadn't wanted to go with any of them because they hadn't been the right ones.' Darcy has stopped looking at me. She's staring ahead at the white wall, but I can tell she's seeing somewhere else. A different time and place.

'So,' I say, 'we have something in common. We were both in the care system.'

'Pftt,' she says, snapping her head around to face me. 'You were in care for all of two minutes. I got to spend most of my childhood there. You don't know what that's really like.'

'I'm sorry,' I say. 'I really am sorry you had a crappy childhood. But so did I. Until I was adopted, my life was like walking on a tightrope over hot coals.'

'Oh, poor you,' she mocks. 'But this isn't about whose childhood was the worst. This is about you. And how you stole my childhood from me. How you stole my family.'

'What?' I have no idea what she means. For a start, she's American . . . How could I have stolen her family?

'Back then, at Ashlands,' she says, 'do you remember the girl in the room next to you?'

'I don't really remember much. Like you said, I wasn't there long. Not more than a couple of weeks.'

'Yes,' Darcy says. 'You were there for twelve whole days before you were adopted. *Twelve days*, whoopee doo. *I* was in and out of Ashlands for years.'

'You were there?' I gasp. 'At Ashlands? At the same time as me? Why didn't you say something before? Did I do something to upset you back then? Is that what this is about? I can't remember anyone from America being there.'

'Oh, for goodness sake, don't you get it? I'm not really American. My name's Nicole Woodward and I'm from Bristol, *okay*.'

I'm sure my jaw has never dropped this low before. 'Your name isn't Darcy? You're not from America?'

'That's what I just said, isn't it. Keep up. And that's my brother, Callum. He was there for a while, too, until he got fostered long-term . . . without me.' She glares across at him and he flinches.

I'm still reeling from her revelation, trying to process the fact that she's not who I thought she was. That we met when we were kids – even if I don't have any memory of her from back then. 'That still doesn't explain why you have me here now,' I say. 'Why you've gone out of your way to destroy my life.'

'Cal and I had been at Ashlands for a few months,' she says, still talking in her fake American accent, 'and there was a family that came to visit. This really nice couple with a daughter. They talked to me and Cal for ages. They were interested in us. Really interested. I was actually excited for the first time in my life. They should have been the ones. They should have been our new family. Then they left and I never saw them again. And I found out later that they'd adopted *you* – Miss Perfect. If you hadn't come along, I would be living your life. They would've been my family. Mine and Cal's.' Her face is white and strained, her fists clenched against her thighs.

She actually blames me for this. She thinks that as a ten-year-old child I wilfully stole the parents she designated for herself. I mean, yes, I can see how at that age, you would be devastated, but now as an adult surely she can see it was nobody's fault. Maybe the care home should have taken some of the blame for raising her hopes, but no one else is to blame. Certainly not me.

'So,' she continues, 'I made it my life's mission to take it all back. To get back the family that should have been mine all along.'

I shake my head in disbelief. 'You're an adult now. An adult with a pretty enviable life. Surely you're past that point in your life.'

'Doesn't matter,' she says. 'When I set out to do something. I always have to finish it. Otherwise, what's the point of anything?'

I give a shiver at her words, taking a guess at what she means by "finish it". I desperately need to keep her talking, so I can figure out how to get out of here.

'What does Callum have to say about all this?' I ask. 'Does he think the same way as you?' I look up at her brother. 'Do you, Callum? Do you think it's right to punish me for something I had no control over?'

He shifts from one foot to the other, glancing across at his sister, and then back down at me. 'Nic said you ruined everything for us. She's my sister. I look out for her. You hurt Nic, I'll hurt you. She looks out for me, too.'

I realise that Callum isn't the sharpest tool in the shed. Nicole must have been using and manipulating him for years.

'I finally tracked you down to Poole a couple of years ago,' she continues, shifting her attention back to me. 'And so I persuaded Mike to leave London and move here. Told him it would be better for Tyler to grow up by the sea, or some such crap. I found out your sister's kid was in the Kindergarten at Cerne Manor. My plan was to get to you through her. Then, imagine my delight when you enrolled Joe at the same school. In the very same class as Tyler. What luck!'

I'm still reeling from what she's telling me. To have spent the whole of her adult life trying to find me so she could ruin my life is insane.

'Your life was so perfect,' I say. 'Surely you already had

everything. You had Mike and Tyler, your beautiful house, your business.'

'I never loved Mike,' she says without emotion. 'He was a means to an end. I needed his money to track you down, to take everything from you.'

'And Tyler?' I ask, my skin crawling in revulsion at her revelations. I have to get out of here. *Shit*, how am I going to get out of here?

'Tyler is everything to me. He's the only good thing in my life. I've been doing this for him as well as me.'

'What about his dad? You killed Mike. You killed Tyler's father. How do you think he'll feel when he finds out what you did?'

'He will never find out. Never – do you understand me?'

'How does ruining my life get you what you want?' I ask. 'Sure, it might make you feel good, if that's how you get off, but apart from that—'

'It's simple,' Darcy says.

I wait for her to elaborate.

'You stole mine and Callum's childhood,' she says. 'You stole our family, so we'll take them back. I may not be able to reclaim my childhood, but I will have your parents.'

'What are you talking about?' I say, my heart in my throat. But the question is redundant. I know exactly what she's talking about.

CHAPTER THIRTY TWO

'I have it all worked out,' Darcy says. 'Everything is prepared.' She glances across at her brother, a look of irritation on her face. 'God, Cal, can you sit down or something, it's really distracting having you standing there like some kind of zombie statue.'

'I was making sure she doesn't escape, Nic.'

'She's in a basement, zip-tied to a chair, I don't think she'll be going anywhere right this minute. And how many times do I need to tell you to call me Darcy. I haven't been Nic for years.'

Callum shuffles across the room to sit on another of the chairs. Darcy's shoulders relax as he sits.

'You should know,' Nicole says to me, 'in case you were wondering, you *are* going to die.'

I bite my lip, too shocked to reply. I already guessed she was never going to let me go, but to hear her say the actual words . . .

'I've been doing quite a bit of planning,' she says, leaning forward, warming to her subject. 'The police still haven't found the murder weapon from Mike's death.' She pauses. 'That's because I have it.'

'I knew it was you,' I say.

'Of course you did. Clever you.' She rolls her eyes. 'Anyway, you still haven't heard the genius part of it yet . . . the knife used to kill Mike was taken from part of a knife-block set in your kitchen, and it's covered in your fingerprints. When the police eventually discover the weapon in a shoe box in your closet – I'll put it there later – they'll have found their killer. Too bad you won't end up in prison – you'll already be dead.'

I listen to her words as though from a long way away. It's as if she's talking about someone else. Instead, I focus on the pain in my body. Pain is good – it means I'm still alive. I've almost lost circulation in my hands from where the zip ties are cutting into my wrists. My arms feel as though they're being pulled out of their sockets, my bad knee is on fire and my heart is racing so fast I'm sure my chest is about to explode.

'So,' she continues, 'You, Louisa, are now going to write a remorseful note about how jealous you were of my life, and how you wanted to make me suffer, so you tried to have an affair with my husband, and when he wouldn't touch you with a ten-foot bargepole, you were so angry, you killed him. Obviously, you can't live with the guilt, blah, blah, blah.'

'That's ludicrous,' I say.

'Really?' she says. 'I thought it was pretty believable. Especially as half the moms in Ty's class saw how much you upset me the other day.' She sticks her bottom lip out, faking sadness. 'They all witnessed you taunting me about going to visit Mike. They were outraged on my behalf at how mean you were. Hell, you even made me cry. Anyway, once you've written the note, you're going to drive your car off the quarry in the dead of night, and die.'

My palms begin to sweat and my head swims as I hear the details of what she's got planned for me.

'I suppose I could have simply set you up for Mike's murder without killing you, and left it at that,' she muses, 'but that would've been too much of a risk. You'd still be alive; you would have tried to talk your way out of it. Jared might have ended up believing your innocence. Your parents might have stood by you. This way, you'll be a self-confessed murderer and the knife will be found with your prints. Incontrovertible evidence. You'll be remembered as a deranged suicide and I'll be the grieving widow.'

'You're mad,' I whisper. 'It's an insane plan, and the police will see right through it.'

'They won't. I'll be handing the killer to them on a plate,' she says. 'They'll close the case, and that will be that.'

I shake my head. The terrifying thing is, she's probably right. I need to find a flaw. Something that will convince her to change her mind. Problem is, my brain has come unspooled and I'm having a hard time breathing.

'I'll comfort Jared after the loss of his wife,' she continues.

'And he'll comfort me after the loss of my husband. It's perfect. He'll feel guilty that it was his wife who killed Mike. He'll probably feel partly responsible, like he should've done more to stop you. I'll let myself be soothed by him, and I'll tempt him with my body and my wealth. Eventually, we'll fall for each other. I can help him out with Joe—'

'Joe hates you,' I say. 'He says you scare him. My son may be young, but he's a very good judge of character.'

'He'll get over it,' she says coldly. 'He'll grow to love me like a mommy. Jared and I will bring up our two boys together. They'll be step brothers—'

'You know Tyler bullies him,' I interrupt again. 'Joe will be miserable. You can't do this to him.'

'He's young, his memory of you will fade soon enough. Most importantly, your parents will get to know me and grow to love me. I'll become a daughter to them. I still have Mike's money. We can all go on luxurious family holidays together. It will be perfect, like it was always supposed to be.'

'You're deluded,' I say. 'You're actually mad. You can't write the script to your life. You can't say, if I do this and this, then all these things will definitely happen. Life doesn't work that way. I'd have thought you of all people would have realised that by now.'

She shakes her head. 'I don't blame you for trying to pick holes in my plan. After all, you won't be around to see it all happen. You'll be long gone.' She twists her hair around one side of her neck and then lets it go, running her fingers through the silken strands. 'You stole those years from me, Louisa, but now I'm going to take them back. It's only fair.'

'My parents will see right through you,' I hiss. 'And you're forgetting my sister, Beth. She will never in a million years believe I killed myself, just like she knows I had nothing to do with Mike's murder.'

'I'll win her over. After all, soon she'll be my sister. I want my family to get along.'

I give a bitter laugh.

'And anyway,' she continues, 'if Beth doesn't play nicely, there are ways I can make her change her mind.'

'What are you going to do?' I say. 'Kill her? Kill them all off one-by-one when they don't conform to your twisted game of happy families? That'll work out well – eventually, you'll be back on your own again.'

'You're being melodramatic, Louisa.'

That's rich.

She rises to her feet. 'I've had enough of all this talking. It's time for you to write this goodbye note to your family.' She nods to her brother. 'Callum, cut her hands free.'

Darcy strides across the room towards the window. She reaches up to the deep sill and lifts down a clear plastic A4 wallet. Inside it are a few sheets of paper and a Biro. Callum snips the zip tie that binds my wrists behind my back. Their sudden release prompts spasms of pain up both arms and shoulders, but it does feel better to be able to move them again. I bring my hands around to my lap and rub at the red weals on my wrists.

There's no way I'm writing that note, even if she uses her knife to coerce me. As soon as I write it I'm dead anyway, so if I have to suffer some pain . . . Yet the thought of her slicing through my skin is terrifying. Despite my fear, I take a breath and narrow my eyes. 'I won't do it,' I say. 'You write it. You're quite the expert at forging notes – school notes at least.'

'Ooh, Louisa's got a bit of backbone at last,' Darcy trills. She walks over to me, bends down and puts her face up close to mine. I marvel at her beauty. At her narrow heart-shaped face of perfect proportions. It's almost too perfect, her skin too smooth, her features too regular. 'You *will* write this note, Louisa,' she says. 'Don't give me that look. I have your son. I can always arrange for Joe to disappear along with you. Jared would curse your memory forever if I was forced to take that route.'

I draw in a breath. I don't doubt she would use my son to make me do what she wants.

'Why are you still talking in an American accent?' I ask, trying to delay. 'You just told me you were British, born in Bristol. Do you have a west-country accent like your brother?'

'I've become attached to my US accent,' she replies, 'like

I'm attached to Darcy. I think I'll keep her. Anyway, my son knows me as Darcy Lane. To him I'm American. He's half-American, half-British. Once I kill you, that information about my old life will be buried.'

'What about all the surveillance equipment?' I ask, stalling again. 'Why did Max – sorry, Callum – tell me to buy all that stuff?'

'Oh,' Darcy says airily, 'that was just for fun. I wanted to see if you'd do it. If you'd put your trust in a complete stranger and go into debt just to try to catch me out. Turns out you would. Plus, it's icing on the cake for me. The police will discover you bought a bucket load of surveillance equipment, completing the picture that you'd planned to spy on me because of your jealousy and paranoia.' She's enjoying this. Savouring my confusion and fear. I'm no longer surprised by her responses. I realise she must have some emotional defect. I remember watching a TV programme on psychopaths – or was it sociopaths? – I can't remember the difference. But I'm sure Darcy is one or the other. She has no empathy. She doesn't care about what she's done, or what she's about to do. She wants what she wants and that's it.

'Enough questions,' she says, placing the plastic wallet on my lap.

I shake my head even though I know I have no choice.

'That's right,' she says as I reach into the wallet with trembling hands. 'Take out the pen and one of the sheets of paper and I'll dictate your farewell note.'

I do as she instructs, conscious of my clammy fingers on the pristine page, marking it with my prints, branding myself a killer.

'Lean on this,' she says, passing me a hardback book on Californian wines from the dining table.

I rest the paper on the book and grasp the Biro in my hand.

'*Jared*,' she says. 'Go on, write that. *Jared.*'

I do as she asks, writing my husband's name on the paper. A tear drips onto the centre of the page, soaking into the paper.

'Perfect!' She claps her hands together. 'Tears add that extra touch of authenticity don't you think? So, back to the letter. *I'm so sorry for everything I've put you through these past few weeks. The truth is, I haven't been myself.*

She waits for me to finish writing, the scratch of pen on paper, my tears still dripping, wrinkling the page and smudging the ink.

'Okay, good. Now keep going: '*I blamed Darcy for everything that was going wrong in my life, but I know now that it was all in my head. She was only trying to help. I was jealous. I was mad at you both. I'm ashamed to admit it, but I tried to set Darcy up for Mike's murder when it was me all along. I can't believe I did it, I'm so sorry. If I could change things I would, but it's too late now. I love you, and*

Joe is the light of my life—'

'I can't write any more of this!' I cry, dropping the pen on the floor.

'Fine, fine,' she says. 'It looks better if it's half finished, anyway. Shows how upset you are.' Darcy displays no sympathy towards me at all. No sign that she's even remotely sorry about what I'm going through. She's cold. Dead inside. I thrust the note out towards her.

'Put it back in the sleeve,' she says. 'And pick up that pen. We'll need it for evidence, too –it's covered in all your lovely fingerprints. That's it. Great. Job done.' She takes the wallet from me and places it back on the high window sill.

Despair floods me. My legs and hands shake uncontrollably. I'm terrified about dying, but I'm more torn up by the fact that Jared will really believe I lost my mind. My heart twists, knowing that my beautiful son will grow up thinking his mother was a deranged murderer.

Light suddenly spills through the edges of the blinds. The sound of tyres on gravel outside. *A car!*

'Joe!' I cry. 'Are they back? Can I at least see him?'

'Shit,' Darcy says. 'It can't be them already. It's only—' she glances at her watch '—six fifty-five.'

'Want me to go and see to them?' Callum says.

'No. You keep Louisa quiet. I'll go.'

'Let me see my son. Please!'

'Quiet!' she snaps. The car headlights blink off. Darcy lays her knife down on the table, fluffs her hair and smooths her t-shirt. She crosses the room and turns out the light before she leaves, closing the door behind her. Light from the utility room above drifts down the stairs, so at least we're not in total darkness. Callum guides my arms around the back of the chair again and starts to re-tie my wrists.

'Can you at least tie them in front?' I ask. 'It's so painful when they're pulled back like that.'

'Sorry,' he says. 'I have to do it this way.' Once he's done, he comes back around the front and crouches down in front of me, taking a length of material from his pocket.

I shake my head as I realise what it is. 'You don't need that,' I whisper. 'I'll be quiet, I promise.' The thought of being gagged makes me light headed. What if I can't breathe properly?

'Sorry,' he repeats, pushing the cold, dusty material between my teeth. He straightens up and walks behind me, tying the material tight at the back of my head.

The doorbell sounds, distracting me from my panic. Surely Marianna would have a door key. Is Darcy going to answer it? I hold my breath and strain my ears. From above, out there on the driveway come faint voices, Darcy's laughter. *Who is it? Who is it?* Oh my God, I know that voice.

'Mmmmmhph!' I try to call out, but this bloody gag has done its job of almost silencing me.

'Shh,' Callum whispers. 'No one can hear you.'

I ignore him, writhing in my seat and straining against my gag for all I'm worth. Callum grips my shoulders hard until I squeal in pain.

'I asked you to be quiet,' he says.

The tone of his voice chills me so I quiet down, but I can't stop the tears of frustration running down my face. It's Jared's voice I hear up there. He's so close, he could come in here and save me. He could race down the stairs right now and see what his precious Darcy has done to me.

'If she gets in touch, I'll let you know,' Darcy says, her voice louder now.

Lying bitch. I'm sure she wants me to hear. Jared has obviously come here looking for me. He must have got my message. If only he'd arrived a few minutes earlier he would have seen my car. Now it's too late.

As the front door closes and his footsteps crunch away over the gravel, hope drains from my body. He believed her. He's going to drive out of here and go home. And I'll probably never see him again. He's leaving. And I'm left here with a modern-day version of the Kray twins.

The light comes on, making me squint for a moment. When my vision clears, I see Darcy coming back down the stairs. If only I could rip this gag off my mouth so I could quiz her about what Jared was doing here, about what lies she told him.

'In case you didn't hear, that was your darling husband,'

she says, walking across the room and turning to face me, crossing her arms over her chest. 'Apparently, you left him a garbled message. Something about me picking Joe up from school. It's okay, I told him he wasn't to worry.' She smiles and tosses her hair back. 'I reassured him. Told him I saw you collect Joe. That the children were late coming out of class but that everything's fine now.'

My blood heats up and my heart pounds. If only I could rip the bonds from my body and scratch her evil face off. But the more I struggle, the more the ties dig in, and the more impotent I feel. My muffled cries grow stronger, the gag cutting into the edges of my mouth as I try to yell.

'Oh for God's sake, shut up or I'll shut you up,' Darcy snaps. 'You sound like some kind of sick zoo animal.'

I give one last grunt before abandoning my attempts to yell at her, knowing it's pointless.

Darcy turns away from me, her bright hair swinging, a waft of her perfume invading my nostrils, clinging to the back of my throat. But something distracts me from my misery. My heart gives a small leap as I hear a familiar sound – it's *Mr Brightside* coming from upstairs, getting louder.

'Where the hell is that music coming from?' Darcy says. 'Is that . . . Is that your *phone*?' Her eyes widen with panic as my eyes glitter with triumph. She turns back and grips my shoulder so hard it feels like she's going to break it. For all her planning – she hasn't got everything covered – she forgot about my mobile phone which is sitting in my bag in the hall upstairs.

'Go and turn that bloody thing off,' she hisses to Callum.

He heads for the stairs

My heart thumps as I hear Jared's footsteps approaching the house once more. He's come back! He must have called my phone and heard it ringing inside the house.

'Damn, it's too late,' Darcy cries. 'Cal, wait!'

The doorbell rings. Now, there's banging on the door. 'Louisa!' Jared yells. 'Are you in there? What's going on? Darcy! Open the door! Let me in!'

'You'll have to go and shut him up,' Darcy hisses to her brother. 'Go round the back so he doesn't see you.'

Callum disappears up the stairs, his footsteps receding. Darcy crosses the room and turns out the light. The doorbell is still ringing, the banging continues. Jared is threatening to call the police now.

Good. Do it. I *will* him to call them.

The basement is dark now, aside from the overspill of light filtering down the stairs. Darcy is on tiptoe at the thin strip of window, peering through a gap at the bottom of the blinds.

'Shit,' she mutters. She crosses the room and follows after her brother, leaving me alone.

After a moment, Jared's voice falls silent and the doorbell stops ringing. That can't be a good thing. Can it? What the hell is going on up there? I hear more footsteps outside on the gravel. Then, Darcy's voice – her words like machine-gun fire, angry and sharp. Callum replies, his voice low and pleading, becoming louder as they return to the house.

'You told me to,' he says.

'You could've killed him, you idiot,' she replies. 'Now what are we going to do? Ugh, I should have come up here myself. I'm sure I could have explained her phone being here. Now it's all ruined.'

'Sorry, Nic. I mean, Darcy.'

'I always have to sort out everything myself. Bring him to the basement, then.'

The overhead light flashes on and I blink and squint as my eyes adjust to the brightness. I hear footsteps, and the thud of something heavy being dragged along the floor and then down the stairs. Darcy's tan boots appear on the wooden steps, followed by the rest of her. Callum is following behind her. He's half-dragging my husband. Oh God, Jared looks like he's . . .

'Calm down, he's still alive,' Darcy drawls, reading my worried expression.

I try to speak, try to ask what they've done to him, but this damn gag is doing its job of keeping me quiet.

Darcy sets another wooden chair next to mine and Callum plonks my husband onto it. Jared's head lolls and he lets out a low moan. Darcy holds him steady while Callum binds his hands and feet. Once he's secure, Darcy starts pacing up and down the length of the cellar, tapping her fingernails together, her eyes narrowed, her mouth screwed up. She doesn't know what to do. She's worried.

So am I.

CHAPTER THIRTY THREE

Thank God. I know I shouldn't want Jared to be caught up in Darcy's plan, but now he's here, my stomach isn't churning quite as much. I'm convinced we'll have a better chance of getting out of this together. Darcy has feelings for him, I'm sure of it. She won't let him die, and Jared won't let her kill me.

Darcy paces the floor, a frown on her face.

I gaze at my husband, his eyes closed, his head drooping over his chest, hair falling over his forehead. Suddenly, his eyes fly open. He snaps his head up. Unfortunately, he's already been secured to the chair, his hands tied behind his back. 'What the . . .' He moves his shoulders and jerks his body, trying to figure out what's going on. I can't even warn him about what's happened as I still have this stupid gag over my mouth.

Jared glares at Darcy who's standing in front of the wine rack. And then his gaze lands on me, tied up and gagged beside him. His eyes widen further. 'Lou! What the hell's going on? Darcy? Why am I—'

Darcy holds up her hand to halt his questions but he ignores her.

'Will you explain what the fuck my wife and I are doing tied up in here. And did someone just hit me on the head?' He blinks and swings his head from left to right, catching sight of Callum who walks over to Darcy's side. 'Who the fuck are you?' Jared asks.

'It's unfortunate,' Darcy replies. 'You were meant to get back in your car and leave. If you'd done what you were supposed to, you wouldn't be down here now.'

'What?' Jared sounds woozy. 'Where are we?'

'Mike's wine cellar,' she replies.

'In your house? In the basement?' His voice is clearer now. He blinks and glances wildly around.

'Correct,' she says.

'I don't know what you're playing at,' he growls, 'but you better untie us right now. Are you insane?'

I want to shout *yes she fucking is insane and if you'd listened to me in the first place we wouldn't be down here now.*

He turns to look at me, fear and concern clouding his eyes. 'My God, Louisa, are you hurt? I was calling you. I heard your ringtone.' He turns back to Darcy. 'Take that gag off her mouth! Why do you have my wife down here? God, my head hurts like a bastard. What the hell is going on?'

'If you could be quiet for a minute,' Darcy says icily, 'I'll tell you.'

Jared's face darkens and twists, his eyes are narrow slits.

I don't think I've ever seen him so angry.

'Your wife here was about to commit suicide,' Darcy says.

'What!'

'But then you got all nosey and angry, so now it looks like she'll be taking you and Joe with her. She'll be driving off a cliff into a quarry tonight and you'll all be going along for the ride.'

'What the actual fuck are you talking about?' Jared cries.

'You were supposed to leave,' Darcy yells back, her composure ruffled. She takes a breath through gritted teeth and lowers her voice. 'But you didn't. So now I'm going to have to kill you. Or, more accurately, Callum here is going to kill you. And, to make it look authentic, I'm afraid Joe is going to be part of this family trip to the quarry.'

Jared is shaking his head. I'm starting to hyperventilate. Surely she's not going to include Joe in her psychotic plan. Not my baby boy. I try to yell, try to break free, but it's hopeless.

'Oh my God,' Jared murmurs. 'Louisa was right about you all along. You're mad. You've been targeting her, playing us all. Why didn't I see it before?'

'Because I didn't want you to see it,' she replies.

'Why?' he asks. 'Why did you do it?'

'Oh, I'm not going into all that again,' she says. 'I've already explained it once this evening. Callum, shut him up. Gag him or something.'

Callum starts to protest. 'I haven't got anything to—'

'Use his frigging scarf or something.' She puts a hand to her forehead as Callum quickly does as she asks.

Jared turns to look at me, a mixture of emotions in his eyes – anger, fear . . . an apology.

'What did you mean?' Callum asks, straightening up and turning to face his sister. 'You said I have to kill them.'

'Isn't it obvious?' she says. 'You're going to kill them all.'

'No. Not the little boy,' he says.

'It will be better,' she explains, 'cleaner. More believable. And it will ruin her reputation even further if it looks like she's killed her husband and son along with herself. No one forgives that sort of behaviour.'

'I . . . I can't, Nic. You're the one who does the killing. I can't do it. I always do the other stuff. I'm good at the other stuff.'

'You have to man up, Callum,' she says, her accent slipping. 'Yes, it's always me who does it. Now it's your turn. I have too many other things to organise – planting Mike's murder weapon, leaving the suicide note. Tying up all the loose ends. All you have to do is put on a pair of gloves, knock them out, put the car in first gear and send them off the edge of the cliff. Easy. Jared and Joe will be tied up anyway because she'll be killing them against their will.'

'No, I can't.'

'What do you mean, "no"?' she spits. 'Don't tell me "no"!'

'But these are nice people. They're not nasty. They never did anything bad to us. Not really. Especially not the little boy.'

Darcy shoves his chest with the heel of her hand. 'You're so pathetic,' she sneers. 'Always snivelling and moaning. *I don't want to do it, Nic. Do we have to, Nic?* You're weak. You've always been weak and stupid.'

'And you've always been a bully,' he replies softly. 'Just like Mum.'

'I'm nothing like Mum!' she cries. 'You take that back!'

'No. Because it's true.'

'You ungrateful little shit.' Darcy raises her fist like she's going to punch him. She's obviously not used to her brother talking back like this.

'You always make me do things I don't want to do,' he says. 'And I always do them. I never say no. But not this time.' Callum takes something out of his coat pocket and holds it out in front of her. It's a black and silver Swiss army knife. He flicks open the blade.

Darcy laughs and lowers her fist. 'What are you going to do with that, Cal? Pick your nose with it?'

He ignores her and walks over to Jared.

'Don't kill him now, stupid!' Darcy cries. 'We have to do this properly. Like I planned. Or we'll get caught.'

My heart is in my throat. Surely he won't kill Jared, not after everything he just said to his sister. Jared glances across at me, eyes wide, and I try to convey love and forgiveness in my gaze. Callum moves behind Jared, crouches down and slices through the zip ties around his wrists, placing the penknife in Jared's hand and coming around, back towards his sister.

Darcy now realises what Callum's just done. 'No-o-o!' She launches herself at her brother, kicking him and clawing at his face. He grabs her in a bear hug, trying to restrain her. But she's mad as hell, swearing and lashing out at him with everything she's got.

Jared has managed to slice through the ties on his ankles, and he's pulled the scarf down, off his mouth and around his neck. Now, he's up off the chair and turning his attention to me, cutting through my wrist ties and sawing at the gag, working it free. I'm shaking with relief but I can't take my eyes of Darcy and her brother.

Her thumbs are pressed down into Callum's eye sockets. He's howling in pain and frustration, pulling at her arms, trying to shake her off. Callum is big. He's strong. But Darcy is fuelled by bitterness and rage. Her strength is in her fury. Callum wrenches one of her hands off his face, blood dripping from his eyes. But she gets it free again, makes a fist and punches him in the throat. He wheezes and coughs. Darcy blindly reaches behind. Her hand snakes across the table top, feeling around for the knife which lies just within her grasp. I can't let her get to it, but Jared hasn't cut through my ankle ties yet.

'Jared!' I croak. 'The knife! Get the knife!'

He turns to see Darcy groping on the table for it while trying to fend off her brother who now has her by the throat.

'Go!' I urge.

Jared leaves me with one leg still bound to the chair. But he's too late. Darcy's fingers close around the knife handle. She brings it around and plunges it deep into Callum's chest. Her brother stops howling and releases his hands from around his sister's neck. He drops to his knees and stares in disbelief at Darcy who wears a look of exhausted triumph.

With the knife still protruding from his chest, Callum falls forward, crashing to the ground with a sickening thud, rivulets of blood streaming and pooling across the white marble floor. Silence falls upon the room for a brief moment. And then a wail starts up from within Darcy's chest.

'Now look what you made me do!' she screams. 'Cal!' she yells. 'You stupid idiot! You've ruined everything!' She kicks his lifeless body and crouches down to try to get to the knife out from beneath his hulking body. But before she can get to it, Jared drags her away, standing between her and Callum's body. He holds the penknife out in front of him as Darcy whips around to face him.

'You haven't got the balls to do anything with that,' she says.

'Stay where you are,' Jared says. With his free hand, he

reaches into his jacket pocket and takes out his phone, tossing it over to me. 'Lou, call the police.'

Somehow, I catch the phone without dropping it.

'I'm not going to prison for this,' Darcy says, still eyeing the penknife. 'When the police arrive I'll tell them you killed my brother. I'll tell them—'

'It's over, Darcy,' I say, shaking my head. 'After everything you told me tonight, you've got no lies big enough to cover what you've done.'

She stares from Jared's knife to the phone in my hand. I can see her weighing up her options.

I punch in the numbers 999, but nothing happens. 'I can't get a signal!' I cry.

Jared turns toward me and in that split second as he looks away from Darcy, she shoulder charges past him, knocking him sideways and sprints up the stairs.

'Go after her!' I yell. 'She can't get away!'

Jared nods, uses the penknife to slice through the last zip tie on my ankle, and gives chase, taking the cellar steps three at a time.

I lurch out of the chair, ignoring the bolts of pain shooting through my cramped limbs, and follow him out of the basement. I need to get a signal and call the police. I shouldn't have sent Jared after her. He can't confront Darcy alone. If she can kill someone as strong as her brother, she'll have no difficulty hurting my husband.

Once I reach the top of the cellar steps, the bars appear on Jared's phone screen. A signal! I press *999* again as I hobble out of the utility room and into the kitchen. The bifold doors are open, the freezing night air creeping into the Lane's mansion. But no amount of fresh air will ever cleanse the stench of horror from this house.

'Hello, emergency services, which service do you require? Fire, police, or ambulance.'

'Police,' I say. 'And ambulance. Please hurry.'

'Connecting you now.'

I make out the shape of my husband. He's running towards the open gate at the bottom of Darcy's garden, exterior lights illuminating his dark-suited shape. There's no sign of Darcy. She must already be on the beach, trying to make her escape.

'Hello, where are you calling from?' It's the operator.

'Sandbanks,' I gasp as I jog across the decking. 'Please come quickly.' I give them my name and Darcy's address. Now, I'm running across the icy grass again. At least this time I'm giving chase rather than the other way around.

'Please, *please* get here as soon as you can.' I reach the open gate and limp through it onto the beach, glancing wildly from left to right, trying to see if I can spot them.

'What's the nature of the emergency?' the operator asks, calm in the face of my panic.

'Darcy Lane took my son, kidnapped me and my husband,

and then she stabbed her brother,' I cry. 'I think he's dead. And now she's run off onto Sandbanks Beach. My husband is chasing her. I'm scared for him. She's dangerous. You need to find my son – the maid took him to the cinema – I don't know which one. Please find him. Please.'

The woman tells me to calm down, assuring me the emergency services will do everything they can to locate my son. That they'll be here within a few minutes. I hope that's soon enough.

There! To my left I see a figure running away from me along the shoreline. It's a man. It's Jared. I won't be able to catch him up. My lungs are already burning and I've hardly moved any distance at all. Where could Darcy be? Anywhere, I guess. As I stagger after Jared, I throw panicked glances over my shoulder, paranoid that she's doubled back and is coming after me. But the beach behind is empty.

Ahead, Jared has stopped. He's looking around. I daren't call out in case Darcy is lurking close by in the dunes, or somewhere in between the other beach houses. She could be watching me right now. I give an inward shiver as I finally draw closer to my husband.

'Did you see which way she went?' I pant.

'No.'

'Did she definitely come out the back way?'

'I saw the kitchen doors were open,' Jared says, 'so I assumed she'd come out that way, but I guess she could just as easily have gone out the front.'

'Shit,' I say. 'Shit.' And then my whole body begins to shake. To shiver and tremble. I can't tell if it's because of the cold, or if it's the shock.

Jared takes off his suit jacket and wraps it around my shoulders, pulling me into his body and holding me close. He kisses my hair and lets out a sob. 'I'm so sorry, Lou,' he says. 'I'm really, truly sorry. I let you down badly. I don't know how you'll ever forgive me.'

I don't reply. For now, it's enough that we're alive. Then, my ears pick up the distant wail of sirens.

'What about Darcy?' Jared asks, letting me go, but taking my freezing hands in his. 'Shall we keep looking?'

'Forget Darcy,' I say, my teeth chattering. 'The police will find her. Joe is more important. We need to get Joe. Right now. Make sure he's okay.'

My voice is drowned out by the juddering, whirring sound of a helicopter passing over our heads. Jared and I run back towards the house as its searchlights sweep the beach.

I wonder if they will ever find her . . .

CHAPTER THIRTY FOUR

ONE MONTH LATER

The fire crackles and my eyes are drawn by the dancing, licking flames. Three empty stockings hang over the fire, and the curtains are drawn. I lean back into my husband's chest and he kisses the top of my head.

Joe wriggles his body into my side, all cosy in his PJs and dressing gown. I inhale the scent of him – his clean, soft skin, his freshly shampooed hair.

'What time does Santa actually get here?' he asks.

'Once you're asleep,' I reply, tweaking his nose.

'But isn't there an actual time that he comes? Like a timetable or something?'

'No,' I say. 'He only comes once your eyes are closed and you're fast asleep, snoring your head off.'

'I don't snore!'

'Of course you do,' Jared replies. 'All real men snore.'

Joe looks up at Jared and gives him a crazy stare.

We dissolve into laughter and Joe, already over-excited, starts dancing around the lounge, putting on a mad performance for us, leaping about, pulling faces and singing

When Santa Got Stuck up the Chimney.

After everything that happened with Darcy, I thank God that Joe came out of it unscathed and unaffected. In fact, I think the only good and true thing Darcy said that night was when she told me Joe had gone to the movies with Tyler. They were safely away from the house in town watching some Pixar movie, blissfully unaware of what was going on. When Marianna brought them home, she drove back to a driveway teeming with emergency-service vehicles. Joe thought he'd landed on a movie set. We didn't go into details. We just told him that a man had had an accident and the police needed to help him. He seemed to accept our version of events.

After Darcy escaped that night, I almost died with panic that she was on her way to snatch Joe from outside the cinema. Thank goodness she was too selfish to risk getting caught. Lucky for us, Darcy put her own survival over any plans for revenge. She didn't even return to get her own son. Poor Tyler. He may have been a bully but now he has no parents to care for him. He's gone back to London to live with Mike's sister. I hope, in time, he's able to get over the trauma. That he doesn't end up carrying similar scars to his mother.

So, after all that. After all the police, the search helicopters, the sniffer dogs and TV appeals, Darcy managed to escape. No trace has been found of her. The police are still looking, but I don't hold out too much hope. She's had a lifetime's experience of evading justice, of lying and conning. She only told us a small part of what went on during the years after she left care. It seems Nicole Woodward was also wanted in connection with a string of other murders – mainly of vulnerable elderly people. Now she's disappeared, no doubt with a new identity. She'll have landed on her feet somewhere else, I'm sure of it.

Everyone was shocked when they discovered what had happened. Beth has been her amazing supportive self, and the school mums were suitably stunned and apologetic – sending me flowers, and bringing round cakes and casseroles. Mum and Dad were devastated, feeling somehow responsible. They even remembered talking to the little boy and girl at the care home all those years ago, but felt they were unable to take on siblings, which was why they hadn't asked to adopt Nicole and Callum. It had been nothing to do with them "preferring" me. They had simply wanted to give Beth a single brother or sister, and I happened to be the lucky one.

My heart breaks for the child Nicole was back then. Too bad she let it twist her into a monster. She was consumed by her bitterness instead of rising above it. I wonder if she'll ever let it go or whether it will eat at her for the rest of her life.

'Come and sit back down,' Jared calls to Joe, whose crazy

song and dance is now losing steam. 'The movie's about to start.'

As it's Christmas Eve, we're watching *Elf* – such a wonderfully, funny, feel-good movie. Joe bounces onto the sofa and I count my blessings once again.

I suppose, after everything, I could have told Jared to get lost. I could have kicked him out and felt totally justified. He had believed Darcy – a relative stranger – rather than his own wife. But . . . I know how utterly convincing Darcy could be. How she manipulated him by subtly discrediting me. She played a good game, and it was her intention to make me suffer. To split my family up. Well . . . no way is she getting her wish.

Jared is making up for it. Helping me recover from my ordeal. Making sure I'm okay and that I have everything I need. Well . . . I *do* have everything I need. It's right here in this room.

CHAPTER THIRTY FIVE

TWO YEARS LATER

She stops pushing the wheelchair for a moment, leans down and says something to the old woman, making her laugh. For one worrying moment, I think I might have made a mistake and got the wrong person. But, as she leans, her wavy chestnut hair falls forward over her shoulder and she pushes it back with a casual flick – I'd know that gesture anywhere.

This small Edinburgh park is peaceful and quiet, set in the centre of a residential square, lined with beautiful, four-storey, Georgian houses, a Christmas tree in each drawing-room window. The weather is clear and bright, biting cold. We don't get days as chilly as this down south. I watch the two of them make their slow progress along the sycamore-lined path, stopping now and again to chat and laugh about something or other. You'd think you were looking at a grandmother with her dutiful grown-up granddaughter. I know better.

I'm not sure how I feel about seeing her again. I've been waiting for this day for so long, and now it's finally here, I can't quite believe it. It doesn't seem real. I hope I don't fall apart. I thought I would feel excitement, instead, a fascinated dread clutches at my stomach and a strange numbness overtakes my brain. Yet, there's also a boiling anger deep down. I know it won't go away until I've done this.

'Okay,' I say to myself, striding purposefully across the short grass towards them. I know what I want to say, I've rehearsed it enough times. As I get closer, I note her chain-store clothes, fake leather boots, and cheap dye job. Her designer days are well and truly behind her yet she still manages to look elegant.

She might have changed her appearance but I, on the other hand, look just as I've always done. Perhaps just a little older and a little slimmer. I know she'll recognise me as soon as I draw close enough. I made a special effort today – my auburn curls are tamed into soft waves, my wool coat is stylish and fitted. My boots are soft, expensive leather, as is my handbag. All these trimmings don't stop my heart jangling with nerves.

I finally had the operation on my knee. It went well, and now I lift weights and run every day to keep myself strong. I also enrolled in self-defence and kick-boxing classes. I'm fitter than I've ever been in my life. It makes me feel more empowered. We may think we live in a civilised society where physical strength is no longer necessary. Where the mind alone is all we need to survive. But I know different.

We're all just animals fighting for survival. Struggling for our place in the world. And when we find that perfect place, we'll bite and scratch and hiss and spit to keep it from being taken away. I'm not prepared to lose my place. Not now. Not ever again. I will fight for my family with whatever means I have available to me.

I wasn't about to let my fear of this woman hang over my head for the rest of my life. How could I ever truly relax my guard knowing she was still out there? Still a threat.

I walk in a diagonal line across the grass, drawing closer. I hear her talking to the old woman. She's describing what she's going to cook for supper this evening and – I almost laugh out loud – she's speaking to the old woman in a perfect Scottish accent.

Any second she'll glance up and . . . There – she's seen me. My heart jolts. My stomach flutters. Her expression falters for a moment but she quickly regains her composure. I can almost hear the cogs in her brain whirring and clicking, calculating what I'm doing here and how she should react.

'It took me a while,' I say, coming to a stop in front of the wheelchair, ignoring its elderly occupant and staring instead into Nicole's blue eyes. 'But I finally tracked you down.'

She blinks. 'Sorry, I think you might be mistaken. I've no idea who you are.'

I shake my head. 'You can drop the Mrs Doubtfire act. You sound fucking ridiculous.'

'Well now, that's a bit rude.'

'For God's sake, Darcy – or Nicole, or whoever the hell you are today – I know it's you.' Her face is fuller. Less chiselled. Her brown, wavy hair makes her look less glamorous, more homely. But her eyes are still the same – calculating and hard.

'Well, good for you,' she says in an English accent. 'Five gold stars to Louisa "clever-clogs" Sullivan.'

'It's over, Nicole,' I say.

She gives a dry laugh.

'I found you,' I say.

'So you did. Well done.' She rolls her eyes. 'So, come on then, how did you do it? How did you manage to track me down? I thought I covered my tracks pretty well. And I didn't have you marked as particularly bright, Louisa.'

I smile at her put-down, enjoying the fact that I have her rattled. 'You made the mistake of telling me your real name,' I say.

'Yes,' she drawls, 'but back then, I didn't think you'd be around to use it against me. I had your death all worked out. Such a waste of a good plan.'

'Anyway,' I continue, 'I dug into your past. I was a journalist, remember? I discovered how you spent most of your late teens and early twenties tricking old people out of their money, befriending wealthy, childless widows and widowers and conning them into giving you their cash, or leaving you part of their estates when they died. You were clever about it. Always having an alibi, always moving on before anyone grew suspicious, travelling around the country, acquiring new identities to evade getting caught. With your brother to act as your gopher. And then you met Mike and hit the jackpot . . . until you cocked it all up with your insane revenge plan.'

She scowls and tilts her head slowly from side to side, stretching out her neck muscles. I wince as they click.

'When you escaped from the police, I knew you'd have a stash of money hidden away somewhere. But I also figured you'd burn through it pretty quickly, with your expensive tastes.'

She acknowledges my statement with another small tilt of her head.

'So, once that cash was gone, I guessed you'd be forced to go back to what you do best – namely ripping off rich old ladies for their fortunes. And – what a surprise – here you are reverting back to your old ways, traipsing around a Scottish park sucking up to a ninety-two-year-old widow.'

'Tara, who is this person?' the old woman asks in a genteel Morningside accent. 'What's she talking about? Do you know her? Please ask her to leave us alone.'

I drag my gaze from Nicole's face and stare down at the tiny bird-like woman in the wheelchair. 'You should be thanking me,' I say to her. 'I probably just saved your life.'

'What?' the woman cries. 'What's going on, Tara? She says she saved my life? I don't understand what she's talking about. Take me home. I don't like this woman. Not one bit!'

'Oh shut up, you silly cow,' Nicole says.

The woman's mouth opens and closes like a landed fish.

'So,' Nicole says, turning her attention back to me. 'I suppose I can see how you found out about my past. But how did you find out where I am now?'

'It wasn't easy,' I say. 'I had to be a bit . . . creative. I had help from my journalist contacts. And then I spent days wading through the names of any new carers who had suddenly appeared on registered-carers databases. I tracked down any women who even remotely resembled you, knowing you'd have a different identity. It took me ages, and I went on plenty of wild goose chases up and down the country. Luckily, one of them finally paid off. And here I am. With you.'

'So?' she sneers. 'You're not going to do anything about it. You're weak.'

'You're wrong,' I say.

'Piss off, Louisa,' Nicole says. 'You can't do anything to me now.'

'No,' I reply. 'You're right. I can't do anything. But *they* can.'

Her eyes narrow slightly, and she takes a quick glance behind and to her left and right. 'Who? I don't see anybody.'

'Really?' I reply. 'Oh dear, Nicole. You must be losing your touch.'

She shakes her head dismissing me, but I notice her jaw tighten.

'I called the police, Nicole. You're wanted for multiple murders, not to mention a whole string of cons and thefts. They were very interested and pretty excited to get my call after all these months. I told them you were here with an elderly widow – Sheena Macdonald – and that her life was in imminent danger, so you may have to prepare for a bit of drama.'

Nicole isn't saying anything. Her face gives nothing away.

'I managed to persuade the senior investigating officer to give me a head start, so I could have a few minutes alone with you,' I say. 'But I think our time is almost up.'

She lets go of the wheelchair and glances around, weighing up her options.

'The coppers are already arriving,' I continue. 'They're parked up by the gates and surrounding the park, so be my guest, do a runner like you did last time, I can't wait to see them rugby tackle you to the ground.'

'Rugby tackles?' the old woman says. 'Tara! What's going on?'

Finally, Nicole realises she's not going to get out of this. Her eyes are wide and panicked. She takes in her surroundings. The park is fenced securely with beautiful, wrought-iron, high, spiked railings. And there's only one way in and out – currently blocked off by a good proportion of Edinburgh's finest in police vehicles.

I chance a quick peek through the railings to my left, at the black car sitting directly outside the park. Jared gives me a worried nod from the driver's seat. He insisted on coming along to Scotland. He also wanted to come into the park with me to confront Nicole. I told him this was something I had to do myself. He wasn't happy about it but I put my foot down.

Nicole follows my gaze and spots Jared in the car. She bites her lip.

'You didn't split us up,' I say. 'We're happier now than we've ever been. And his agency is doing really well. He found a nice new suite of offices in Parkstone – so close, he can even walk to work.'

She scowls and looks away.

I glance behind me. Several officers are already heading our way across the park. Nicole doesn't even attempt to run. She knows there's no way out. She understands she's been beaten. Her shoulders drop. Her expression goes blank once more.

'While you're in prison,' I add, 'you might want to read my novel. It's selling pretty well and I've almost finished the sequel. You inspired me to start writing again, Nicole. So thanks for that.'

She doesn't respond. But I can tell she heard me by the

tilt of her head and the tightening of her jaw. My happiness is probably a worse punishment for her than jail.

I move off to the side to let the police do their job. A handful of officers crowd around her. One of them starts reading Nicole her rights, another clicks the handcuffs around her wrists.

I turn away from the scene, push up my coat collar and slide my hands into my coat pockets. I begin walking back towards the park gates, away from Darcy Lane and away from that part of my life. Suddenly, a new sense of freedom hits me. It's finally over and I can't wait to get back home. To start living again.

Acknowledgements

Massive thanks to Pete Boland for giving honest feedback and suggestions along the way. I know it must get tedious when instead of being allowed to relax you have to read another of my chapters.

Once again, I'm very grateful to Hannah Riches, an ex-detective with the Metropolitan Police. And also to Samantha Smith, an officer with the Thames Valley Police. Thank you for your time and patience. Any errors in police procedure are purely my own.

Thank you to my wonderful content editor, Jessica Dall. Your notes, as always, are spot on. I'm lucky to have found you.

Thanks to Simon Tucker from *Covered Book Designs* for creating such an atmospheric book cover. You're a star.

I'm forever grateful to my beta readers Julie Carey, Amara Gillo, Julia Summers and Terry Harden, whose feedback and typo-spotting was invaluable. Thanks also to my fab Street Team – your support is wonderful as ever.

I'd also like to mention the support of several author and reader Facebook groups I belong to: *The Book Club*, *Book Connectors* and *UK Crime Book Club* have all been instrumental in spreading the word and helping with feedback and support. Their members are wonderful and I feel privileged to be part of such a lovely, bookish family. Thank you, guys!

Finally, to all my readers and reviewers, love and thanks always.

~

Also available by Shalini Boland:

THE GIRL FROM THE SEA

A psychological thriller with a wicked twist

Washed up on the beach, she can't remember who she is.
She can't even remember her name.
Turns out, she has a perfect life –
friends and family eager to fill in the blanks.
But why are they lying to her?
What don't they want her to remember?

~

Coming 2017

THE MILLIONAIRE'S WIFE

A twisty psychological thriller

~

ABOUT THE AUTHOR

Shalini Boland grew up in Gloucestershire and now lives in
Dorset with her husband and two young sons.

www.shaliniboland.co.uk